BLADE SINGER

AARON
DE ORIVE

MARTHA
WELLS

Copyright © 2014 by Aaron de Orive & Martha Wells

All rights reserved under International and Pan-American Copyright Conventions

By payment of required fees, you have been granted the *non*-exclusive, *non*-transferable right to access and read the text of this book. No part of this text may be reproduced, transmitted, downloaded, decompiled, reverse engineered, or stored in or introduced into any information storage and retrieval system, in any form or by any means, whether electronic or mechanical, now known or hereinafter invented without the express written permission of copyright owner.

Please Note

The reverse engineering, uploading, and/or distributing of this book via the internet or via any other means without the permission of the copyright owner is illegal and punishable by law. Please purchase only authorized electronic editions, and do not participate in or encourage electronic piracy of copyrighted materials. Your support of the author's rights is appreciated

No part of this book may be reproduced or transmitted in any form or by any electronic or mechanical means, including photocopying, recording or by any information storage and retrieval system, without the written permission of the publisher, except where permitted by law.

Thank you.

Interior format by The Killion Group
http://thekilliongroupinc.com

DEDICATION

To Blythe and Elena, two faerie queens without equal.

CHAPTER 1

Manny Boreaux's gaze darted back and forth between the three large boys advancing on him. They had spaced themselves out pretty well. Given his small, wiry frame, they probably figured he could move quickly when he wanted to. *Guess it had to happen sooner or later,* Manny thought. These boys had been all over him from the moment he had walked into his homeroom class at his new school. Junior high was supposed to be hard enough without adding a trio of bullies eager for fresh meat. They were big but Manny didn't think they looked particularly bright.

The boys must have been lying in wait behind the dumpster. The teachers would all be at the front entrance, shepherding the younger kids onto their buses, so there wouldn't be any witnesses or help for Manny.

"Give it back. I know you stole it, you dirty thief!" Gregory, the leader of the pack, was the biggest seventh grader Manny had ever seen. His huge ears and stooped shoulders made him look like an ape. That was why most of the kids called him *El Chango,* the Monkey. Just not to his face, unless they wanted to get hurt.

"They searched my locker and my backpack," Manny said, exasperated. "I don't have your stupid game, okay?"

The trio had backed him up to the chain link fence

that surrounded the dusty gravel lot. Manny's fingers curled around the sun-warmed metal links. He shot a glance up at the six foot fence. As fast as he was, he'd never be able to scramble over the top before one of the bullies got their hands on him. And if his pants caught on the loose links at the top, it would all be over.

"You're a stinking liar!" said Gregory. The idea that somebody had actually stolen from him, like he stole from the smaller weaker kids, had obviously made him furious. "You probably just hid it somewhere so you could get it later. Now hand it over and I won't beat the hell out of you!"

Manny knew Gregory would beat him up either way. *He probably lives for that sort of thing.* "Just go cry to your daddy," Manny said, making his voice deliberately nasty. "I'm sure he'll buy you a new one. He wouldn't want his precious little boy to be sad and cry."

"At least I have a dad, jerkbutt!" Gregory sneered. "You gotta settle for whatever lowlife drunk your crazy aunt drags home."

Manny gritted his teeth, his ears burning like they always did when he wanted to hit something. He knew he'd get quite a beating from Gregory and his knuckle-dragging monkey-boys if he fought back. But seriously, what kind of insult was "jerkbutt" anyway? "Shut up, Gregory," Manny said, though his voice came out rough from holding back his anger. "Just leave me alone."

Gregory laughed and smacked his friends on their chests. "He's so easy." His minions cackled like hyenas while Gregory's smirk grew into a twisted smile.

Well, maybe Manny could try hitting something...

Using the fence as a springboard, Manny launched himself at Gregory. He hit the larger boy square in the stomach with his shoulder, and knocked him flat. Gregory landed hard on his back with Manny on top. The monkey-boys stood there stunned for a few seconds, then lunged forward at Manny. But Manny rolled over Gregory and shoved to his feet.

Manny sprinted for the open gate, gravel crunching under his feet. He grabbed the fence and slid on the gravel, swiveling onto the street. He had run only a few yards when he heard the horn honk. He glanced over his shoulder and saw a familiar blue tow truck with black lettering on its side that said *Gutierrez & Sons*.

Beto! Thank God! Manny slowed to a jog.

The truck pulled alongside him and stopped. Beto, wearing his usual dirty cap and oil-stained overalls, frowned at Manny. "Where you going in such a hurry?"

Manny yanked the truck door open and hopped inside. Beto continued to study him, sucking his teeth. Of his aunt's recent boyfriends, Beto was definitely Manny's favorite. He never seemed to mind having Manny around, and he knew more about cool cars and motorcycles than anyone else.

"What's up, jefe?" Beto asked. He always called Manny "boss," another point in his favor.

A look out the window toward the vacant lot confirmed that Gregory and his friends had disappeared. "Nothing." Manny relaxed back on the worn vinyl seat. "I thought Tia Licha was picking me up. Is she okay?"

"She's fine, jefe," said Beto. "She had a last minute customer and had to stay late. She called me to come get you. But from the sound of her voice, you better be glad she didn't come. Do I even want to know?"

Manny slipped out of his backpack and dropped it on the seat next to him. "No, not really." He reached for his seatbelt, then frowned at Beto when he noticed he wasn't wearing his. "Uh, forget something?"

"Oh, right, sorry!" Beto fumbled for the belt and buckled in. Satisfied, Manny settled into his seat.

Beto merged back into the traffic. "Gotta pick up a car and drop it off at the shop. I'm late, so you're coming with me. I'll let you off at the corner as usual. Cool?"

"Sure, okay." Manny looked out the window. This was an old neighborhood, with big brick houses and yards with summer-dry oak trees and yellowing grass. It shouldn't be this hot so early, even for Austin, but there had been a drought all Spring.

He liked it when Beto let him ride along in the tow truck. He'd picture himself as an FBI agent impounding some dangerous criminal's vehicle, one that always ended up having a stash of weapons in the trunk. He knew Beto could get in trouble with Old Man Gutierrez for letting him ride in the truck during work hours. That's why he always got dropped off at the corner.

"After that, we can pick up dinner and wait for your tia to get home," Beto said. "And it better be something she loves because we need to get her in a good mood."

"Pizza?" Manny said, though he didn't think Beto would go for it. Never hurt to try, though.

"Something Licha loves, jefe. And it's gotta go good with margaritas. I'm making a pitcher when we get to the house." Beto winked. "Ammunition."

"Easy. Chicken mole," said Manny.

"Órale, now you're talking." Distant thunder rumbled and Beto squinted up at the sky. There were patches of gray clouds building to the south, a dark contrast against the hot blue afternoon sky. "We could sure use some rain."

Manny unzipped his backpack and pulled out Gregory's Sony Vita. He stared at the dark screen. Gregory had been right — Manny had stashed the game in the boys' bathroom until it was safe to retrieve it. *That jerk deserved it,* thought Manny. He stole from other kids, he deserved the same to happen to him. The tiny Vita screen flashed as he powered it on.

"Nice toy, jefe." Beto glanced at the game. "Where'd

you get it?"

"A friend gave it to me." Manny kept his eyes on the screen, worried Beto would sense the lie if he looked at him. "He got a new one."

Beto whistled. "Good to have friends like that."

"You're telling me," muttered Manny, punching buttons. He was determined to enjoy Chango's little toy.

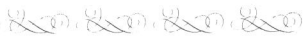

Sitting at the kitchen table, Manny kept stealing glances at his aunt. The chicken mole hadn't cheered her up. In fact, Licha hadn't eaten very much at all. The phone call from Principal Ortiz had made for a quiet, uncomfortable dinner, and she was watching Manny intently between sips of her margarita. Even Beto's attempts to dance with her in the kitchen while the food was heating in the microwave hadn't resulted in a single smile.

And to make matters worse, her hair was now red. She was a stylist at a hair salon, and changed her hair color whenever she was stressed out about something, like a bad breakup with a boyfriend. But Beto was sitting right there, so that left only one other person who might be responsible for it.

Way to ruin dinner, dork, Manny cursed himself silently. He didn't like making his aunt upset, but it just seemed to turn out that way a lot lately.

Dinner used to be Manny's favorite part of the day. As far back as he could remember, family dinners had been fun, full of stories and laughter. One of Manny's favorite memories was of helping his dad make his famous gumbo. Passing on the family recipe had been a big deal and his dad had sworn Manny to secrecy. His mom had watched the entire affair with a big smile.

But that seemed like a long time ago and his parents were gone, lost in a terrible wreckage of twisted metal. Manny had moved in with his aunt just after the accident, almost six months ago. Things had been okay at first, even though Manny knew he had been hard to live with. He would go from furiously angry to so depressed he didn't want to get out of bed, and he couldn't seem to control it.

He had barely made it through his last year of middle school, and had almost been forced to repeat the sixth grade, which would have been a nightmare. At first, his aunt had said nothing. But when his grades had gotten worse and his fights more frequent, she'd asked him if he wanted to talk about it. But what could Manny say that would make any difference? No amount of talking could change what had happened. He knew his aunt was hoping that a new school would be a chance to get back on the right track, but it wasn't turning out that way.

Licha set her glass down. "What are we gonna do, mijo?"

Manny had been stirring the rice on his plate with a fork for the last fifteen minutes. He hadn't eaten much either. He kept his eyes downcast, too embarrassed to look his aunt in the eye. "I don't know," he muttered.

"Did you take that boy's game?" Licha asked.

Manny shot a quick glance at Beto. He didn't know if Beto had told Licha about the game Manny had been playing in the truck. Beto was leaning back in his chair, enjoying his beer and listening to the music playing on the stereo. His eyes were closed. Beto had been to prison once, years ago when he was barely out of high school, for stealing a car. But he hadn't done anything since then. *You're no help,* Manny thought.

"I asked you a question, Manny. Did you take it?" Licha's tone made it clear she expected an answer and fast.

Manny chewed his lip, then shook his head. "No, I

didn't take it." He knew the hesitation just made him look more guilty. *Because you are guilty,* he reminded himself.

"And that's the truth? You better not be lying to me, Manny." Licha's voice was tight with anger.

Manny glanced again at Beto, who had opened his eyes and was now looking straight at him. Beto's face betrayed no emotion, no hint of what he was thinking. As if he was just going to sit there and let Manny make his own mistakes. Manny looked at his aunt and said, "Yes, that's the truth." His stomach was churning as he waited for Beto to call him on it, but Beto said nothing. Manny felt even worse, like he had made Beto a liar, too.

"And what about you skipping class and fighting with the other boys?" said Licha.

"I don't do that!" Distracted, Manny protested it a bit too quickly.

"Which part?" Licha looked skeptical. "The skipping or the fighting?"

"It's that idiot Gregory. He hates me for some reason. He's just bored, I guess." Manny grimaced. He sounded whiny even to himself. And Gregory really was a bully; someone just needed to cut him down to size. *And there's a whole lot there to cut, too.*

"Mijo, this principal doesn't know you like the old one. She didn't sound very sympathetic. And you're not like this, Manny. You're a really smart kid." Licha rubbed her forehead as if she had a headache.

Given that he'd only been at his new school for a few months, Manny had been called into the principal's office a lot, but he had ignored most of the warnings. He just found it difficult to care about all the stuff the school insisted he care about. He remembered when school had been fun more often than not, but it was like remembering something that had happened to somebody else, in another lifetime.

"I want you to talk to Father Diego," said Licha,

breaking his train of thought.

Manny sighed. "Tia, I don't wanna talk to him..."

"Why not?" Licha held her hands out in appeal. "He knows this has been a hard time for us. Maybe he can help you. What would it hurt just to talk?"

The truth was that Father Diego was pretty cool. Everyone seemed to like him. Manny thought he had a great voice, really deep for such a small guy. His aunt called him Father Antonio Banderas. But Manny just didn't want to talk about it to anybody.

Manny slumped in his chair, picking at a worn spot on the wooden table top. "Why do I have to talk about it, Tia?" Licha had told him how she had talked to the old priest who used to be at the church, a long time ago when Manny's grandmother had died, and how it had helped her. But he still didn't see the point of it.

"Well, for one thing," Licha replied, her brow furrowed in worry, "you don't seem to think that your mom and dad are really gone. That's not good, mijo."

"They are gone. I've told everybody that." Manny felt his ears burning. He really didn't want to talk about this. He would rather admit to stealing the game than talk about this.

Licha shifted her chair over to put her arm around Manny. "Mijo, you tell everyone that they've gone away, not that they're dead." Her voice was quiet and serious. "I know it's painful. I miss them too."

Manny looked away, biting his lip until it hurt. "I know they're dead," he said, and it was like the words were forced out of him. "I'm not stupid." Outside the dining room windows, he could see distant flashes of lightning. It was like the weather was just as upset as he was.

Licha sighed and looked over at Beto for help. He studied both of them, his face creased in worry. "What difference does it make what he thinks, Licha? He just needs more time." He drained his beer, then set the bottle on the table. "We should plan a trip down to the

Alamo. Maybe go see a Spurs game."

Licha watched Manny. "Well, I've already invited Father Diego over for coffee tomorrow. You only need to talk to him for a few minutes."

Manny pulled away from his aunt. "Why did you do that? I didn't say I'd talk to him!"

"It's for your own good, Manny," Licha said firmly. "Talk for a just few minutes and we'll all go to the River Walk next weekend. Deal?"

Manny threw his fork down. "No! No deal! I can't believe you did that, Tia!" He pushed away from the table and stormed into the kitchen. "I'm not going to talk to anybody!" he yelled over his shoulder.

Licha got up and went after him. "Manny, get back here. I'm talking to you. Sit back down here!" But Manny had already marched through the living room and down the hall toward his room. He slammed the door once he got inside, locked it and pressed his back against it.

Licha knocked so hard he could feel the vibration through the door. "Father Diego comes tomorrow at ten, Manny!" Her voice was muffled, but Manny could tell how mad she was. "And I expect you to talk to him when he gets here! Do you understand me? I've tried to be patient but that's not working!"

Manny heard Beto gently try to coax his aunt back to the dining room. Then he heard Licha crying. Her voice thick with tears, she said, "I miss them, too, Beto, so much. I have to do something to help him."

"I know, chulita, I know," Manny heard Beto murmur.

Manny winced and slid to the floor. He knew he wasn't the only one who was hurting, and he knew the way he was acting was just making it worse for Licha.

He knew all that. But he couldn't seem to make himself do anything about it.

CHAPTER 2

Manny didn't get much sleep that night, and was awake when the dawn light first started to show gray behind his window blinds. Thunder still rumbled occasionally in the distance, but when he opened the blinds, it didn't look like it had rained yet.

The rest of the house was still silent when he got up, went to the bathroom and got dressed. He wandered back to his room and sat down on the bed. It was Saturday morning, and he could do anything he wanted. But with the threat of Father Diego's visit looming over him, it was hard to think of anything else.

Trying to distract himself, he picked up the framed photo of his parents propped on his bedside table. After the accident, it had taken a long time for him to be able to look at it again. It had just hurt too much.

They were hugging, cheek to cheek, wide smiles on their faces. They were like night and day sharing an embrace. His father's blond hair and pale eyes contrasted with his mother's black hair and dark eyes. His aunt had called them "El Sol y La Luna," the Sun and the Moon. It fit them perfectly.

There was a painful tightening in his throat and an ache in his chest, and his eyes stung with tears. How could they be dead? Horrible things like that just didn't happen. What if they had gone somewhere and were waiting for him? He hadn't seen their bodies in the closed coffins. What if they were empty? What if someone just didn't want to tell him the truth? Part of him knew those thoughts didn't make sense, but he had stopped listening to that part months ago.

And there was no way he was talking to Father Diego.

He got his shoes on and grabbed his backpack, opened the window and climbed out into the backyard. The air smelled dusty and electric, like it might pour down rain at any moment, and heavy gray clouds filled the sky. An old oak tree shaded the yard, making the grass sparse even when it rained enough for it to grow, and helpfully blocked Manny from view if anybody looked out the windows in the neighbors' houses. A dog barked somewhere when he reached the chain-link fence, but he climbed over it and hurried down the empty gravel driveway of the house behind theirs, then he was out on the street.

He walked, with no clear idea of where he was going. He just knew he wanted to go.

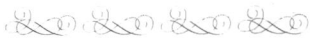

Manny had been wandering for a few hours when he ended up at the old strip mall.

It was a quiet morning. He had watched part of a junior league soccer game at the park, and scraped together enough quarters from his backpack and his pockets to pay for a breakfast taco from the tamale van. It was past ten o'clock, so he figured he had at least a couple more hours to go before Father Diego would leave and he could safely head for home. Tia Licha would probably kill him, but then he probably deserved it.

Thunder rumbled again, close and threatening, and Manny glanced uneasily up at the sky. If he came home soaking wet, maybe she would go easy on him.

Manny snorted to himself. *Not likely.* He knew he'd crossed a line by even temporarily running away.

Then he saw Beltran's Discount Books, with the friendly "open" sign in its window.

The store used to be one of his favorite haunts, but he hadn't been there for months.

The bell above the entrance jangled a welcome as Manny pushed the heavy glass door open. The familiar cool, dusty air of the small shop greeted him like an old friend. Manny took a deep breath, thinking of secrets and adventures in strange worlds.

There were only a few customers scattered around, skimming books on the old wooden shelves that divided the cramped space into a series of narrow corridors. The shop had more in common with a garage sale than with the polished interior of a larger bookstore, but that was what Manny liked about it. It had what his Tia Licha called "personality."

Manny glanced at the front counter, expecting to see Mrs. Beltran smiling and waving to him. But an unfamiliar clerk was ringing up a customer's purchases. Manny studied the tall, thin man's wispy silver hair and well-trimmed salt-and-pepper goatee. Round, gold-framed glasses perched just above his forehead. When the man turned and looked at him, Manny looked quickly away and headed to his favorite section, the fantasy aisle.

Positioning himself so he could keep an eye on the new clerk, Manny dumped his backpack on the floor and scanned the titles crammed into the bookshelf. He used to have most of them memorized, but he spotted several new ones and pulled them out to see their covers and read the blurbs on the back. Dragons, wizards, robots and spaceships, the four staples of all good fiction. He couldn't remember now why he had stopped coming here. He had always loved that feeling of slipping away into a fictional world, the moment when the printing on the page seemed to dissolve away and you were lost in the story, in the characters and their adventures.

Maybe the real world got too...real, he thought. Maybe everything had gone so wrong, he just assumed his favorite books would betray him, too. That the magic wouldn't work anymore.

That was too depressing to think about. Then one cover caught his eye. It showed a flying person with dragon wings and claws. He automatically glanced at the first page, and before he knew it, he was reading the book.

"Can I help you, young man?"

Manny jumped and turned around. The tall clerk, his glasses now over his pale gray eyes, studied him with raised brows. He didn't seem very happy.

"I was just looking," muttered Manny. He replaced the book back on the shelf.

"Looking is allowed," said the clerk, but he didn't smile to show he really meant it. "Let me know if you need any help." He spent a few more uncomfortable moments staring at Manny, then turned to go.

"What happened to Mrs. Beltran?" Manny asked.

The clerk stopped and glanced back at him. "She decided to retire due to health reasons. I'm taking over the store. My name is Mr. Gray, if you should need anything." He gave a curt nod and made his way back to the front counter where another customer waited to be checked out.

Health reasons? Manny knew what that meant, and it was never good. Mrs. Beltran had always seemed old and a bit frail, but he had no idea she had been sick. What if he never saw her again? Now he really regretted staying away for so long. He was pretty sure the new owner wouldn't hand out bubblegum with every purchase.

It had been a mistake to come in here. He didn't like Mr. Gray and if the bookstore was his now, maybe he didn't like it anymore either. He started to replace the paperbacks he had pulled out, but the shelf was so full the other books had pushed into their space. Gritting his teeth in annoyance, he tried to squeeze them back in.

He was about to give up when he saw the problem. There was a big oversized hardcover with a faded leather spine jammed in sideways on top of this shelf of paperbacks and it was pushing everything over. It was weird that he hadn't noticed it before. He grabbed the book with both hands and pulled it out.

It was a very old book, out of place among all the bright colors of the paperbacks. The worn, leather-bound cover was as soft as suede. It had faded to a dull red, but still showed patches of bright crimson here and there, and in the grooves of the binding. That had probably been its original color. There was still a slight tinge of gold visible on the top pages, while the rest had worn down to a dirty mustard color. On the spine, in faded gold letters, the title read: *Blade Singer*. And at the top, the author's name: *Auberon Fae*. Manny was familiar with a lot of fantasy authors but he didn't recognize the name. *Probably some old, dead British guy.*

He opened the book to the scarlet letters of the title page, running his fingers across them. The publishing information at the bottom said: *Avalon, Alberich and Sons*. And under that were the following numbers: *1662*. He did the math in his head. *This book is three hundred and fifty years old?* He had never held anything that old in his hands before. Well, there had been that Indian arrowhead he'd found a couple of years ago while hiking with his dad, but it had just felt like a plain old rock. This book felt old.

He gingerly leafed through the stiff pages, listening to them crinkle. The strong musty smell triggered a memory of himself as a much younger boy riding on his dad's shoulders. His dad went up and down the book aisles and read the titles aloud to Manny, who would get to pick the one that would go home with them.

Thunder rumbled outside again, much louder than before. The door's bell jangled as somebody left, and a cool breeze swept through that smelled of rain-splashed dirt and concrete. Manny forgot about leaving the store and leafed through the book. Spaced out about every fifty pages were black and white illustrations. The drawings featured dashing cavaliers in various dramatic acts of derring-do. Manny studied the figures carefully. Some of them didn't look human. The lightning that flashed outside the store's windows seemed to make the images move: swords clashed, muskets fired, and horses reared with each new flash.

He turned a page, looking for the next illustration, when something fell out of the book and bounced off his shoe. It glinted in the light as it rolled to a stop on the carpeted floor.

A coin?

Manny bent down to pick it up. It was a coin, all right, heavy and gold. Stamped on one side was the head of a young man with a smooth face and shoulder-length hair. His face was turned to the right and he seemed to be wearing a laurel wreath, like the Roman emperors in the history books. There was some sort of writing he couldn't read around the edges.

He turned the coin over. An emblem made up of three interlocked spirals was stamped on that side. Each of the spirals was the neck of a snake or a dragon. That was a triskelion. His mom had owned a silver pendant in that shape. It had been a gift from Manny's dad.

He hefted the coin in his hand. Something like this had to be worth a lot of money. It would be in a safe or a museum, not in an old book. He should probably tell Mr. Gray it was there, even though he didn't like the guy.

Then he realized the coin felt strangely warm. It

was making his skin tingle.

He held it on his open palm and poked it gently. *That's weird.*

A blinding flash of lightning lit up the store and the overhead lights went out. Thunder shook the walls like an earthquake.

Manny flinched. He thought he heard Mr. Gray call out from the front of the store, asking if he was okay, but the coin in his palm had started to glow, and Manny couldn't look away.

He cupped his hands around it, making sure it wasn't a trick of the lightning or his imagination. The coin shone with an inner light, a golden radiance that bathed his face. He heard a distant ringing. Then suddenly it wasn't so distant, it was loud enough to drown out the rumbling thunder, the rain and the wind. He felt dizzy, and something...someone...wanted him to flip the coin into the air. It seemed a crazy thing to do. There was no way he was going to...

Manny watched his hands, shaking badly, position the shining coin on the back of his thumb and side of his forefinger.

With a gasp, he flipped the coin high into the air.

CHAPTER 3

Manny's ear rang as the coin flipped end over end, as if he was inside a giant bell. It went into slow motion as it tumbled upward, until finally it hung suspended in the air, flaring like a miniature sun.

A great wind struck Manny with the force of a hurricane. Like some giant had flipped him high into the air just as he had flipped the coin. He tumbled head over heels, the world melting around him.

The ringing of the coin blended with the tolling of the bells and his panicked yell. The sound became deafening. He had the gut wrenching sensation of falling, only he was falling upwards, faster and faster. His vision blurred, and he started to fade.

"You there! Filthy thief!"

The shrill voice snapped him back to consciousness. A host of unfamiliar shapes bustled around him. A cacophony of strange sounds blasted his ears. An overpowering miasma of odors assaulted his nose.

"Oh, man," was all he managed to say. He would have fallen on his butt if someone hadn't grabbed his wrist. That someone was shaking him now. Hard. Manny focused on his assailant.

A round-faced man with a large moustache that curled at the edges scowled down at him. "He's got my purse! See?"

Dazed, Manny glanced at his own hand. He was

clutching a large, black pouch tightly in his fist.

The man's feathered wide-brimmed hat kept bumping Manny in the head, but he was too stunned to do anything but stare at the man's clothing. The stranger wore a bright blue doublet and breeches with a lace collar on his shoulders and lace cuffs at his wrists. They were like the cloth napkins his grandmother used to collect.

"Drop my purse at once, you thief!" the man shouted.

Manny looked around. *What. The. Heck?* He blinked, shook his head, and looked again. Every year, starting when he was four years old, his parents had taken him to a Renaissance festival. It was his favorite place in the whole world. People dressed up like pirates, wenches, beggars, nobles, and cavaliers, and they ran around a huge wooded park filled with stone cottages, small castles, courtyards, and horse-drawn wagons.

That's what Manny was seeing now, except that the buildings weren't small, they towered into the sky, the stone worn and stained. The streets weren't paths of clay and grass, they were brick and cobblestones. And there were absolutely no tourists in shorts, t-shirts, and sunglasses anywhere in sight. Everyone was dressed in costumes.

"Drop my money purse, I said!" The man continued shaking Manny, his face flushed with anger. "Or I'll have my man thrash you!"

"Hey!" Manny stammered. "Quit shaking me. I didn't take anything."

"No? Then what have you got in your hand?"

Dropping the pouch, Manny pulled free and backed away. "This isn't happening," he muttered. "I'm dreaming. That's what this is. It's just a crazy dream."

"You'll wish this was a dream soon enough. Gunthar, thrash that boy," cried the man, pointing at him.

The creature that stepped forward made Manny's jaw drop. He was shorter than Manny, probably four feet tall, and had wrinkled, nut-brown skin. He wore a bright green jacket, yellow pants, enormous black boots, and sported a bright green cap. A bulbous, ruddy nose as big as a summer squash sprouted from the center of his face, and his dark, wiry beard was braided with beads. But most alarming of all, he was carrying a wooden club.

"I'll teach you to steal from your betters, you pointy-eared goblin," Gunthar barked.

What did he just call me? Manny just stared, even more confused. But Gunthar swung the big club at him and he didn't have time to figure it out.

As the club crashed down, Manny darted aside to avoid the strike. He had a heartbeat to realize he had moved way faster than he ever had before, then Gunthar swung the club again, this time like a baseball player determined to hit a home run. Without thinking, Manny dove away from the blow and rolled clear, coming gracefully to his feet. He turned and hissed at Gunthar.

Manny blinked and took a step back. *I just hissed. I've never hissed at anything before in my life.*

"You can dance all you want, goblin," growled Gunthar. "But I'll get you eventually." He hefted the club to show he intended to have another go.

"You there, sentry!" the man was shouting, waving at someone behind Manny. "Do your duty, stop this thief!"

Manny ducked away from Gunthar, just as something grabbed at him from behind, tearing at his shirt. He whirled around to see a huge man standing over him, broad-shouldered, heavily muscled, so tall he had to stoop to reach for Manny. He wore a rough leather tunic plated with metal rings, and had shaggy hair, gray-tinged skin, and an angry expression.

Then he showed jagged, pointed teeth and growled,

like an enormous angry bear. *Trow,* something in Manny's head whispered. *That thing is a trow.*

The trow grabbed for him again and Manny backpedaled, dodging another blow from Gunthar in the process. Manny pointed at him. "You're a spriggan!"

"He's a sharp one, ain't he?" Gunthar snorted at the trow.

"How do I know that?" Manny said, his voice tight with panic.

People on the street were starting to stop to watch and point. *I've got to get out of here,* Manny thought, throwing a desperate look around the street.

Across the way, there was a two-story stone building, with a big window on the second floor sealed by wooden shutters. A thick beam stood out from the wall just above it, with coiled ropes and a block and tackle attached, for lifting heavy things up to the second story opening. It looked like the Renaissance Festival version of a warehouse. Manny bolted for it.

The trow charged after him, its growl reverberating in Manny's bones. Manny leapt atop a barrel next to the closed street door, then jumped toward a wagon laden with hay, and landed on the side of the soft bales. He scrambled to the top of the pile, looked up at the ropes hanging from the beam. They were looped up, dangling nearly ten feet above his head; there was no way he could reach it.

Even as he thought that, he crouched and leapt.

He caught a loop of the rope, clutched at the rough coils, and hauled himself up until he could get his foot onto the loop and push. He climbed up to the beam, scrabbled up onto it, then ran along it until he could jump up to the roof. It was steeply pitched and he slipped and slid on slate tiles greasy with soot as he ran toward the back of the warehouse.

The roof of the next building was lower down, an easy jump. The shouts from the street were already fading as he fled from that roof to the next.

CHAPTER 4

Manny ended up on a stone ledge below the small round attic window of a narrow four-story house, panting more from exhilaration than exertion and trying to think.

Okay, this is crazy. I'm crazy. And, he reluctantly admitted to himself, *I'm different.*

His bare feet didn't hurt from running; under the dirt they had a thick callus that was as tough as the soles of his sneakers. His hands... His skin was the same familiar light brown, but his fingers were way more callused, and he didn't remember them being that long. He was wearing different clothes, a shabby pair of brown canvas pants that were torn off below the knees, and a light cotton shirt. His pants were held up by a rope belt around his too-skinny waist. He felt weird inside his own skin. Like maybe it wasn't his skin.

Swallowing in a dry throat, he turned toward the window. With his sleeve, he scrubbed at the dirt on the glass until he could see his reflection.

He stared, bit his lip and looked away, then turned back to stare some more. *I'm not me.* He didn't even think he was human.

Manny had always been a skinny kid, and he had lost weight in the past few months, but now he was skinnier than he ever had been in his life. And his arms and legs seemed longer than they should be. The sleeves of his shirt were rolled up, showing forearms that looked like they were all bone and muscle. But the worst part was his face. His eyes were like a cat's, the familiar brown turned to luminous green and the pupils weirdly slender. Then he pushed his mop of hair back. His ears were long and pointed, just like an elf's, just like in the movies.

He sat back, swallowing down a lump in his throat. *It's a dream. But how come I can't wake up?*

"What's he doing?" a high-pitched voice said, from somewhere not far above Manny's head.

"I don't know," a similar voice replied. "He's just staring at himself."

Uh oh, Manny thought. Cautiously, he stood, looking up. Peering down at him, from the top of the dormer over the window, were two little people. They were no bigger than kittens, and had high pointed ears, sharp little features, and hair like puffs of cotton blossom. One had green skin, and the other was blue, and they were wearing tiny little clothes made out of leaves.

"Now he's staring at us," the blue one said.

"Maybe he's gone mad." The green one pointed significantly at his or her head.

Manny didn't think he could argue with that. "Who are you guys?"

"We're the Pixie Troupe of Elder Asphodel," the green one said. "This is our roof."

"He don't know where he is," the blue one said.

The green one shushed him. "Hush, he might rampage."

"No, no, I won't do that," Manny said. *Pixies? Like Tinkerbell?* Except they didn't seem to have wings. At least they were answering his questions and not trying to hit him. "What do you mean, 'your roof?' You live up here?"

Their pointed ears twitched in outrage. "Of course

we do!" the green one said, making an expansive gesture back.

It seemed to be an invitation, so Manny gripped the edge of the dormer, found a foothold in the rough wooden siding, and pushed himself up. What he saw made him gasp in astonishment.

Nestled in among the chimneys and steeply-pitched dormers of the roof was a forest and a miniature city. Green plants, vines, and flowers grew on every surface, surrounding elaborately constructed buildings made of scraps of wood and trash, like broken bowls, rusted metal pots, bent spoons, and old ratty boots and shoes. Lots of shoes. They were made into individual houses, apartment buildings, castles. There were blue and green pixies everywhere, sitting on the balconies and windows of their makeshift city, carrying thimbles as if they contained something very important, thrashing around in the plants, chasing each other. "Wow," Manny breathed. "Wow."

"He's mad, all right," the blue one said. "Acts as if he's never seen Sidhe before."

"Yes," the green one agreed. "It's probably the you-know, the change." It pointed a spear at him that was made from a knitting needle. "Move along now, mad creature, move along!"

"Uh, okay." Manny was too floored to argue any further. He sank down, back to the ledge below the window. *This place just keeps getting weirder.* Taking a deep breath, he looked out over the city.

It stretched out all around him, big stone buildings with steeply pitched slate roofs and little round towers, interspersed with timbered houses with white plastered walls and gables. Farther away there were stone buildings that were much bigger, standing high above the city, with real towers like castles. Smoke spiraled up from hundreds of chimneys, and it was noisy with the sound of horses' hooves on the cobbled streets, the creak of wagon wheels, shouts of street vendors.

The day itself was also different. Instead of evening, it was early afternoon. The blue sky was lightly dotted with clouds, but there was no sign of the evening storm from back home. It was cooler here, too, more like early spring than summer.

So, there are pixies and other weird things here, and I'm like an elf, or something. That would explain his ability to jump like somebody in a Ninja movie. *But why did that spriggan keep calling me a goblin?* He was a rather freaky-looking elf.

He decided to ask the pixies, turning to pull himself up to look over the edge of the roof again. But when he did, a bunch more of them were closer to the edge, menacing him with knitting needle spears and little bows and arrows. "Move along, move along!" one of them said. "We don't want your kind here."

"I just wanted to ask—" Several needle points jabbed at his face. "Okay, fine," Manny said hurriedly, lowering himself down again as the pixies brandished their weapons.

Back on the ledge, Manny took a deep breath. It was all too strange. If he wasn't crazy and this wasn't a dream, he was really in a different world. He'd read books, seen movies and TV shows about people being sent to strange fantasy places through closets, mirrors, and holes in the ground. *But those are just stories.*

Maybe they weren't just stories.

He had been a little scared of El Chango and the other bullies at his school. But he was beginning to realize there might be whole dimensions of scared that he hadn't known existed. But it was exciting, too. A different world, with magical creatures. It was scary, but also kind of awesome.

The only thing he could think of to do was look around, check out the city, see if there was anything that could make sense of all this. It was clear he wasn't Manny Boreaux anymore. He was someone else entirely. Maybe he could figure out where his new self lived and find somebody there who could help him or at the very least tell him where he was.

Having a plan, even if it was a vague one, made him feel less helpless, more like he knew what he was doing. He walked along the ledge, balancing easily, and jumped lightly down to the next gabled roof. This one was free of pixies, though flowers grew in the nooks and crannies between the shingles. Climbing to the peak and then sliding down, Manny heard loud voices ahead and ducked instinctively, then eased forward to look down into the alley that ran along the side of the house.

There were three men below, facing down a little wrinkled brown man with a big nose. He looked like Gunthar, the club-wielding spriggan, except this creature was dressed in muted colors, wasn't as muscled and broad, and he didn't look anywhere near as mean. He was glaring up at the human men, angry and scared.

One of the men said impatiently, "Come on, Moret, just pay the price. You filthy Sidhe are all liars and cheats. We know you've got hidden gold."

"Do I look like I have hidden gold?" The little man waved his arms in frustration. "Why would I sell tin if I had gold? You humans are the ones with all the—"

The words cut off abruptly as one of the men backhanded him across the face.

Manny jerked back from the edge of the roof, his heart pounding. The casual violence of it made his stomach hurt, reminded him that he could have gotten beaten up in the street if he hadn't escaped, over money he hadn't stolen. He had to remember this place might be exciting and magical but it was also dangerous, in a very real way that could involve broken bones and other unpleasant things.

A low grumbly voice said, "Humans, they're all alike."

"Huh?" Manny flinched away. There was something — someone — sitting nearby on the roof. It was a mottled gray color, fading into the slate shingles, with rough knobby skin. It looked like a rock with arms and legs, and two small dark eyes. "Did you just say something?"

It nodded. "I said you can't trust 'em, and if you're caught eating 'em, you're the one gets blamed."

"Uh, yeah, sure." Manny edged away, heading for the far side of the roof. He didn't know what that thing was, and he didn't want to know. The house was backed by another narrow alley, and he crouched and made the leap to the next roof easily.

From there he had a good view of a major street, much wider than the one he had been on before. It looked about the same, except that there were more well-dressed people. The men wore short breeches and boots, or shoes and white stockings, with doublets and lace collars and big feathered hats, just like in the Musketeer movies. The women wore long dresses with big skirts, carefully holding them up to keep the fabric from brushing against the dirty cobbles. Two hulking trows passed by, city sentries like the one who had chased him.

There were poor people, too, wearing rougher clothes of brown or gray or other dull colors, walking along, pushing handcarts, or carrying other burdens, sweeping the street, selling things out of wooden cases they carried slung over their shoulders. But most of them weren't human. They had green or gray or brown skin, pointed ears, were way too short or way too tall. *Sidhe.* The pixies and the men in the street had both used the word. The name did seem strangely familiar. There were humans who looked poor, too, and a few obviously rich people who weren't human, but most of the Sidhe looked like they had all the bad jobs.

Great, Manny thought sourly, putting that together with what he had seen in the alley, and what the creepy rock thing had said. *What if I really am a thief here?* Which probably meant there was no one living with him, no elf-people like Licha and Beto. No home to go to. That thought made his skin go cold.

He watched for a while, but he couldn't hear much talking over the noise of the wagons. *I can't stay up here if I'm going to find out what this place is and what happened to me.* But so far the rooftops had been safe and he was reluctant to leave them. At least he knew he could get back up there fast if he had to.

He found a deserted alley and climbed down onto the roof of a small wooden shed, then dropped the rest of the way to the muddy cobbles. The smell was much worse down here at street level; wincing at it, he followed the alley out to the street, and cautiously joined the crowd.

He walked, keeping his head down, his shoulders hunching involuntarily. But none of the busy passers-by paid any attention to him, so after a while he started to relax. He passed a kid mopping the steps of an expensive stone house, a kid who looked like a miniature version of Moret, the Sidhe in the alley. *Brownies, they're brownies,* Manny thought suddenly, not sure where the knowledge had come from. He was looking around, trying to think of the names for the other types of Sidhe, when the street turned into a wide open square filled with little market stalls.

There were all kinds of things for sale: bolts of fabric, polished cooking pots, baskets of fruit, vegetables, loaves of bread. Everywhere money changed hands and people bargained with vendors, human and Sidhe alike. Looking up, he saw there were pixies there, too, climbing purposefully back and forth along the tops of the stalls. From the bundles of scraps and trash they were carrying, they must have their own version of the market up there.

There were also stalls selling some pretty strange stuff that must be meant for the Sidhe, though sometimes the merchants looked human. Manny saw one that sold nothing but mushrooms, dried and fresh, of more varieties than he could remember seeing at even the fanciest grocery stores. Though he was pretty sure even the most expensive stores back home didn't sell glowing mushrooms. There was another that sold pine cones and all different kinds of nuts.

Then Manny saw several Tinkerbell-like fairies trapped inside a birdcage, hanging from the eaves of a stall selling ironwork. They were even tinier than the pixies, with translucent wings like dragonflies, and were dressed only in flower petals and leaves. He stared, wondering if they were prisoners, why the pixies or some of the others didn't try to rescue them. Then one slipped easily through the bars of the cage and flew off, and another one climbed out to sit on top of it. Manny rolled his eyes and moved on.

He came to the edge of the market, stopped next to a table with trays of buns crusted with almonds and glistening with honey. A short brownie woman with a big nose and pointed ears was packing some into a basket for a couple of well-dressed human women. Manny wasn't hungry; all the craziness of his arrival had made his stomach queasy. But he knew he would be hungry later and wished he had eaten more for breakfast.

"Hey, you! Get away from there!"

Manny spun around to see three men striding toward him. They were dressed like the trows, in leather armor, but the clothes beneath were finer quality, and they all seemed to be normal humans. This would have been reassuring, except they were glaring at Manny. *Oh no, not again.*

"Hey, I didn't touch anything, okay?" Manny held up empty hands, backing away. "I was just looking."

He thought they would lose interest if he moved on, but as he turned away a big hand grabbed his shoulder and yanked him back around. "Hey—!"

The sentry shook him like a rag doll. "You little scum, you keep away from here."

At the pastry table, the human women were staring, startled, and the brownie woman looked alarmed, but no one was saying, "Let that kid go!" or looked likely to.

"Take it easy, will you? I'm just trying to find other elves like me—" Manny started to explain.

But the man drew back a fist, and Manny reacted instinctively, kicking him in the kneecap and wrenching away. The sentry let go with a curse and Manny staggered back. Grabbing the chance to escape, he ran.

Bolting between the stalls, Manny heard shouts and the crashes of heavy bodies slamming into boxes and tables and other people. The sentries were right behind him.

He spotted a street leading off through a tall archway between buildings, and dashed for it. Running lightly over the dirty cobbles, he glanced back to see if the men had followed him.

He slammed into someone, bounced off and nearly fell, but strong hands caught his shoulders, holding him up. Manny heard the sentries pounding down the alley behind him and gasped, "I gotta go! They're after me—"

A voice, dry with contempt, said, "What brave sentries, only three of you to take on this fearsome creature."

It was a familiar voice.

Manny stared up at the man who had caught him, his jaw dropping in astonishment. He was tall and slender, dressed just like a cavalier, in a dark doublet and breeches, boots, lace collar, and a wide-brimmed feathered hat. He also wore a forest green tabard with a big gold triskelion embroidered on the chest.

But the man's face... They were the same handsome features, the familiar dirty blond hair, those instantly recognizable pale blue eyes.

"Dad!" Manny gasped, and threw his arms around the cavalier.

CHAPTER 5

Manny smiled up at his father. "Dad, what are you doing here?" Then realized his father had pointed ears. *Holy crap, he's an elf!* Wait, that actually made sense, since Manny was an elf here too. Well, it didn't actually make sense, because nothing about this made sense, but it fit with the crazy way this world seemed to work.

"What did you call me, boy?" The elf-man frowned.

"Dad, it's me, Manny!" Manny's throat went tight with emotion and he bit his lip, trying to stay in control. He was standing there talking to his dead father and he couldn't believe it.

One of the human sentries laughed. "Have you taken to siring little thieves in the streets, Etienne?"

The elf called Etienne set Manny aside, gently but firmly, telling the sentries, "If I had, would any of you gentlemen wish to take exception to it?" He added, with steel in his voice, "If so, speak now, for I've another appointment and must make quick work of you."

The sentries hesitated, their amused expressions giving way to wariness. Two of them started to stroll back toward the street, trying to look casual about it. The one who had laughed backed a few steps away before he said, "We've no time to bother with you. Be on your way, then!"

Etienne laughed, sounding as if he thought this was really funny, and the last sentry hurried to join the others. *This has to be a dream,* Manny thought, watching him, still dazed. Here he was, in a strange magical world, standing next to an elf cavalier who looked just like his dad. It was too strange to be real. *But if it's a dream, I can't get hurt, even if I don't wake up. I think.* The pain sure felt real, though. Maybe it was better not to test that theory.

With a shake of his head, Etienne started away down the side street.

"Dad, wait!" Manny called after him. "You have to tell me—"

Etienne waved a hand without looking back. "I've no time, boy."

He doesn't recognize me? Manny started after him. He hung back, staying close enough not to lose him, but not close enough for Etienne to notice. He didn't know why this man would look like his dad but not recognize him. It didn't...

The answer made Manny stop in his tracks, stunned by a possibility.

Maybe his father had gotten transported to this world, the same way Manny had, but he had lost his memory. That would explain a lot. Well, it would explain everything except how they had both gotten turned into elves. *But it might mean Mom is here, too, somewhere.* Though maybe she had also lost her memory. Maybe there hadn't been an accident at all. *They disappeared, and nobody could explain it, and so everybody lied to me and told me they died.* It sounded too bizarre to be true; he couldn't see Licha doing that. But there was his dad. Manny jolted into motion again, hurrying to catch up. He had to find out what the hell was going on.

Etienne stayed on the smaller less crowded side streets, which made him easier to follow. Manny didn't see any more sentries, which was a relief. Most of the people he saw were Sidhe, and seemed occupied with their own tasks.

Etienne finally turned down a narrow street that led through an archway into a big open courtyard, part of a large three story building made of sandy-colored stone. One wall had long galleries with archways and pillars looking down on the court, but no one seemed to be up there. Vines potted in troughs climbed the courtyard walls, and there was a fountain with a wide shallow pool to one side.

Four other men waited there. Three of them looked human at first glance, and they were wearing black tabards trimmed in silver. The contemptuous glares the men gave Etienne told Manny they were not friends. *A rival faction, I bet,* Manny thought, edging around the wall for a better view. *Just like the Cardinal's Guards in the Musketeer movies.*

Etienne ignored the three men standing by the fountain, crossing the court toward the man waiting near the shade of an ivy-covered trellis. The man stepped out of the shadow to meet him. As they greeted each other, Manny squinted, feeling like there was something different about the guy but he couldn't quite see...

Whoa, Manny thought, staring in amazement. The guy was short enough for his head to come just above Etienne's shoulder, and he had curly hair and pointed ears. He was dressed like the others in doublet and knee breeches, but he wasn't wearing boots or shoes. But the weird part was the legs below the breeches were covered with chestnut brown fur, the same color as his hair, and they ended in hooves, like a deer's hooves.

A faun, just like in Greek Mythology. Manny wished he had paid more attention to his English and Literature classes, now. He had been more interested in the battles and warriors of mythology, and all he could remember about fauns was that they played pipes or flutes or something.

The faun called toward the human swordsmen, "It appears you were wrong, Desmarais. Cowardice and a lack of punctuality are not the same thing. However, you still have time to run away, if you run very fast."

"Funny, Rabican." One of the men stepped forward, a big man with dark hair and big mustachios. "We were about to retire to a tavern, Etienne, since the hour was growing so late." With an unpleasant grin, he added, "Did fear slow your steps?"

Etienne snorted, amused. "If you think this was the most important appointment I had today, then you're truly as ignorant as I had originally pointed out. I'm afraid this little duel ranks far below matters of real import."

Desmarais put his hand on the hilt of his rapier. "You'll pay for your insults."

Rabican the faun swept off his hat. "Yes, yes, then you're determined to go through with this act of suicide? There's still time to make peace and avoid bloodshed." He said this part with a grin, clearly not expecting the larger human to take him up on the offer.

"If Desmarais apologizes for being a colossal buffoon, I'd be satisfied," said Etienne. "Oh, and for having an ugly mustache, too," he added, tracing his opponent's offending characteristic with his finger in the air.

Desmarais' hand went reflexively to his mustache, then he angrily drew his rapier. "Enough! Draw your sword, elf!"

Rabican shrugged and stepped aside.

"A duel," Manny breathed, torn between excitement and fear. This wasn't a movie, this was the real thing, and his dad might get killed.

Then Etienne drew his sword, and Manny gasped. It caught the light like a glass prism, a long sharp translucent needle of crystal. *That has to be magic.* It seemed crazy for a moment, but then Manny just shrugged to himself. If you could have Sidhe, there was no reason you couldn't have magic swords.

There was a murmur from the other human swordsmen, as if they were unwillingly impressed. Even Desmarais eyed the blade warily.

"Feeling a bit nervous?" asked Etienne.

"Of what? A worthless piece of faerie glass?" Desmarais snorted.

"But just think how lovely it'll appear stained with your blood," Etienne said, and for an instant his face was way more dangerous, and he looked much less like Manny's father. Manny blinked, and the image was gone. Etienne was again the elf-version of his dad.

"Do you really think you'll ever get that sword to sing, Etienne?" Desmarais countered. "Who's the colossal buffoon?"

Etienne's smile faded.

Desmarais chuckled, and seemed pleased he had struck a nerve.

Get the sword to sing? Manny wondered. Maybe it was a metaphor.

The two men circled each other, ignoring the shouts and encouragement of the other men, focused only on each other. Then Desmarais lunged forward. Etienne parried, and the clashing swords, steel against the strange crystal, a sharp ring that resonated in Manny's bones. The flurry of thrusts and parries was almost too quick to follow. The men broke apart, Desmarais panting and backing away a few steps, then they came together again as Etienne attacked. Etienne wasn't even breathing hard.

He wasn't just bragging, Manny thought, watching the two men intently. Etienne wasn't the least bit worried, and didn't look as if he had any reason to be. He was faster than Desmarais, more focused, more accurate.

With a sudden flourish, Etienne disarmed

Desmarais. The elf vaulted over his stunned opponent, caught his rapier in mid-air, then slapped Desmarais' backside with the flat of his own blade. Manny snorted and Rabican laughed appreciatively.

"That was quite a jiggle," said Etienne, spinning to face Desmarais again. "More marching, less pastry I think."

Desmarais took an angry step forward but froze when he was met by the sharp points of two rapiers, one metal, one crystal. "You would attack an unarmed man?" snarled Desmarais.

Etienne grinned, then tossed Desmarais his sword. "Not hardly."

Desmarais attacked again and the duel resumed, but by now it was clear that Etienne was only toying with his opponent. The scowls Desmarais' companions were giving Etienne confirmed it. Even Rabican seemed to be tiring of the sport.

"End this, Etienne," said the faun with an exaggerated sigh. "You've humiliated him enough for one day."

Taking that as his cue, Etienne's blade darted in. Desmarais staggered away, his blade clattering on the pavement, one hand pressed to his arm where blood stained his white shirt sleeve. Manny whistled in admiration. It had been so fast; if he had blinked he would have missed it.

Etienne stepped back. "Do you yield?"

Desmarais glanced at his companions, both of whom nodded. "Yes, damn you, I yield," Desmarais said grudgingly. Then with a sneer, he added, "But this duel has proven me right. The sword didn't work for you, Etienne. Again. The legend says it only works for one who fights with true courage. Perhaps the sword knows something you don't."

Etienne's expression hardened, the long line of his jaw tightening. He strode forward and placed the tip of his sword an inch from Desmarais' alarmed face.

"Magic or not, it's still a blade, and it does its duty just the same." With a flick of his wrist, he sliced off the ends of Desmarais' mustachios, then sheathed his sword.

Rabican laughed again, a sound that was far more of a bleat than anything else. "It doesn't take true courage to defeat the likes of you, Desmarais. Obviously, the sword's magic wasn't needed. Although your barber may disagree." The faun clapped Etienne on the back and they both left the courtyard.

Manny darted from his hiding spot and hurried after the Sidhe cavaliers. He couldn't help grinning. He was stuck in this weird place, but at least his dad alive and well, and an amazing elf swordsman to boot.

"That was amazing, dad," said Manny, falling into step beside Etienne.

The cavalier stopped and frowned at him. "You again. Your jest has gone far enough, boy. Stop calling me that."

Rabican studied Manny with some amusement. "Who is this, Etienne?"

Etienne sighed. "I saved this boy from a severe beating at the hands of some sentries. He's most likely a thief. He claims I'm his father. Poor lad is clearly addled."

Rabican chuckled. "Wouldn't that be something. Are you sure he's addled?" The chuckle turned into a belly laugh.

"I'm not in the mood, Rabican." Etienne's expression was clearly unamused. "Desmarais left a sour taste in my mouth."

"Bah! He is a buffoon and unworthy of further thought," Rabican said. He glanced at Manny. "He does look like a thief. Away with you, lad."

"Look, this is going to be hard to explain, but you must have lost your memory," Manny told Etienne. "You have to listen to me. I'm your son, Manny." He grabbed the cavalier's arm. "And I'm not a thief."

Etienne pulled his arm free. "The change is upon you, boy. You didn't get that way by selling flowers in the streets."

Change? What change? Manny thought desperately. "I'm not really an elf, dad. And neither are—"

"That's clear by looking at you, boy." Etienne seemed even more annoyed. "You're halfway to a goblin. But I agree with Rabican. Away with you now. I'm tiring of your game." He turned away.

"No, you've got to listen to me!" Manny shouted. He raced to Etienne and again tried to grab his arm. "Isn't it true that you just woke up here last year, you don't remember where you were before that? I know you, you're—"

Etienne grabbed Manny's shoulder, so hard it hurt, and stared him in the eyes. "Stop this nonsense, boy. I've lived in this city since I was a boy and Rabican and many others can attest to that. There's nothing wrong with my memory or my wits. I don't know who put you up to this, but I'm not amused. Now be on your way or I'll toss you into the Foundry."

The look in Etienne's eyes choked Manny's protest off in his throat. To his horror, he felt his eyes well up with tears. He jerked away and dashed his sleeve across his eyes. Etienne released him. Even Rabican watched him grimly now.

Etienne hesitated, then reached into his pouch and pulled out a coin. "Here, boy. Take it. My anger should not have been directed at you." He held out the coin.

Manny wiped his eyes on his sleeve. The ache in his chest made it hard to breathe. Ignoring the coin, he looked away, and tried to swallow the enormous lump in his throat. Finally, Etienne took his hand and planted the coin in his dirty palm. Without another word, the two men turned and walked away.

Manny watched them go. He wished that this was just a bad dream, wished it as hard as he could. This wasn't like the fantasy worlds he'd read about. He wasn't a king, or a wizard, or a hero prophesied about in a legend. It was bad enough that he was here at all, but to see someone so much like his father, who didn't know him at all...

He shook his head, shying away from the thought. He was all alone here, and this was no place for him. *I just want to go back home.* But the fear that he would never find his way home burned in the pit of his stomach like a red hot stone.

CHAPTER 6

The sun had begun to set. Manny had no idea how long he had been wandering. The streets all started to look the same after a while, the buildings indistinct, the people just a sea of unfriendly and unfamiliar faces. The wind was getting chilly as the light failed and the streets grew more shadowed, and the cobbles were cold under Manny's sore feet. He was careful to hide whenever he saw anyone, Sidhe or human, in the distinctive armor and uniforms of city sentries. He had no destination and no clue what he should do.

Feeling an ache in his hand, he looked down and saw he was still clutching the coin Etienne had given him. He managed to make his stiff fingers uncurl and stared at the coin, now streaked with sweaty grime from his palm. Maybe if he tried flipping the coin, it would send him back. But this coin was silver, not gold. And it didn't feel the same as the gold coin had felt in the bookstore. It didn't sparkle, there was no glow, and the only heat it gave off was the heat of his own body.

What could it hurt? Manny placed the coin on the back of this thumb. He held his arm rigid, wanting desperately to flip the coin but dreading the likely result. He took a deep breath, closed his eyes, and flipped it into the air.

His eyes snapped open, tracking the flash of silver.

He barely caught it before it could bounce on the cobblestones. His heart was pounding, his breath short. But aside from that, there was no effect.

Manny slumped against a building, staring at the coin. *This has to be a dream,* he thought. *This can't possibly be happening.* But Manny had never had a dream that felt so real, with details so vivid. He had never felt hungry, tired, cold, or sick in a dream. Dreams didn't make your feet hurt. *Maybe Tia Licha was right. Maybe I should have spoken to Father Diego sooner. Maybe I have finally gone crazy.* Thinking of Licha made it even worse. Had she and Beto noticed he was gone, and thought that he had run away? Had they called the police?

Oh. Or... He wasn't in his own body. Maybe it was lying there in the bookstore, and they thought he was dead. Imagining what that would do to Licha made him want to curl up into a ball and shut out the world.

"Well, isn't this a fortunate turn of events." Manny looked up to see the three sentries Etienne had saved him from earlier closing in on him. He scrambled to his feet, his back pressed against the wall.

"Did I see a glint of silver in your dirty palm?" said the leader of the pack, the one Manny had kicked in the kneecap, a redhead with a pockmarked face. "Did you think I'd forget you? We have a score to settle."

"Leave me alone," Manny muttered.

Redhead was studying Manny as if deciding what part of him to break first. "Etienne isn't here to defend you, pickpocket. So much for a *father's* love, eh?" he chortled. "Now hand over the coin."

Manny's first instinct was to do exactly what this man wanted him to do. Handing over the coin seemed the wisest course of action. He knew that this sneering sentry would not be content to simply punch him in the face a few times like Gregory back home. No, the predatory look in his eyes, and the way he gripped the hilt of his dagger, convinced Manny that he wouldn't hesitate to kill him. In fact, he would enjoy doing it.

But a thought took root in his head, like a voice that said, *Don't give him what he wants! You're faster than him. You're smarter than him. You can beat these men!*

"No." Manny's gaze locked with the sentry's.

Redhead's eyes widened in surprise at Manny's single, defiant word. "Oh, so I'll have to take it from you then, will I?" He drew his dagger. The blade flashed in the dying light. "I was hoping you'd resist."

Manny balled up his fists and tensed, waiting for Redhead's knife to come slashing forward, waiting to feel the painful bite of its edge.

With a cry, one of Redhead's companions went sprawling to the ground. The other spun around, reaching for his rapier. A figure crouched behind the fallen sentry, holding a staff. Manny peered around Redhead, who had turned to face the attacker.

The figure was dressed in form-fitting leather and had a high leather collar pulled up over the lower half of its face. The startled sentry drew his sword but before he could come on guard, the figure rammed the end of the staff into his stomach. The sentry staggered and dropped his sword, the wind going out of him in a gurgled cry. The figure spun gracefully, twirling the staff in the air and bringing it crashing down against the other sentry's temple. The sentry collapsed like a sack of potatoes. The whole thing had taken only a couple of seconds.

Redhead blinked, holding his dagger out. Apparently realizing he was woefully under-armed, he switched his dagger to his left hand and began to draw his sword. The staff slapped the dagger of out of his hand, and the figure advanced, raining a flurry of savage blows on Redhead's body. The way the figure moved and used the staff reminded Manny of the kung fu movies he and his dad had watched together.

Redhead was driven back against the wall. Manny sprang away, ready to run if the attacker turned its attention to him. The figure held the end of the staff a few inches from Redhead's eyes.

"You sentries disgust me," the figure hissed. "You're the biggest thieves on the streets." Manny's eyes widened. The voice was high and strangely familiar.

"You will pay for this," snarled Redhead. "I swear to you!"

The figure cocked its head. "Yes, someday I'll pay for what I've done. But not today." The staff pulled back and slammed Redhead in the mouth. He cried out, clapping a hand to his bloodied lips. He leaned over and spat out rotten teeth. He glared at the figure, drooling, "You miserable, little—"

The end of the staff caught him just above the nose. Redhead slid to the ground and slumped over onto his side.

The figure glanced around, making sure the other sentries posed no further threat. It straightened, turned, and jogged down the darkened street. Manny just stood and stared. The figure stopped, looked around as if expecting someone to be with it. The someone was evidently supposed to be Manny, because it turned back to him and pulled down its collar, revealing its face for the first time. But Manny already knew who it was. The way the figure moved, the way it impatiently planted its hand on its hip. The voice, warmly familiar and unmistakable.

"What are you waiting for?" asked his mother. "Remy, come on, before more sentries arrive!"

Manny sprinted to her side. He gazed up at her, studying her face. She was human, not Sidhe like him. And she was exactly as he remembered: dark eyes, sharp features, smooth olive skin. Manny smiled at her. He had no idea who Remy was, but right at that moment, he didn't care. His mother could have called him a stupid idiot, it would have made no difference.

She frowned and brushed the hair from his eyes. "Are you all right?"

Manny managed to say, "I'm fine. I'm just tired and hungry." He slowly wrapped his arms around her and hugged her tightly. "And I'm really happy to see you."

His mother squeezed him and kissed the top of his head. "I'm happy to see you, too, but now is not the time for sentiment." She grabbed his hand and pulled him along. "I need to go see Heinze and unload some goods. For both our sakes, I hope you've earned your keep today, Remy. Morrigan's been in a particularly foul mood of late. And we both know how dangerous it is to upset her."

Manny had no idea what she was talking about, but he was content to let himself be led along. He knew in his heart this was no more his mother than Etienne had been his father. But whoever Remy was, it was clear this woman had some sort of connection to him. And if Manny was supposed to be Remy, he needed to find out what that connection was. Maybe she could help him get back home.

CHAPTER 7

The speed and ease with which his otherworld mother navigated the city impressed Manny. She seemed to know every alley, every hiding spot, and the easiest accesses to the rooftops. She moved like a cat — quietly, gracefully, like a living shadow. And here Manny thought he was supposed to be the stealthy elf.

As they leapt from one rooftop to land on another, Manny stopped and stared at a distant building that glowed like silver in the moonlight. It was huge, with a domed roof, a spire rising up from the center, and a blocky but elegant double tower on one end. Arches along the outside seemed meant to support the walls. *I wonder what that is,* he thought. *Maybe an old church?*

Then Manny noticed that there were figures moving along the parapets. He squinted, trying to make them out. Their movements and shapes seemed inhuman and somehow strangely familiar. *Could those be...?* His suspicion was confirmed when one of them launched into the air, spread jagged wings and soared over the city. Gargoyles. Real, living gargoyles.

In the darkness, he could also see sparks of colored light, red, green, blue, yellow, like Christmas lights or colored fireflies, flickering all over the near and distant rooftops. The whole city was alive with it.

Then the bells of the church began to toll. It was a strangely haunting sound, that somehow reminded him of the golden coin. If he concentrated, he could still hear the ring of the tumbling coin. It was as if the sound had been permanently burned into his memory, but had retreated to the back of his mind, waiting there for... he wasn't sure.

"Do you find the Basilica particularly fascinating tonight?"

Manny blinked, realizing his mother had come back to stand beside him. "Is that what that is? It's really cool," he muttered.

"Remy, I'm asking again, are you well?" She drew him down the roof a little, and swiveled him toward the street. In the reflected glow of the torches outside the noisy tavern below, he could see her worried expression. She turned his face this way and that. "Is it the change? Do you feel different?"

"The what?" Manny frowned at her and touched his own face. "Am I changing? Do you know what's happened to me?" His heart gave a jump. Did she know he was not who he seemed to be?

"Of course I know what's happened to you," she replied, her look of concern deepening. "It's happening still."

It suddenly dawned on Manny that she was talking about his unusual appearance. Apparently he didn't look right, even for an elf. "Someone called me a goblin today," he admitted.

"Is that surprising? It's more obvious every day, Remy." She knelt by his side. A tiny glowing Tinkerbell fairy, like an animate flying flower, tried to land in her hair and she brushed it away impatiently. "What's wrong? You can tell me."

He wanted to tell her everything. Right there, right then. But he knew it wasn't the right time. He needed to get her trust first. He couldn't just tell her that the elf she clearly cared about was no longer Remy but some human kid from Austin, Texas, named Manny Boreaux.

"I... uh, fell," he finally blurted out.

"You fell?" Her look was beyond incredulous. "You? Fell? When did this happen?"

"Earlier today, when the sentries were chasing me."

"I see." She studied him thoughtfully. "And what happened when you fell?"

"I, uh, hit my head. Here, see?" He turned his head and pointed to a spot just below the curve of his skull.

She ran her fingers through his hair, feeling around for a bump. "I don't feel anything."

He pulled away, brushing his hair back over the spot. "Well, it hurts. My vision got blurry and everything. I think I've forgotten some things." He bit his lip. He had meant to sound much more convincing. Even he wouldn't have believed that one.

She stood up and crossed her arms. "What sorts of things?"

Manny glanced around, shrugging his shoulders. "I don't know, all sorts of things, I guess."

"Like what?" Now she really sounded like his mom.

Manny met her gaze again. "Like... your name?"

She stood perfectly still for a moment, just staring at him, then she burst out laughing. "What? My name? Oh, Remy, please tell me this is some sort of game."

If only it was a game. He said miserably, "No, it's not. I fell and hit my head and now I can't remember anything."

"Oh, so now it's anything? You can't remember anything?" She planted her hands on her hips. Uh oh, his mom used to do that when she was getting really angry.

"Well, almost anything," he mumbled.

"You really don't remember my name?"

Manny shook his head, not daring to look her in the eyes.

"It's Adriana, Remy. Adriana." She smacked her forehead. "Powers above, I can't believe this! What are you playing at, Remy?"

"I'm not playing! I told you I hit my head and you treat it like a joke." He turned his back on her and crossed his arms. He hoped he was more convincing this time. It was depressing confirmation that no matter how much this woman looked and sounded like her, she wasn't really his mom. His mother's name was Raquel.

Adriana stepped closer and squeezed his shoulder. "I'm sorry." Manny suppressed a grimace of relief. He had been more convincing. "Let's finish my business and get some food. I'll have a better look at your head in the light. I can't see as well as you can in the dark."

Manny turned back to her. "Okay, that sounds great."

Adriana sprang lightly to the edge of the roof, glanced down, and then leapt over the edge. Manny darted to the roof's edge and looked down. Adriana had bounced off several canvas awnings and landed in a wagon full of hay. She waved at Manny to follow. Manny hesitated, then thought, *yeah, I can do this*. He followed Adriana's path, jumped and bounced and landed gracefully on his feet in the street next to the wagon.

Adrianna looked surprised, and Manny grinned at her. *Now that was smooth.*

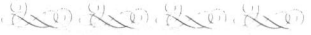

Heinze turned out to be a type of Sidhe called a kobold. He couldn't have been more than two feet high, with skin as blue as a ripe blueberry, and rows of tiny, sharp teeth. He was dressed in brown woolen knickers and a baggy cream-colored shirt, over a blood-stained apron. He sat on a high stool, using a jeweler's glass to study a gold medallion inlaid with small gems. He grunted and hummed to himself as he turned the medallion in his grimy hands. The gems glittered in the candlelight. There were several other pieces of jewelry sitting on a gore-encrusted table that had been recently littered with fish heads.

Manny glanced around at the various gutted sea creatures, most of them unrecognizable, that hung from several cords crisscrossing the room. He'd never heard of a fishmonger nor had he ever been in a fishmonger's shop, but if they were all like this he was very grateful for that. The smell was enough to knock the spots off a cheetah. *Man, how can anyone stand this?* Pinching his nose, he concentrated on breathing through his mouth.

Adriana winced and rubbed the bridge of her nose, obviously not happy about having to spend time in this stinking place either. "So are you going to take all night, Heinze? I have places to be."

Heinze dropped the medallion back on the table. He smacked his lips and considered it. "You're the finest cat burglar in all of Lutetia, my dear. Nay, all of Aquitania, surely. The Hands of Shadow are lucky to count you among their number." He held up his hand and wiggled his dirty fingers.

Manny frowned. *The Hands of Shadow?* He glanced at Adriana, whose expression was grim.

"Flattery bores me, Heinze," she said, crossing her arms.

"Of course. Two hundred livres, then." His voice, despite sounding squeaky, had an odd gravelly quality to it, making it seem as if he were growling instead of speaking. Manny thought it made him sound like a Chihuahua his Tia Licha had once owned named Hercules.

"Two hundred?" Adriana looked like someone had just spat in her mouth. "The workmanship alone is worth two hundred."

"Only to the right buyer, my dear," Heinze said. "I'm sure you realize my position. I can't just traipse down to the market with this, now can I?" He made an expression like an exaggerated pout, shrugged his small shoulders and shook his head.

Adriana glared, but Heinze only smiled, showing off his needle-sharp teeth. "Fine." She set her jaw, looking as if she would rather punch Heinze than take his money. "It seems I have no choice."

Heinze reached under the table and produced a small box. He pulled a key from a chain he wore around his neck and unlocked it. He counted out several golden coins into a pouch, pulled the drawstrings tight, then tossed the pouch on the table.

Adriana scooped it up and stuffed it into her vest. "How can you sleep at night, Heinze?" she asked.

"Warm griffin milk," he replied. "I recommend it."

Adriana stood up. Manny followed suit, happy to be leaving the house of stench. "I'll have more goods soon," Adriana said. "But I'll need to unload them quickly. If you're having trouble with buyers..."

Heinze hopped off his stool and limped to the door. "Have I ever let you down, my dear? Besides, where else are you going to find someone with the courage to cross Morrigan?"

"You mean the greed?" Adriana walked to the door, Manny in tow.

"Your mistress' reputation is well known in my circles," Heinze continued. "The only thing worse than an Unseelie witch is a vengeful one. We're both aware she knows nothing of this side business and nothing of the money you've been keeping from her. We both also know what I'm risking by buying these stolen jewels, which should rightfully be hers. She would not take it well if she discovered it."

"We both also know the profit you're making," said Adriana. "I don't come here for the pleasure of your company, Heinze. Just do your job." She pushed open the door and walked out into the cold night.

Following her, Manny glanced back at the kobold, unable to repress a wince of disgust. Heinze smirked at him, and said, "Come back when you're a goblin, boy. Perhaps then I'll have some work for you." Then he slammed the door in Manny's face.

Back out in the dark alley, Manny hurried after Adriana. Ramshackle stone and wood buildings loomed over them, blotting out the moon and starlight, and even with his improved night vision, he could barely see her. "Hey, what did he mean by that?" Manny asked. "'When I become a goblin.' I'm an elf, right?"

Adriana stopped and turned to him. "Remy, you haven't forgotten that, as well?" She sounded startled.

"Uh... I'm an elf," Manny managed, uncertain. The goblin thing was starting to freak him out. When they were up on the roof, he had told Adriana that someone had called him a goblin, and she had said it was more obvious every day. He had thought she just meant that he was acting like a goblin, by stealing things. He thought about the goblins in books and movies, with fangs and claws and bugged-out, scary eyes. He added in a little voice, "Can we say I've forgotten about that and you explain it to me?"

Adriana hesitated, then shook her head. But she said, "If you're playing a game with me, Remy, I'll clout you so hard you will lose your memory."

Manny swallowed hard. "I promise, no games. I really just can't remember. Please?"

Adriana sighed. "Sidhe who are done ill, or who do ill by others, start to change, their appearance reflecting what's inside. Little elves like you become goblins." She squeezed his shoulder sympathetically. "But it's not your fault, Remy. It's this city, and the way your people are treated, and what we've both had to do to survive." She paused and looked away. "And it's Morrigan, her influence over both of us..." She shook her head, as if it was something she didn't want to think about. "Once I get us out of here, you'll go back to your old self, I promise."

"Oh." Manny nodded numbly. "Right, I will, thanks." Adriana started back down the street again, and Manny followed her, his head reeling. All he could think was, *Oh great, I'm turning into a monster.*

CHAPTER 8

Adriana led Manny through the dark streets, and he was glad neither she nor anyone else could see his face. He was pretty certain he looked confused and on the verge of freaking out, because that was how he felt. The idea that his body was changing made cold sweat break out all over his skin. He didn't want to be a goblin, he didn't. Whatever this Remy kid had done, Manny hadn't, and it just wasn't...

Wait a minute. Manny stopped abruptly in the middle of a damp narrow street. *Remy's the one turning into a goblin, not me.* He let out his breath in relief. *You're Manny, not Remy, just remember that.*

But he thought about Gregory's Sony Vita. Manny was a thief just like Remy. And he had been done ill by, and done ill to others, lying and making Tia Licha feel terrible. *And you can do things like jump and climb like a ninja, that comes from Remy.* Maybe Manny's bad things were combining with Remy's bad things... *No,* he told himself firmly. There was a big difference between jumping and climbing skills and wanting to eat people with your nasty pointy teeth.

Adriana called softly, "Come on, Remy!" He hurried to catch up with her.

Finally they reached the place that was apparently their home, a couple of rooms in a big, tumbledown tavern. The tavern was two stories tall, with a steep pitched roof, built around a courtyard for horses and carriages, though there weren't many in residence now. Most of it seemed divided into rooms for long-term occupants, like an old hotel turned into apartments. The main building across the court was lit up and noisy, with singing, occasional crashing noises, and some very scary drunks staggering out of it. Manny was glad that his and Adriana's place was at the far opposite end, reached by a small door in the stone wall just inside the gate to the courtyard.

They had two small rooms, the first with a rickety table and chairs, and the second with a couple of low beds piled with mismatched blankets. It looked pretty bad, but it wasn't dirty, and it didn't smell. Adriana bolted the door behind them, then went to a battered cupboard, saying, "We'll eat, then we'll go see Morrigan and give her tonight's tribute." In a lower voice, she added, "And won't I be glad to get that over with!"

"Okay." Manny's stomach grumbled and cramped, and he remembered how long it had been since he had eaten. The food Adriana piled onto the table was simple, just crusty brown bread, apples, and a hunk of cheese that he was relieved to discover tasted much better than it smelled. Using a belt knife Adriana handed him, Manny made a big cheese and sliced apple sandwich for each of them and sat down to eat.

Chewing, Manny looked up to see Adriana watching him with a bemused expression. She had taken apart her sandwich to eat the pieces individually. He swallowed and said, "What?"

She lifted a brow. "I've never seen you eat like that."

"Really?" He chomped into the sandwich again and said around a mouthful, "I don't usually get hungry?"

Adriana set down her cup with a thump. "Remy, just how bad is your memory?"

"Uh..." Manny picked up his own cup and took a drink to wash the last of the bread down. It wasn't water, and he just managed to swallow before he had to cough. He coughed again and told Adriana, "That's wine!"

"Of course it's wine! What's wrong with you?" Adriana sat back, staring at him in worry. "Oh, Remy. That must have been some knock on the head. I should take you to an apothecary..." She tapped her fingers on the table, distracted. "If I can find an honest one willing to look at you in your current state. And if I can, he's unlikely to open his shop to us at this hour. Not unless I pay for the privilege." She pulled Heinze's money pouch out of her jacket and weighed it thoughtfully. "I've barely enough for the tribute for both of us as it is."

Manny slumped at the table and miserably ate another piece of cheese. He wasn't doing very well at pretending to be this Remy character. He couldn't even get through a normal meal without making all kinds of mistakes; how was he going to get through the next day of Adriana's complicated life?

Suddenly he just didn't want to lie anymore, not to this woman who was so much like his mother, not to the only person who had been really nice to him since he fell into this crazy place. "Adriana," he said slowly. "This is going to sound strange... But I'm not really Remy."

Adriana looked up from the money pouch. Brow furrowed with worry, she said, "Just try not to think about it right now. I'll find help—"

"No, really, no, I lied about falling," Manny said urgently. In a rush, before he changed his mind, he said, "I didn't hit my head, but I didn't know how to tell you... I'm not an elf at all, I'm just a kid. My name is Manny Boreaux, and I'm from Austin. That's in America," he added, as it seemed unlikely that she would have heard of it before. "I got here by magic, or something, I don't know."

Adriana pressed her lips together, angry, and said,

"So this is a game, a bad joke on me. I told you, Remy, I've no time for that!" She swore under her breath, frustrated. "I suppose it's the goblin coming through, changing your nature, making you do these things—"

"I'm not lying!" Manny shouted. He had started to pride himself on being such a good liar, on fooling his teachers, the principal, Tia Licha, Beto — well, maybe not Beto — and now here he was, unable to convince someone he was telling the truth, when it was really important. "I swear, I'll swear on anything, I'm telling the truth. There was a coin in an old book, it was really weird and glowing, and I tossed it in the air and it was like I went with it, and I came down here."

Adriana was staring at him in shock. "Gods above. There is something wrong with you." She squeezed his hand. "It will be all right, do you understand? I'll think of a way to take care of everything."

Manny just nodded. She didn't believe his crazy story, obviously, but maybe she had just gone back to believing that he had had a bad knock on the head. But it was hard to resist the lure of the words "everything will be all right."

Adriana pushed her chair back and stood, still watching him with concern. "Remy, I have to take the tribute to Morrigan, I can't put it off any longer. You stay here; I can say you're injured. That would be true, she'll sense that. She would accept that excuse."

Though Adriana was trying to seem confident, Manny got the feeling that his staying behind wasn't exactly a good idea. And all it sounded like they had to do was go to this Morrigan person and hand over some money. "No, it's okay." He got to his feet. "I'll go with you. You shouldn't go out alone in the dark, anyway."

Adriana said, "Remy, whatever has happened to you, you're in no condition to face Morrigan. If she sees you in this confused state... there's no telling what she might do."

"I'm not confused," Manny insisted. "I'll keep quiet,

I promise. Please don't leave me here alone. I don't think I could take it right now." That wasn't quite true, but he really wanted to stay with Adriana. What if something happened to her and she never came back?

Adriana paced a few times, biting her thumbnail and muttering to herself. Manny couldn't help but smile. His mom used to do the same thing when she was really worried about something.

Adriana stopped pacing. "Very well." She knelt in front of him and squeezed his shoulders. "But you've got to promise you won't say a word, not a word." Manny nodded, hugged her tightly, and wished with all his heart that this was really his mom.

Adriana led him away from the tavern, through the twisting alleys and narrow winding streets. They passed a looming stone building with lots of candlelit windows, and torches out in front of the wide doorway to welcome visitors. As they hurried past it Manny could hear snatches of music and laughter. The music sounded vaguely like some he had heard from the folk and bluegrass musicians at music festivals, as if it was played on old-timey instruments. *It probably is,* he reminded himself. *Very old timey.*

They reached an area where the buildings were mostly wood and dingy white plaster, where there were fewer people out and not so many lit windows. Manny could smell foul stagnant water and dead fish. Finally they came out of a narrow street onto a walkway that ran along the river's bank, the water a dark expanse glittering under the moonlight. They were heading toward a big stone bridge, lit with torches, going across to a place with stone towers and turrets. Manny saw shapes crossing it, people on foot and some on horseback, and a wagon or two. He thought that was their destination, but Adriana turned off before the bridge, climbing down a slippery set of uneven stairs until they were even closer to the water.

They made their way along a stone wall, their feet slipping in the wet grass and cold mud, until they were deep into the shadows under the bridge. Adriana found a nearly invisible opening in the crumbling rock and dirt beside one of the arched supports, and slipped through it. Manny, who was beginning to wonder if this was such a great idea after all, stubbed his toes on the rocks as he hurried to keep up with her.

The tunnel was dark, slimy, and smelled of dead things and pee, and it made Manny's skin itch. What little light there was from outside faded rapidly. Firelight glowed from some point ahead, and as they drew closer, Manny saw it was a smoky torch set into a rusty bracket. Adriana stopped beside it and crouched down to poke around in a pile of what Manny would have assumed was just garbage. She stood again, holding a piece of wood the size of a bat with something black on the end of it. She held it to the torch, and after a moment the black stuff lit up and they had a torch of their own.

Oh, so that's how that works, Manny thought, following her again. He had always wondered why the fire didn't burn all the way down to your hand.

The light made it easier to make their way down the tunnel, but seeing what was in there didn't do good things for Manny's stomach. The air was cold and damp, and the rocky walls were wet and sticky. He wished he wasn't barefoot. In fact, he wished he was wearing galoshes, or maybe a spacesuit.

After what seemed a long distance, the tunnel ran into a bigger tunnel, not quite so cave-like, with rounded smooth stone-lined walls. There was a channel down the middle of it, filled with rushing water that smelled even worse than anything else had so far.

I bet that's the sewer, Manny thought. He didn't want to ask any questions, because Adriana looked worried. But it was what Manny had always imagined a sewer would look like. They went along the walkway next to it, then crossed a narrow bridge over to the other side. A little way down there was a rough hole in the wall, and they went through that into another dirty cave-like passage.

Manny's feet were hurting from the rough rock, and he was trying hard not to ask how much longer this was going to take. Finally he couldn't stand it a moment more. "Adriana, are we almost there?"

"Remy, you know—" she started to say impatiently, then stopped. "Or maybe you don't. Yes, we're almost—"

A big shape suddenly lurched out of the darkness and loomed over them. Adriana jerked backward with a startled cry, nearly dropping the torch, and Manny froze in horror. It was a monster, with green wart-ridden skin, giant clawed hands, and a wide, gaping mouth full of horrid teeth. The name popped into Manny's head. *Oh my God! It's a troll!*

The troll's piggish red eyes glowed like embers. Then it roared, flashing its sharp, yellow-stained tusks and a slimy, purple tongue and lunged for them.

CHAPTER 9

A huge troll charging at him, claws clutching and slavering jaws snapping, should have frozen Manny in terror. But once again his otherworld instincts took over, so instead of being glued to the spot, he dove straight at the troll.

He had just enough time for the panicked thought *What the hell am I doing?* before he tucked and rolled underneath the monster. Manny came to his feet behind the creature, crouched low and ready to spring away again.

The troll spun around, its face a terrible grimace. And then it did something Manny didn't expect.

"Oi! Ya slippery sewer rat." Its voice was a deep rusty growl that hurt Manny's ears, like Beto's old Harley Davidson motorcycle. "Stay still so I can eat ya!"

Manny blinked in surprise. *It can talk!* And its breath smelled about as bad as the motorcycle's exhaust. Worse, actually. It made another grab for him and Manny leapt clear.

"Blast ya!" snarled the troll, swinging around to face him. Then Adriana appeared in front of the creature, still gripping her torch. She hit it hard across the face, sending a shower of sparks into the air.

"Ow! That bloody hurt!" The troll reared up to its full height, which Manny guessed to be around seven feet, and rubbed its squat nose with a huge warty hand.

"Back off, Lothair!" Adriana brandished the torch like a club. "I don't have time for your stupid games!"

Manny gaped at Adriana. *She knows this thing?*

Lothair glared, and Manny thought he would charge again, but he bellowed out a guffaw instead. "Easy, darlin'." He chuckled in a particularly nasty tone. "Don't go gettin' yourself all in a tizzy. I wasn't gonna harm the little blighter." He turned and winked a red glowing eye at Manny. "After all, he'll be one of us soon. Won't ya, runt?"

Oh no I won't, Manny thought. He'd almost rather be eaten.

Adriana lowered her torch but kept her gaze on the troll. "All your roaring is going to bring the city watch down here. Wouldn't that make Morrigan happy."

"Oh, I ain't the one's been drawing attention to myself," replied Lothair.

Adriana tensed. "I don't know what you're talking about."

The troll eyed her coldly. "No, I 'spose you don't." He turned to Manny. "You're unusually quiet, runt. What's wrong? Fae cat got your forked little tongue?"

Manny darted to Adriana's side. "Stop calling me runt!" Then he froze, aghast. *Who said that? Oh, it was me.* He hadn't meant to say anything, especially not to a seven foot monster. His mouth was leading a life of its own.

Lothair seemed less surprised but still took a few menacing steps forward, drawing his lips back from his impressive tusks. "What was that, runt? Did you just give me an order?"

Adriana raised her torch again. "I'm warning you, Lothair!"

"Now, now," said the troll, raising his hands in mock fear. "Is it my fault I'm just a tad on the intimidatin' side?"

"The most intimidating thing about you is your smell," said Adriana, wrinkling her nose. "And given that we're in a sewer, that's saying a lot."

Lothair sniffed his armpits, then waggled his eyebrows. "Perhaps you should give me a reason to wash more often."

"How about as a kindness to your fleas," offered Adriana.

"It touches my heart to hear you worry so about my fleas," Lothair said.

"I feel sorry for the poor little things," said Adriana, her voice dry.

"They ain't little." The troll snorted then turned and lumbered down the dark tunnel. "Hurry up, she's waiting," he called over his shoulder.

Unclenching his aching fists, Manny sighed and leaned against Adriana. She cupped his chin and studied his expression. "Are you all right?" she whispered.

Manny managed a nod and a smile. "I'm glad I'd forgotten about him."

That drew a wry chuckle from Adriana. "See? Perhaps that bump wasn't entirely a bad thing. I wish I could forget that stinking monster. But you'll remember our agreement, won't you? Not a word when we see Morrigan."

"My lips are sealed." Manny mimed closing an imaginary zipper on his mouth.

Adriana tapped his nose, then followed the troll down the tunnel. Manny followed close on her heels.

Lothair took them through a series of twisting tunnels, all of them leading farther down. The torchlight caught crumbled remnants of walls and strange formations of rock and even stalactites, all of it dripping with oily moisture. It was like Inner Space Cavern, where Manny's parents had taken him once, only it was more scary than pretty.

The passage widened out and the ceiling vanished,

as if they had walked into a much bigger space. Manny saw it was blocked ahead, and sneaked a wary look at Adriana, wondering if Lothair was leading them into a trap. She didn't seem more worried than before, though.

As they got closer, the torchlight revealed that the obstruction ahead was a gate. A big wooden one, with the crumbling remnants of small stone towers to either side and the face of something dragon-like carved into the rock above it. Lothair pushed on one side and the heavy wooden door swung silently open.

Adriana followed him through, and Manny trailed after her. He wasn't sure he wanted to see what was coming next.

On the other side of the gate was a huge chamber, most of it cloaked in darkness. The remains of a wide set of stairs spiraled around the outer wall, leading down to a space that looked as if it had once been the great hall of a castle. Manny thought he could see a throne at one end. Torches threw leaping orange shadows on broken pillars and statues lining the stairway, their shapes so crumbling and stained with mold it was hard to see if they had been images of humans or Sidhe.

"What is this place?" Manny whispered to Adriana. He remembered his promise, but they hadn't reached this Morrigan person yet.

She whispered back, "This is part of the Undercity, an ancient Fae city that Lutetia was built on top of, hundreds of years ago. It's mostly abandoned now, although it's said that a few Fae creatures still live in the lowest levels." She squeezed his shoulder. "No more talking now."

As they followed Lothair down the stairs, Manny saw a fire sputtered in the center of the vast chamber, with a haunch of meat suspended on a spit over the flames. The firelight cast shadows on a raised dais just beyond it. The throne Manny had seen stood there, a stone chair covered in furs.

Several sinister looking Sidhe squatted around the fire, tossing dice, drinking, or fighting over scraps of food. Manny spotted a couple of fauns like Rabican, only these were larger and looked much more feral. Several short, twisted, black-skinned creatures shared a large mug of some sort of foul-smelling drink. But most disturbing of all were a trio of pale, willowy, snaggletoothed monsters that wore dirty red berets, creatures that Manny thought could only have been goblins. They stopped their dice game to glare at him as he crossed the chamber with Adriana, their hungry, predatory eyes glittering in the firelight.

As they reached the fire, Lothair grabbed the spit, the flesh of his hand sizzling where he gripped the blistering hot skewer. He tore chunks of flesh off the haunch, chewing noisily, the hot juices running down his horned chin.

"Such carelessness," said a velvety voice from the darkness. "Caught picking someone's pocket, chased by the city watch, consorting with the King's Chevaliers. The Hands of Shadow cannot afford such attention."

At the sound of that voice, Manny shivered as a bone-chilling cold blossomed in his chest. He managed a glance up at the ceiling. A dark shape hung in the murky top of the chamber. Glowing emerald eyes blinked to life in the gloom as the ominous shape spread inky wings and dropped.

A hideous bat-winged Sidhe hag alighted on the dais in front of the throne. She locked a baleful gaze on Manny, with a smile so wide it seemed to split her long, smooth face in half. Manny could not look away, although he desperately wanted to. The hag wrapped her wings about herself like a tattered cloak and seated herself gracefully in the chair.

Adriana stepped in front of Manny, breaking the hag's mesmerizing hold on him. "No harm was done,

Morrigan. I made sure of that."

Morrigan arched an eyebrow. "This time, perhaps."

"There won't be a next time." Adriana sounded calm, though Manny could hear the tension in her voice. "You have my word."

"You're quite correct," said Morrigan, scrutinizing Manny as if she were studying an interesting insect.

Adriana pulled Manny closer. "Morrigan, please, you don't have to—" Morrigan laughed, a high-pitched, chilling cackle that echoed throughout the chamber like breaking glass.

"Always so protective, my pet." Morrigan's voice was dry with amusement. "Your devotion is commendable. But we must keep our eyes on the prize. Soon, the Hands of Shadow will pass into legend, and I will finally get what is rightfully mine."

Sliding an arm around Manny's shoulders, Adriana smiled, as if trying to make it seem everything was okay. "Of that I have no doubt. So when do you bring me into this secret scheme of yours?"

Morrigan tut-tutted. "This is no ordinary job, my dear, it's the culmination of a life's work."

Adriana lifted her chin. "I thought I was your best burglar."

"Without a doubt, my sweet," Morrigan agreed easily, "you are a master of the craft. My finest pupil. And a human, at that."

"So you don't trust me?" Adriana cocked her hip, planting her fist on it. Manny was still pressed against her and could feel her heart pounding.

Morrigan's mouth split into another of her ghastly smiles. "That remains to be seen. This particular job will demand my personal attention. And you know I hate to be upstaged. If I bring you in, it must be for a good reason. And I must have your complete confidence."

"Does this heist have anything to do with the secret meeting at Gassot's?" asked Adriana.

The hag's eyes widened and she darted a scowl at Lothair. The troll shook his head vigorously. "No, no! I didn't say nothing to her! I swear!"

"He didn't," agreed Adriana. "I'm afraid you're becoming predictable, Morrigan."

"I prefer to see it as cleverness on your part, my pet." Morrigan flexed her claws. "Prominent figures lurk in the shadows on this job. Everything must be perfect."

"Who did you cut a deal with now?" Adriana asked a little warily. "The chief magistrate?"

Morrigan chuckled. "That's what I like about you, my delicate blossom, always thinking big. But it was ever my intention to share. After all, when have I not taken care of my beloved children?" She cocked her head at the Sidhe thieves, raising her brows. The ragtag group cheered her, lifting their dirty cups in a toast.

The hag's gaze went to Manny. "Ah, but as all of you well know, I can't abide when my love is not reciprocated. Few things vex me so." She uncurled a long, bony finger and wagged it at Manny, beckoning him forward. "Come give Auntie Morrigan her due."

Adriana slipped a pouch from her vest and began to step forward, "I've got our tribute—" She stopped when Morrigan held up a hand.

"Give it to the boy," insisted Morrigan, her gaze locked on Manny. "I want him to present the tribute, by way of apology for the day's events."

Adriana hesitated, then slowly handed the pouch to Manny. "Go ahead, Remy."

Lothair suddenly tossed the spit aside and lumbered over to stand behind Adriana, his piggish eyes gleaming hungrily.

Manny could sense more than see Adriana's body tensing again. He swallowed hard and took the pouch, uncertain what to do.

"Everything will be fine," Adriana said, but her

voice was tight. "Just give Morrigan the pouch and come back to me."

Manny slowly walked toward the dais, keeping his eyes down, not daring to look at Morrigan's face. He stretched out his arm to offer the pouch, his heart thundering in his ears. The distant voice in his head yelled, *Don't go near her! Don't let her touch you!* Manny had to fight the urge to drop the pouch and bolt.

With an explosive flutter of leathery wings, Morrigan lunged forward, caught Manny's wrist, and snatched the pouch from his hand. He cried out and tried to pull away, but the hag's grip was like iron. Adriana started forward but Lothair grabbed her arms, holding her back.

Morrigan yanked Manny effortlessly onto the dais, looming over him. "You showed such promise, lad," she hissed. "Soon you would have joined the fold. But now you endanger us all and put my careful plans at risk. This is how you repay me for taking you in and raising you as a son?"

"I'm sorry! I'm sorry!" Manny stammered, leaning as far away from the hag as he could. Her teeth were pearly white and as smooth and sharp as knives. Her eyes shone like ghostly green will-o-wisps. But despite all of that, there was something inexplicably attractive about Morrigan's features, as if once, long ago, she had possessed the face of an angel. It made Manny want to look at her, even though she terrified him.

The hag sniffed at him, as if trying to identify spoiled meat. "What has happened to you, dear boy?" she whispered, her gaze searching Manny's face.

"Morrigan!" snapped Adriana. "Can't you see he's sorry? He can make this up to you!"

The hag held Manny at arm's length. "I think not, my sweet. He's a liability now, nothing more."

"No!" cried Adriana, struggling in Lothair's grip. "No, he's not! He's still useful! Give me a chance to prove it to you!"

"And how exactly will you do that?" asked Morrigan, turning to look at Adriana. She motioned for Lothair to release her. Adriana ran to the base of the dais.

"The Dupre Estate," said Adriana, almost breathless. "I've scouted the hotel and discovered a way in. But I need Remy. I need his size and his stealth. I'll take him with me tonight and we can do the job. The haul will be worth hundreds of thousands of livres, Morrigan. And it'll all be yours. What do you say? Certainly a prize like that can buy a worthless pickpocket one night's reprieve? And if he doesn't prove useful, I'll take care of the problem myself. Do we have a deal?"

Morrigan studied Adriana's face for several tense moments, then dropped Manny. He landed on his feet and scrambled to Adriana's side.

The hag weighed the pouch in her hand before it disappeared into the dark folds of her wings. She smiled, her voice once again a purr. "Why not? I am in a magnanimous mood, after all. But this prize had better be everything you claim."

"It will be, you have my word," said Adriana. "You won't be disappointed."

Manny looked up at Adriana but she would not meet his gaze. She took his hand and pulled him toward the stairs, the Sidhe thieves sneering and snarling as she passed. They reached the steps and climbed as rapidly as they could toward the gateway that led out to the tunnel. Stumbling on the rough stone, Manny's skin felt hot and his stomach wanted to turn.

Adriana said she'd take care of the problem if I didn't prove useful. That couldn't mean what it sounded like it meant. That his only friend in this strange new world had just promised a Sidhe hag that she would kill him if he failed to help her break into someone's house.

CHAPTER 10

They made their way back through the dark streets to the rooms off the tavern courtyard. The pokey little place didn't feel like a homey refuge anymore; it felt like a trap. Manny dropped into a chair, warily watching as Adriana got the lamp lit and then paced back and forth. She looked frustrated and angry. He said, "Are you going to kill me?"

"What?" She halted, staring at him. "Remy, of course not! I had to tell Morrigan that to buy us time."

Manny wasn't sure he believed her. He said, stubbornly, "I'm not Remy. I told you, my name is Manny, I'm not from here, and I'm not the one she wants to kill. I didn't do any of the things she said, that was him."

Adriana turned away, pushing her hair back. "Remy, I have to think, there's no time for this nonsense."

"It's not nonsense!" Manny stood. "I'm not lying or crazy or anything else. Look, if you don't want to kill me, then help me. Help me look for a way to get out of here and go home."

Adriana snapped, "Remy — Manny — whatever you want to call yourself, be quiet so I can think! Or we'll both be dead."

Fuming, Manny folded his arms and stomped away, back into the little bedroom. He was a great liar; why couldn't he be as convincing when he was telling the truth? Maybe being such a good liar had somehow wrecked his ability to tell the truth. *That would be just my luck.*

For a moment, Manny was so homesick he wanted to die. He could see his room so vividly it was like he could reach out and touch the wall. Feel himself lying in his own bed, practically smell the faint clean scent of the sheets. He blinked and it was gone. *I want to go home*, he thought miserably. He wondered what time it was there, if Licha and Beto were still up watching TV in the living room or if they had gone to bed.

Then Manny felt a prickle on his neck, like something was staring at him. He looked worriedly around, then spotted a cat perched on a shelf, watching him intently. He guessed it had snuck in from outside. There were a lot of chinks and cracks in the walls, letting in cold air. And it wasn't exactly a normal cat, either. It had feathery silver fur that sparkled in the candlelight, and its eyes were an oddly bright crystalline blue. It had spikes of hair standing out from its ears that glittered like real silver. *It's a faerie cat, I bet,* Manny thought, distracted for a moment from his troubles.

"Hey, who do you belong to?" he asked it softly. It twitched an ear at him. Making clucking and kissing noises that were usually effective in getting cats to come and be petted, Manny stepped closer. He held out his hand and the cat sniffed it cautiously. Then it suddenly pulled back, yowling as if mortally offended. Manny flinched, startled, and jerked his hand back as the cat took a swipe at him.

It jumped from the shelf up to one of the ceiling beams, then wound its way out through a gap in the wall.

Feeling rejected, Manny turned around. Adriana stood in the doorway, staring at him. He shrugged, flustered. "Guess it's not a pet cat."

She said, "It's your pet cat. It lives here at the tavern and it's always been attached to you. It sleeps with you sometimes."

Manny grimaced. "Remy, not me."

Adriana stepped slowly forward, her brow furrowed, regarding him as intently as the cat had. She said, "Could it be true? This incredible story of yours?"

"Of course it's true." Manny waved his hands helplessly. "Why would Remy make up this stuff? It's not stopping you or Morrigan from wanting to kill him!"

"Lady of the Light," she muttered. "If this is true, then where's Remy? Is he dead?"

"I don't know!" Manny glared, then the obvious answer occurred to him. "He's probably in my body, or something. Where else would he be?" *Yeah, he probably is in my body.*

Manny had wondered if his body was just lying there like a dead person, but this made more sense. Or as much sense as anything did. *If he found his way home, I hope he's not messing with my stuff.* He hoped Remy didn't get Tia Licha and Beto in trouble by stealing everything that wasn't nailed down. What if Remy got Manny's body arrested and sent to juvenile detention? That would be about all Manny needed. And if Remy didn't tell Licha and Beto the truth, they would think Manny was a criminal.

Adriana lunged forward to grab Manny's arm and shake him. "Tell me where he is! What are you, a Fae sorcerer?"

"No!" Manny struggled; her grip on his arm was painfully strong. For an instant she didn't look like his mom at all; she was a stranger, her face thinner, her features harsh. He wrenched away and stumbled backward. "I don't know where he is! And I told you who I am! I don't know how to make you believe me. Why would anybody want to be Remy? He's a thief and a liar and that freaky monster Morrigan wants to kill him." His throat went tight, all the fear and anger and frustration welling up, and he had to force the words out. "Why would anybody want that?"

Adriana stood there, watching him as he took a sharp breath and wiped a hand across his nose. He stared hard at her, but the moment had passed and her face was the same as his mother's, again. Mostly. Maybe her features were a little too sharp, like his mother's would have looked if her life had been much harder. She shook her head finally. "It would certainly explain everything, wouldn't it? Your memory, the strange way you've been behaving, the cat. But why? How did this happen?"

Sudden hope made Manny's heart pound. If she believed him... It wouldn't make everything better, but it would be one less battle to fight. "It was the magic, the coin in the book, like I told you. It must have been just an accident. I mean..." He shrugged helplessly. "We don't have magic where I come from, or faeries, or monsters or sorcerers. We have stories about them, but they aren't real. At least I thought they weren't real. Whatever made it happen, it must have been something from this world."

Adriana frowned, but this time she looked more thoughtful than angry. "And you don't know where Remy is?"

"No. I guess he's in my body. Otherwise I'm in a coma, and maybe he's in somebody else's body. Though then where would the person whose body he's in—"

Adriana held up a hand. "Enough. If this is true—"

"It is true!"

"Then the only way to help him is to help you. Which means speaking to someone learned in magic. And unfortunately, I don't know anyone like that I can approach." She grimaced. "Except Morrigan."

"That would be a bad idea," Manny agreed.

She let her breath out in resignation. "And if it is just some spell-caused delusion, then it doesn't change the fact that we have to get away from Morrigan."

Manny nodded in relief. "Getting away from her sounds good to me."

"My plan was for us to take ship to Hispania, where we can get help from my family. But I can't afford passage yet, so we'll have to go through with the burglary tonight." Adriana looked sharply at Manny. "I'll need your help, Re— Manny. Can you do that?"

He started to say yes, then something occurred to him. It would be stealing, even though stealing in a magical world felt less real than stealing from bullies like Gregory. "If I do, will it make me turn into a goblin faster?"

Adriana looked down at him, and her expression was sad and worried. It made her look even more like his mother than before. "I don't know. It might. But perhaps not enough to make a difference before we leave here."

He was glad she hadn't lied, or tried to sugar-coat it. "Okay. It's better than getting killed, I guess, and it's not like we have a choice."

With a wry smile, she said, "True enough."

Adriana loaded a small bag with some tools, including a big coil of dark-colored rope, and they set out into the night.

It was even quieter than it had been earlier on the way to Morrigan's lair. They were heading into a rich neighborhood and everybody seemed to be asleep, tucked behind the solid stone walls of the big houses.

They reached the house, visible only as a huge looming bulk, the whitewashed stone gleaming faintly in the starlight, the windows all dark. They crept through a back courtyard with a well, between the house and a smaller two-story building that smelled strongly of horse. Manny didn't see any windows in the ground floor of the house, and the two doorways that faced this courtyard had heavy wooden doors.

Adriana stopped, and pointed up to the third floor. In an almost voiceless whisper, she said, "There, you see it?"

Luckily Manny had elf eyes that could see in the dark, and he saw the fourth window from the corner. It was a small one barely wider than his shoulders, with a broken pane at the bottom. He nodded, not trusting himself to speak. Adriana had warned him that the servants who took care of the horses would be sleeping nearby in the stables, and any noise at all might wake them.

She gave him a little push to get him started, and Manny went to the wall of the house, careful to step quietly on the paved ground. He ran his hands across the wall and was relieved that Adriana had been right: the stone was old and pitted, with gaps in the mortar between the blocks that made good handholds for strong little elf fingers.

He took a deep breath, gripped the stone, and started to climb. He fumbled a little and slipped once, but the window was getting rapidly closer. In his own body, Manny could never have done this, but as Remy, it was easy. If he could do this, he could do anything. It was like being in a Spiderman comic. Except Spiderman had still gotten beaten up and nearly killed a lot. Manny gritted his teeth and reminded himself not to get too confident.

He reached the wide wooden sill, pulled himself up onto it, and clung tightly. He put his ear to the broken pane and listened, but he couldn't hear any snoring or movement. He carefully reached through, found the metal latch, and pushed it. The window swung back into the room with a faint squeak.

Manny climbed inside the pitch dark room, feeling cautiously to make sure he didn't knock anything over.

There was a wooden floor underfoot, that was about all he could tell at first. The room felt empty and smelled of dust, and it wasn't much warmer here than it was outside. He pushed the window shut and locked it again.

His eyes adjusted, and he saw he was in a narrow stairwell, a little light falling from the landing above where there must be another window. *Okay, this is good,* Manny thought. The stairwell was narrow and plain, with no carpet and bare plaster walls. Adriana had said the window must lead to a corridor or stairwell used only by the servants, since it was so small and no one had bothered to fix it yet.

Following Adriana's directions, Manny went down to the second floor landing, stepping softly to keep the boards from creaking. There he opened the door just enough to peek out. The corridor beyond was dark, too, but he could see the shapes of tables against the walls, upholstered chairs, big paintings, unlit candelabra, vases with flowers, and the glitter on silver and glass. He stepped out, shutting the door behind him, feeling the thick softness of a runner carpet under his feet. Manny slunk down the corridor.

He made his way toward the far side of the house, passing through a confusing maze of dark corridors and big shadowy sitting rooms filled with furniture, his nerves so tense he felt like he was made out of high tension wire. The place was so quiet, so still. He made himself pretend this was just an empty building, that there weren't people sleeping on the floors above.

He reached a room at the end of the house that smelled flowery and held dozens of vases and containers filled with plants and even small trees; this had to be the right spot. He found the outside wall, and two double wooden doors. He fumbled for a lock and found a bar, and lifted it away. Easing the door open and wincing at the creak, he found a second door made of glass with tiny diamond-shaped panes. He got it open, and stepped out onto a narrow balcony. He looked over the rail down into an empty side courtyard, filled with the dark shapes of trees and bushes and the sound of a trickling fountain.

Then a rope flew up out of the shadows, the padded weight on the end catching on the railing. Letting his breath out in relief, Manny grabbed it and quickly tied it off. A moment later Adriana climbed rapidly up hand over hand and swung herself over the rail. Manny helped her pull the rope up; they left it coiled on the balcony but still tied to the railing.

They slipped back inside, and Adriana handed Manny a big bag. Following her out of the garden room, he fished around inside it but it was empty. He belatedly realized it was for carrying the stuff they stole.

Adriana led the way, not back the way Manny had come, but around toward the front of the house. On the way, she had explained that the richest objects would be in what she had called the public rooms, where the people who lived here gave parties and balls and big dinners. It made sense to Manny.

They passed through a series of cold dark rooms with high ceilings. Light from the windows gleamed off silver and crystal and finely polished furniture. Manny held the bag for Adriana while she moved swiftly through, scooping up heavy silver candlesticks, fruit bowls, goblets, plates, a couple of small boxes studded with what felt like jewels, and a little miniature painting with an elaborate metal frame. It felt a little creepy and disturbing, like stealing from a museum. Manny's parents had always taught him that museums were sacred territory — no touching, just looking. He reminded himself these were rich people, that they could replace it all, though oddly that didn't help much. It still felt uncomfortably wrong.

But maybe that was a good thing. Maybe it meant this wasn't helping turn Manny into a goblin.

The bag was getting heavy and Manny thought they must surely have enough by now. He tugged on Adriana's sleeve, and whispered, "Let's go."

She nodded, then hesitated. They had paused in an archway opening into another big room. It lay towards the center of the house, with no windows, and looked like just a dark cave. But there was just enough light to see a big table holding a statue about four feet high. Manny couldn't make out much detail in the dimness. It looked like an animal, something sinuous, like a snake or a dragon, and even in the dark it gleamed with jewels. "Just a few of those gems, and then we'll go," Adriana whispered back. She drew a slim knife from her belt and stepped toward it.

Watching her, Manny suddenly had a bad feeling, and it wasn't just about the stealing. He didn't know what it was: the half-hidden shape of the statue, something about the way the light gleamed enticingly off the jewels even in a windowless unlit room. "Adriana," he whispered urgently. "Wait, something's wrong—"

She stopped, but she had already put the tip of her knife to one of the jewels.

A low hiss echoed through the room. Adriana froze, then backed away slowly as the statue started to move.

CHAPTER 11

Light glittered along the metal curves as the statue flowed sinuously down off the table. It landed on the wooden floor with a faint metallic click of claws. Manny clutched the bag, heart pounding, riveted to the spot. A foul odor drifted out of the room, a smell like matches striking, like a recently repaved street, sulfur and tar and something sharp like acid. The light around the creature brightened, as if its scales glowed. As it turned toward them he saw it was like a little dragon, with wings and a long reptilian tail, except it had feathers, and there was something weirdly birdlike about its legs and head.

Still backing away, Adriana bumped into Manny, reaching back to grip his arm.

The creature stalked toward the doorway on two legs with clawed feet, cocking its head to eye them in a predatory, bird-like way. Her voice low and tense, Adriana said, "When it draws breath, run."

When it draws breath...? Manny wondered, but then the creature's chest expanded as it whooshed in air. Adriana snapped, "Run!" and pushed him down the corridor.

Manny stumbled, glancing back to see Adriana ducking away from a sparkling cloud that smelled so bad his stomach nearly turned. His lungs ached just from the scent of it. Covering her mouth, Adriana staggered after him, waving him on.

Manny ran, looking back to make sure she was following. She was, and the monster was following her, loping down the corridor after them.

Clutching the heavy bag to his chest, Manny dodged through the next doorway, hoping he remembered the path back through the darkened rooms to the balcony door. The house was just a big square block, so he knew which direction it was in, but if he took the wrong turn and ended up running into a dead end... *It'll be a dead end for real,* he thought desperately.

Manny heard a whoosh sound behind him a moment before Adriana shouted, "Manny, down!"

He ducked and a stream of the poison gas shot right over his head, blocked the doorway he had been about to plunge through, and hung in a big sparkling cloud. Running through it would be a bad idea. He looked back, saw Adriana crouched behind him. The monster was about twenty feet away, braced to leap after them. At least it couldn't seem to run and breathe poison gas at the same time.

Manny gasped, "This way," and grabbed Adriana's hand as he pushed to his feet. He took the doorway opposite to the blocked one, heading around the front of the house.

They ran flat out through the big rooms, the creature's claws clacking against the polished wooden floor behind them. Manny heard thumping and yelling upstairs; the whole house must realize they were here now.

He knew that for sure a moment later as they bolted past the landing of the main grand staircase. Light glowed down it from candles and lamps, and someone yelled, "There they are! After them!"

Just run, Manny told himself. They barreled through two sitting rooms, Adriana pausing to pull a tall cabinet down behind them to block their pursuers' path. But Manny heard footsteps pounding from the other direction and figured someone was coming from the servants' stairway too.

He dodged through a passage and then into the garden room, relieved to be so close to the way out. He reached the doorway, fumbling at the catch, and flung the wooden shutters open. Adriana caught up with him a moment later, and together they dragged the glass doors open. Colder air streamed into the room, and safety was so close Manny could taste it. He lifted the bag of loot to pitch it over the balcony railing.

An explosion rang out behind them as the bag ripped out of Manny's hands, scattering its contents across the floor of the balcony. He staggered, saw a man standing in the garden room doorway holding a smoking musket, framed by the dim starlight from the open doors.

Adriana grabbed Manny's arm, catapulting them both forward over the rail of the balcony. As they jerked to an abrupt halt, he realized she had grabbed the rope first. Manny gasped and caught the rope too, helping her support their weight. Together they half-slid, half-fell to the ground, tumbling down to the paved court.

Shouting from the back of the house told Manny the men sleeping in the stables had been alerted. "Come on!" Adriana said, shoving to her feet. As Manny leapt up, his foot knocked against something metal. He snatched it up a cup from the torn bag of loot. Then a noise from overhead made him look up at the balcony.

The silver creature was up there, coiled around the railing, its narrow bird head turned to glare down at him with one jeweled eye. Then it tilted its head back and its chest expanded as it took a deep breath. Manny bolted after Adriana.

Musket shots ricocheted all around them, shattered paving stones. They banged through the courtyard's gate and ran down the street.

They made their way back to the tavern on the darkest, most quiet alleys and streets. Every nerve alert and jumping, Manny listened hard for sounds of pursuit, and flinched at every noise. When they were far enough away from the house to have a little breathing space, he asked Adriana, "What was that thing?"

"You didn't recognize—" She frowned, then said, "That's right, I keep forgetting you really don't know. It was a cockatrice, enspelled to look like a statue. And to trap fools like me. I'm sorry, I've made a ruin of our plan."

"No, it's not your fault," Manny said. "I knew something was funny about it; it gave me a weird feeling. I should have warned you faster." He had tucked the cup under his shirt, and the metal was cold against his skin. As they paused under a lit window, he pulled it out and studied the twining, delicate etchings that covered its shining silver surface, then showed it to Adriana. "You think this will be enough to get us to Hispania?"

"I don't know," she admitted, taking the cup from him. "I hope so."

Manny guessed it was good that she was being honest with him. Though at the moment, a comforting lie would have been nice.

They took a last turn down an alley that opened into the street where their tavern was. As they got within sight of the building, Adriana stopped abruptly, motioning Manny to stay back. He poked his head out to see around her.

At first the tavern looked normal, the courtyard lit by oil lamps, light still showing from the drinking rooms in the main building. It was more quiet than it had been before, but Manny figured it was pretty late at night, even for drunks and carousers. He whispered, "What's wrong?"

"The door to our rooms is open," she said softly. Manny looked and bit his lip. Now he could see it. She was right, the door was standing open against the dark wall. She said, "Wait here."

Adriana slipped across the street, and Manny lost sight of her as she ducked behind a wagon and a stack of barrels. He waited impatiently, staying back in the shadows. The rest of the wood and stone buildings along the street were quiet. He heard a dog bark somewhere, and a baby crying sleepily in the house next to the alley. Finally Adriana returned, easing back around the wagon and walking quickly across the street toward him.

"Our rooms have been searched," she said as she reached him. "From the smell, at least one of Morrigan's Redcaps is still inside, lying in wait for us. She must have got word already of our failure. We can't stay here tonight."

Manny nodded, but his heart sank as he remembered the goblins in Morrigan's chamber. Standing still this long had also given him a chance to realize how cold and tired he was. His feet felt like blocks of ice. This had been a very, very long day, and he felt like he had spent most of it with various people and monsters trying to kill him. "Where do we go?"

He had meant to sound brave, but a little of his despair must have crept into his voice, because Adriana squeezed his shoulder reassuringly. "It's all right, I know a place."

"Okay." As Manny followed her back down the alley, he told her, "I don't like stealing anymore."

She sighed. "I admit, neither do I."

The place Adriana led him to turned out to be in the cellar of an empty house that had been destroyed by fire years ago. It was dark, dank, mossy, and smelled funny. When Adriana dug some candles out of a hiding place near the door and got them lit, Manny saw it also had spiders in the corners. Big spiders. Maybe they were faerie spiders, because Manny didn't think there were spiders that big outside of Australia or South America. The only furniture was some broken ceramic jugs and empty barrels, singed and blackened by the long-ago fire. A passage in the wall led to a room with a collapsed ceiling, and a stairway up to the ruins of the house was blocked by rubble.

Adriana tossed her satchel on a pile of old blankets, and said, "It's not much, but it's served Remy and me well in the past. The rumor is that a powerful Fae sorcerer lived here and was killed in the fire; fear of his ghost keeps everyone away, human and Sidhe alike."

"Oh." Manny looked around uneasily. "So it's really not haunted?"

She hesitated just long enough to make him nervous. "No, no, it's not haunted."

Manny shook out the blankets to get rid of the beetles and dirt and dragged them into the center of the cellar, as far away from the spiders as possible. As he piled them up to make a softer if not very clean bed, Adriana went through their belongings. They didn't have much, just her burglar tools minus the rope. The only loot they had managed to hold onto was the silver cup. It wasn't studded with gems, but it was heavy and obviously the work of a very skilled craftsman. "It looks really expensive. Do you think it's worth a lot?" Manny asked her as she examined it.

"It won't buy regular passage on a skyship, that's for certain. But I might be able to negotiate for space in the cargo hold, or better yet, for berths as part of the crew."

"A skyship?" Manny liked the sound of that.

"Yes, a vessel that sails through the air," replied Adriana. "Don't they have things like that wherever you're from?"

"Actually, they do," said Manny, "but I didn't think you guys had them here." He wondered if leaving the city and going to Hispania would put him further away from finding a way home. He didn't know for certain that whatever had brought him here was somewhere in this city, but it was the assumption that made the most sense. And he really, really wanted to go home. It might be morning there now, and Tia Licha would be getting ready to go to work. She always made sure Manny got up on time, and stood over him until he at least ate a bowl of cereal. Sometimes Beto got up early and went to get breakfast tacos from the cafe a few blocks away.

Adriana tucked the cup away in the satchel. "I'll take this to Heinze in the morning and see how much I can get for it."

Manny sank down on the blankets, watching her expression carefully. He thought there was a good chance she was lying to make him feel better. "What if it isn't enough? Can we walk to Hispania?"

Adriana sighed and took a seat on the edge of the blankets. "We'd never make it. Morrigan's Redcaps are like hounds. They would track us. Why do you think we need a skyship? We have to get as far away from here as quickly as we can. Out on the open road or even on a slower sea-going vessel, we'd be an easy target. Morrigan's reach is very long."

"Oh." Manny bit his lip. Adriana looked weary, her face drawn. In the flickering candlelight, he could see the faint lines at the corner of her eyes, just like his mother had had. Except she wasn't his mother, any more than Etienne was his father. *Your parents aren't here. They're dead, back home. And you could be stuck here forever.*

The exhaustion of the very long, very strange day began to claim him and he yawned.

Adriana glanced at him. "Perhaps it's best if you get some rest."

He nodded and turned away from her, curling up on the blankets and squeezing his eyes shut. "Good night, Adriana," he murmured.

Adriana sat there in silence. Then she started to sing softly. It was a song Manny hadn't heard before, and he didn't recognize all the words but it seemed to be about a maiden and the moon. His mother had sung him to sleep when he was little, and it made him remember that vividly. Her tender touch, her breathy voice...

As he drifted off to sleep, the room grew blurry, dissolved, and transformed into his old bedroom in his parents' house. For a few precious heartbeats, he was back home, his mother near him, singing him to sleep. He was in a place where the terrible accident had never happened, where his life had not been turned into a painful mess, where his troubles were minor and easy to overcome.

Manny smiled as he fell asleep.

CHAPTER 12

The creature was stalking him.

Manny crept along the dark, mist-filled halls of his old school. Pale moonlight poured through the windows, gathering in ghostly pools on the floor. Manny slipped past them to hide in the shadows. He tried to be as quiet as possible, but he was afraid the creature could sense him. It was ravenous for his blood, yet it enjoyed the hunt and Manny's terror.

The mist clung to Manny's legs like webs, pulled at him, slowed him down. The creature's shadow scuttled along the walls, spidery legs like skeletal fingers tasting the air, scenting him.

Manny pressed himself against the wall beside a bank of lockers. His heart hammered in his ears. The cold mist chilled his bones and turned his sweat to ice.

Then he realized someone stood near him. Manny turned to stare at the dark figure. It was so close its shoulder touched Manny's. It was just a featureless dark shape, but Manny wasn't afraid of it. The figure leaned close to whisper.

"Don't panic," it said, and its voice was familiar. "It feeds on that. You can hide from it, trick it. It can't catch you if you use your head. Trust your instincts."

The words reassured Manny, made him bold. He looked away from the figure and scanned the halls. He could smell a heavy stench and hear the click of the creature's claws as it skittered along the linoleum.

His shadow companion whispered desperately, "You've got to keep moving. If it corners you, all will be lost. Go!"

Manny darted down the hall toward the gym. Again he stuck to the patches of darkness. He wasn't afraid of the shadows. He knew the creature hid there, but so could he. The darkness could protect him. He hurried to the gym's doors, his shadow companion right on his heels.

"That's it," it urged. "You're fast, you're clever, a shadow dancer. It knows you can hurt it. Remember that." Manny knew its voice. He had heard it his entire life. It was his own, even though the words were not.

Easing open one of the push bar doors, Manny slipped into the empty gym. A large, tattered tarp lay in a heap in the center of the basketball court, like a jagged wound in the floor. He glanced at the bleachers. They would provide good cover and give him the freedom to move around. But something about the dirty tarp made him nervous.

Carefully edging around it, Manny kept his eyes on the wrinkled canvas. Its surface was slick and oily and it had a weird musky odor. As he stumbled, Manny's toe nudged the edge and the canvas recoiled, curled in on itself. Manny froze. He knew exactly what this was.

The canvas erupted into flapping leather. Manny jerked back, his sneakers squeaking on the polished floor, and bolted for the bleachers. The bat-winged horror that was Morrigan lunged for him with a savage snarl, her sharp teeth bared.

Sharp claws scooped Manny up and carried him, kicking and struggling, to the Sidhe hag's nightmarish face.

"I know where you come from! I know who you are!" Her gnashing teeth made a sound like knives being drawn across metal, her breath made Manny retch.

She held Manny a few inches from her rictus of a mouth and licked her cracked lips with a snake-like tongue.

"You can't hide from me, boy!" She squeezed Manny until he gasped for breath, her talons digging into his skin.

"Manny!" Morrigan shrieked, her bloodshot eyes burning into his. "Your name is *Manny*!"

* * *

Manny woke flailing and kicking at the shape leaning over him.

"Manny, it's me!"

The room swam into focus. Adriana knelt beside him, shaking him awake. He glanced around, disoriented, still feeling the painful press of Morrigan's claws on his ribs. They were in the abandoned cellar. Adriana and let go of his shoulders, relieved. "You were dreaming."

He sat up and rubbed his eyes. They burned, like waking up with a bad fever. "Sorry..."

"That must have been some nightmare." Adriana reached for a small basket sitting next to her. "Here, maybe a little food will make you feel better. I brought some roasted pork and bread." She pulled back the cloth covering the basket.

The smell of the freshly baked bread helped to clear Manny's fuzzy brain. The basket held steaming rolls that resembled the bread used to make sub sandwiches. The sweet aroma smelled like a real bakery, much better than the one at the grocery store.

She set the basket in front of him and took one of the rolls, then picked up one of the slices of pork. "How do you like to eat again? Show me."

Manny held out his hand. "Your knife." Adriana put the pork back into the basket and handed her knife over. He took her roll and sliced it in half, then sliced another for himself. He handed her knife back. "Now observe carefully." Taking several of the pork slices, he made two sandwiches and offered one to Adriana. She took it but kept watching him closely.

"It's called a 'sandwich'." Manny pronounced the word slowly. "Or as my aunt calls them, a 'torta.'"

"A torta," Adriana repeated and took a bite. Juice ran down her chin and she wiped it away with her sleeve. "Good way to keep your fingers clean."

"Exactly," Manny replied, his mouth full of bread and savory meat.

Adriana uncorked a bottle, and took a deep drink. "It's wine, in case you were wondering." She offered the bottle to him.

Manny took it, sniffed the opening, then took a tentative sip. "Ugh, I don't know how people can like this stuff," he said with a grimace. "I'd kill for a black cherry soda." He took another drink from the bottle then noticed Adriana looking at him quizzically. "It's wine for kids where I come from," Manny explained.

As they ate, Manny asked, "So did you sell the cup?"

Adriana shook her head. "Heinze's shop was closed. There was no one about and the house seemed abandoned. I fear Morrigan's Redcaps paid him a visit."

Manny's looked down at his half-eaten sandwich. "Oh..." He hadn't cared much for the scheming kobold but the thought of him in Morrigan's claws turned his stomach. He didn't want to see that happen to anyone. "So what do we do now?"

"I know a few other fences," said Adriana, not seeming disturbed by Heinze's probable fate. "But I wanted to make sure you were safe first. I'll go see someone else when we're packed and ready to go."

"I'm ready to go," replied Manny. "Most of our stuff is already packed, except for these dirty blankets. And I'm totally okay with leaving them behind." He glanced at the spiders, which had retreated into the corners of their webs. "The spiders might like them." He felt a chill as he remembered his dream.

Adriana brushed her hands clean and stood up. "Fine, but you're staying here while I conduct this business."

"What? No way!" Manny pushed to his feet.

"It's too dangerous, Manny. We're being hunted by some of the most deadly Unseelie in the world." Adriana rooted around in one of their packs.

"Un-what?" said Manny.

"The Redcaps," answered Adriana. "They're Dark Fae, the Shadow Folk, the Unseelie."

Manny muttered the word under his breath. He did know it, or rather Remy did. He was Seelie, one of the Light Fae, the cousins and the bitter enemies of the Dark Fae. Or was he? He wasn't sure if there was a name for someone like him, a Sidhe who was in transition between Light and Dark. *That's Remy, not you,* he reminded himself.

Adriana pulled a short-barreled pistol out of their pack, along with a tarnished brass container shaped like a bulb and a leather bundle. She unrolled it, revealing several luminous, silver ball bearings and a couple of long, thin metal rods and brushes.

"Wow," said Manny, reaching for one of the ball bearings. "Is that a musket ball? Why are they glowing like—"

Adriana smacked his hand. "Don't touch. That's Fae silver. It'll make you sick." She loaded the pistol, pouring gunpowder from the brass container down the barrel, then wrapping one of the musket balls in a small square of dirty cloth. She rammed the ball down the barrel with the rod.

Manny watched the procedure with fascination. He had seen muskets being loaded in various movies, but never in real life. "Will a Fae silver bullet kill a Redcap?"

Adriana tucked the pistol into her vest, her expression preoccupied. "Redcaps are easy enough to kill with ordinary weapons. This is for tougher enemies. Like Lothair."

"Or Morrigan?" Manny asked hopefully.

Adriana shot him a sharp look, then stood and took up her walking staff. "I'm not sure what would kill her, or even if she can be killed." She rubbed her reddened eyes. She didn't look as if she had slept much, and he wondered if she had sat up all night, waiting and watching for someone to come after them.

Manny hesitated. "We need help, Adriana. We can't take all those guys on by ourselves." It seemed obvious to him, but he wasn't sure if she could bring herself to admit it.

Adriana thumped her staff on the floor, exasperated. "And who do you think is going to help us?" But there was a desperation in Adriana's voice that she couldn't hide. Maybe she wasn't even trying to anymore. "No one is coming to our rescue."

"Etienne." The elf cavalier's name along with the image of his father popped into Manny's head. "He'd help us. I know he would."

"The King's Chevalier?" Adriana snorted. "Now you're jesting."

"He's some kind of royal guard, isn't he? They're like the FBI," Manny insisted.

"The what?" snapped Adriana. "You're not making sense."

"Where I come from," said Manny, "the FBI are like special police—"

Adriana's confused scowl deepened and she shook her head, moving toward the door. Manny hurried to block her exit. "Police are like guards." He held out his hands to stop her. "They hunt criminals and stop crimes."

"We are criminals," Adriana said, obviously trying to hold onto her patience. "We're members of the

Hands of Shadow, wanted thieves. We can't go to the Chevaliers for help, we'd be arrested. Or worse, shot on sight." She took Manny by the shoulders. "I know it's not like that for you where you come from, but you're here now, and you have to listen to me. I can get us out of Lutetia today but I need you to stay in hiding. I don't want to push our luck."

Manny started to protest but Adriana shook him gently. "Manny, you must remember that this body does not belong to you. Neither one of us knows what would happen if you were to be killed. Would Remy be forever trapped in your realm? Would I ever see him again? If you place yourself in danger, you risk Remy as well."

Pulling away from her, Manny frowned. "So you don't care about me. You only care about getting Remy back."

"Manny..." She rubbed her face, then grabbed his shoulders, her expression serious. "Remy has been my friend for a long time. I'm practically his— I'm the closest thing to family he has. But I want to see you returned to your family as well. They must be as worried about you as I am about Remy."

Manny walked back to the blankets and dropped down, his back to Adriana. He folded his arms. *I'm practically his—* she had started to say. Manny knew how that sentence ended. *Practically his mother.* He knew he was jealous of Remy, and he knew it was stupid, and childish, but he couldn't help it. "Do whatever you need to do," he said, but couldn't make himself sound happy about it.

Adriana was silent. When she spoke, her voice was distant and Manny wasn't even sure if her words were meant for him. "I'll be back soon. I will never abandon you. I promise."

When he finally glanced back, she was gone. Manny's shoulders slumped and he sighed. Maybe she was right. He thought about his unpleasant encounter with Etienne. The Chevalier had threatened to throw Manny into the Foundry if he kept pestering him. Manny had no idea what that was but it sure didn't sound good. But he couldn't shake the image of his father's smiling face or forget the sound of his laugh. He closed his eyes. *He's not my dad. Get that into your thick head. Just like Adriana is not my mom.*

But he heard the shadow voice in his head again, the voice from his dream, the one who had tried to help him. It was louder and clearer than ever. *You can't let her take all the risks. You have to help her. If Morrigan found her, think of what she would do.*

Manny opened his eyes, grabbed one of their packs, and searched through it. He pulled out a sheathed knife, drew it, and studied the sharp edge. Allowing himself to be guided by his shadow voice, he tested the weapon's balance. Flipping the knife over and catching it by the blade, he threw it at one of the charred beams. The tip sunk into the wood precisely where he had aimed it. *Whoa.*

Bouncing to his feet, he pulled the knife out of the wood and sheathed it again, then tucked it into his belt. He knew what his shadow voice wanted him to do, what he had to do. From now on, he was determined to listen to that voice. He realized it had always been there, helping him move past his fear, encouraging him, showing him what his elf body was capable of. And he knew who it was.

From now on, he was going to listen to Remy.

CHAPTER 13

Being determined to act and having a plan of action, Manny quickly discovered, were not at all the same thing. After leaving the cellar, he wound his way through the streets, sticking to the alleys. He was comfortable in the shadows and knew he had to stay out of sight. His previous encounter with Etienne had happened by chance, although the more he thought about that, the more he became convinced that maybe it wasn't just a coincidence. Etienne looked exactly like father, and that had to mean something. It had to be a kind of magic, and maybe it was somehow drawing them together. But how was he supposed to find the man again?

In the movies, the Musketeers always had a headquarters of some sort. Why should the King's Chevaliers of this world be any different? He figured it would be a fancy mansion like the one he and Adriana had broken into. But even from the little he'd seen, there were probably hundreds of houses like that in the city.

Crouched by a stack of vegetable crates, he studied the faces of the passers-by. He could ask someone for directions but he had no guarantee they'd tell him. Maybe they'd sic the city watch on him. A half-goblin asking for directions to the Chevaliers' headquarters would probably seem a little suspicious.

On the bright side, he discovered by accident that he was more than just good at moving quietly and staying out of sight. He figured it out when he was walking down an alley and two city sentries suddenly turned the corner ahead and started straight toward him. Then some other instinct took over and he stepped back against the dirty stone wall, freezing into place.

The two men passed him without even a glance. *Huh,* Manny thought, watching them walk away down the alley. *That was almost like magic.* Maybe it was magic.

He started testing it on the street peddlers and other passers-by. If he managed to freeze before they got a good look at him, people simply did not notice him. It helped if he cleared his mind and didn't think about them or anything else.

Maybe he was turning invisible, like a ghost. After all, wasn't anything possible in this place? In the stories he'd read or seen on TV, lots of faeries had the power to turn invisible. But like everyone else, the Sidhe walked right past him when he was "ghosting," as he started to call it. If it worked on Morrigan and the Redcaps too, it would definitely come in handy.

Finally Manny spotted two Sidhe Chevaliers, each wearing the same forest green tabard that Etienne had worn, walking along a street. He started to follow them. They had to be Chevaliers and he figured that eventually they would have to go to their headquarters. And if he ghosted, they would have no idea he was following them. At least, he hoped so. He had no idea what special powers or senses some of the Sidhe had, but he still had to take the chance.

The velvet tabards worn by the Chevaliers were distinctive and made them easy to follow in a crowd. They were shaped like a poncho that had two flaps of fabric where sleeves would normally have been. The tabards were trimmed in gold and bore a gold triskelion on their chests and at each shoulder. Manny thought they looked pretty cool, and the swaggering Chevaliers displayed them to great advantage.

The two Chevaliers he followed were especially dashing in their tabards. One had aqua hair, webbed hands, and his skin was covered in iridescent scales. Black, unblinking eyes and gill slits at his neck further accentuated his fish-like appearance. *That's a merrow,* his shadow voice whispered in Manny's head. The merrow's hat, doublet, shirt, pants, and boots were all various shades of blue and green, and gave the impression that the Chevalier's clothes had been spun from the sea itself.

By contrast, the colorful merrow's companion was a short, bald man whose skin gleamed like polished obsidian. His spiky beard and eyebrows were needle-thin filaments of purple crystal, and his eyes glittered like amethysts. He was dressed entirely in black velvet and leather, making him look like a living silhouette. *A gnome,* said his shadow voice.

Manny began following them, sticking to sections of the streets and walkways that provided plenty of cover. Whenever the crowds got too heavy, Manny would ghost until they thinned sufficiently, always being careful to keep his quarry in sight.

As he passed more Chevaliers, he realized something he hadn't before: all of them were Sidhe. Once he had made this observation, he began actively looking for humans wearing the green tabards, but he saw none. Given the treatment of the Sidhe that he'd witnessed, it surprised him they would occupy such prestigious positions. After all, the Chevaliers seemed to be an elite royal fighting force.

Then when he stopped to ghost out of sight from a group of city sentries, it finally hit him. *The Sidhe all have special abilities.* He smiled at the obviousness of it. *Any king would want soldiers with those kinds of powers. It'd be like having an army of superheroes.*

He wondered what abilities Etienne possessed. He knew the Chevalier was amazingly fast; his duel had been fairly one-sided. Could he ghost as well? Or was that more an attribute of Manny's goblin nature than his elfish one?

He wondered what abilities distinguished the two Chevaliers he was following. He figured the merrow could probably breathe underwater and possibly swim really fast. *Like Aquaman,* he thought, picturing the merrow in the superhero's orange and green costume. *Nah, I like his clothes better,* he decided. The gnome looked pretty strong. He knew from an old storybook that gnomes had something to do with mining and the earth but wasn't sure exactly what.

Manny's hopes of being led quickly to the Chevaliers' headquarters were soon dashed. The pair stopped at several shops, once to measure the gnome for new boots, another time for the merrow to pick up a pair of flintlock pistols that were carved into the shape of dolphins. A lunch stop at a tavern resulted in a long wait as the Chevaliers ate their fill of roasted chicken and fresh bread, and drank several bottles of wine. Manny watched them from behind a barrel near a window. At this rate, it might take all day to find Etienne.

What if Adriana comes back to the cellar and finds me gone? She might be there now. Manny winced as he imagined her getting angry with him. Or she might be afraid that he had been caught by Morrigan. He knew he was taking a big risk. He thought about returning to the cellar, but he had come so far. *Just a little while longer,* he promised himself. If they didn't go to their headquarters soon, he would give up.

Manny's stomach growled as he glumly watched the Chevaliers feast. He glanced around at the other tables. Maybe there was something he might be able to liberate... *No! No more stealing! The last thing I need is to help goblinate myself.* He sank his chin into his hands and sighed. He was in the process of selecting other Chevaliers to follow among the tavern crowd when the bells of the Basilica began tolling.

His Chevaliers reacted immediately to the bells. They tossed some coins on the table and hurried away down the street. Manny watched them go, staying put. *Maybe they're late for work? Or maybe they're off to do more shopping.* He sighed and stood up. *Oh, what have I got to lose? In for an inch, in for a mile,* he thought, recalling what his dad used to say. He hurried after the Chevaliers and hoped for the best.

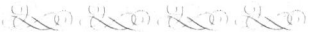

Manny studied the outside of the Chevaliers' headquarters from a garden courtyard across the street. He had scrambled up a tree and hid himself in its branches, watching the comings and goings for the last twenty or so minutes. The stone mansion wasn't the most impressive or even the biggest in the neighborhood, but it had a big walled park with trees around it. The entrance was barred with wrought iron gates, but Manny was high up enough to see over the wall and watch the Chevaliers going in and out of the house. The merrow and the gnome had led Manny to the mansion after departing the tavern, but now that he was here, he wasn't sure what his next move should be.

He doubted that he'd be able to sneak into the walled grounds, not with so many Sidhe around. Given all the abilities he remembered being attributed to faeries, he was pretty sure someone would be able to spot him, even if he was ghosting his heart out. He couldn't risk being seen, or worse caught, by the royal guard.

And boy were there plenty of Sidhe soldiers. There must have been over a hundred of them, of every size, color, and description he could imagine. Elves seemed the most common, or at least Manny was pretty sure they were elves. Most of them were tall, some fair-skinned and some a dark chestnut brown, and all had flowing manes of hair that shimmered like gold, silver, bronze, or copper, and long, curving ears.

His shadow voice echoed in his mind and he repeated the names in a whisper: *dwarf, selkie, faun, gnome, spriggan, merrow, brownie, trow.* All of the Sidhe were humanoid and they ranged in size from giants to kids. The trow towered above their fellows, easily seven or eight feet tall and muscled like titans. The dark-skinned brownies were the smallest, only three feet or so tall, but they were long-limbed with thin, delicate fingers. Manny wasn't sure how effective they'd be as soldiers, then noticed most of them carried slender muskets. *They must be really good shots,* he mused. *Size doesn't matter much if you can shoot somebody through the eye before he gets near you.*

And there was not a single human among them. As far as he could tell, it was an exclusive Sidhe club. That gave Manny no small measure of pride and he allowed himself a smile. *I guess I could be a Chevalier.* But as he continued to scan the crowds, his smile slowly faded. Along with a lack of humans in their ranks, he also noticed that all of the Sidhe were Seelie. There were no Unseelie among them either.

But each of them could be, he thought. *All Seelie can turn into Unseelie if they...* He looked at his ragged clothing, his dirty feet, and thought about the way Remy and Adriana lived. *Is that all it takes here? If you live like this you turn into a monster?* But he'd seen poor Seelie working in the streets, so there had to be more to it than that. Thinking of the dangerous Unseelie thieves in Morrigan's lair, he recalled their predatory looks, their cruel sneers. They were twisted on the inside as well as on the outside.

So what's Remy really like? Manny found it hard to

believe that the young elf was anything like the Unseelie in those sewers. Someone like Adriana could never be so devoted to a vicious creature, could she? And the fact that she was desperate to get Remy away from Morrigan must mean that she saw something worth saving.

And then when she looked at him there was her expression of worry and exasperation and affection. Adriana loved Remy like a son. He had no doubt about that. The thought gave him another pang of jealousy. He gritted his teeth. *Focus, Manny, you dumbass! You have a job to—*

The crowd near the front doors to the mansion began to stir. Manny flattened himself on the branch for a better look at the cause of the commotion. *There!* Etienne was walking toward the gates of the house's compound, surrounded by his comrades, many of whom clapped him on back or shoulders. *Well, he's definitely a popular guy.*

He slid off the branch, hung on by his hands, then dropped to the ground. Pressing himself against the tree's trunk, he was ready to ghost. The Chevalier had worked his way out of the courtyard and past the gates and now hurried down the street. *Perfect,* thought Manny, *I'll be able to talk to him alone. I'll make him believe my story. I've got to.*

He was about to dash across the street when he got a strange sensation. It was a prickling at the back of his neck, a feathery touch like a spider's web brushing against his skin. Manny twitched and shrugged then shot a glance over his shoulder, goose pimples breaking out all along his arms and shoulders.

Someone was in the courtyard, hidden by the trees and hedges, watching him. Manny scanned for any movement but saw only doves and squirrels, flying and scampering away from—

Manny froze, his jaw dropping open. A figure detached itself from a large, gnarled oak tree a few yards away. It seemed to simply materialize into existence. It stared straight at Manny, its yellow eyes wide and unblinking, its sharp teeth flashing in a triumphant sneer.

The Redcap raised its skeletal fingers and waggled them at Manny, its sneer widening into a hungry smile.

CHAPTER 14

If Manny tried to climb the tree again, the Redcap would be on him before he could get halfway up to the first branch. He could run through the trees at the back of the courtyard, try to reach the alley behind it... The creature was still smiling at him, teeth bared, waiting for him to make the wrong decision.

A crazy impulse seized Manny and he ran through the open gate of the courtyard and into the street. He heard the Redcap snarl just behind him and ducked barely in time; its clawed fingers grazed his back. He pivoted to the left. The heavier Redcap took another swipe at him, staggering past with a hiss.

Manny put on a burst of speed and whipped around a parked wagon, grabbing onto the stout wheel to help him make the turn. He spotted an elf woman peddler walking along the street in front of the Chevaliers' mansion. Manny sprinted toward her, trying to ghost, thinking "Don't see me" with all his might. It probably wouldn't work on the Redcap, but he didn't think anyone else on the street had noticed him yet.

He ducked around the elf woman and crouched down, making himself as invisible as possible. The single-minded Redcap pounded across the street toward him — and toward the elf woman. She saw the creature charging toward her, intent on murder, and screamed, dropping her tray of trinkets.

And a dozen Chevaliers burst out of the front gate. They saw the Redcap apparently about to attack the helpless peddler, and all of them drew their swords. The Redcap jolted to a halt, staring in dismay. As the Chevaliers charged it, it bolted away toward the garden courtyard.

Manny bounced to his feet and hurried up the street after Etienne, pleased with his own cleverness.

He quickly caught up, though he was careful to hang back, taking cover behind some brownies who were carrying baskets to market. He didn't want Etienne to see him right away. The Chevalier seemed to be in a hurry, and being stopped by that crazy goblin kid who kept calling him "dad" probably wouldn't put him in a receptive mood.

I have to think of a way to get him to listen to me, Manny thought. *I can't mess this up.*

He followed Etienne down the street, then around a corner. The neighborhood was all big mansions with courtyards and stables, shaded by a few large trees, but they seemed to be busy places. Manny kept a nervous eye out for more Redcaps or other threats, but everybody on the street was in a hurry to get somewhere, and no one looked twice at him.

Etienne didn't go far, stopping at a smaller stone house squeezed in between the walls of two larger mansions. It had a little cobbled court in front and vines climbed up to the second story and the steeply pitched roof. Etienne strode through the big open double doors, and after a moment Manny followed him.

He found himself in a small foyer with barrels stacked up against the walls, but archways led into bigger candlelit rooms where men were sitting at tables, eating and drinking. It was a tavern, though much nicer than the one Manny and Adriana lived at. It smelled of roasting meat, and fresh bread and wood smoke, and Manny's stomach growled. He stepped into the first archway, taking a closer look at the patrons.

They were a mix of Sidhe and humans, mostly men who looked fairly prosperous in their velvet clothes and starched lace collars. At a table in one corner, there were even some swordsmen with the black and silver tabards that Etienne's opponent had worn. *There he is,* Manny thought as he spotted his quarry.

Etienne sat on the far side of the room from the men in the black tabards. He wasn't alone, but the figure with him had his back toward Manny. Manny could tell it was a burly man with long red hair and a fiery red beard that had been elaborately braided with a golden cord. A pottery jug sat on the table and a plate with a round of bread and some cheese, but neither man was eating. They were both leaning forward, Etienne speaking and his companion listening intently.

A barrel-chested man in a stained apron strode in through the outer doorway, the wine cask he carried over one shoulder temporarily blocking any view of Manny. Thinking "Don't see me" as hard as he could, Manny slipped into the room, taking cover in the shadows along the walls. Fortunately the room was rather dark; the windows were set high, not letting in much light, probably because of the towering mansions to either side.

Manny reached the big stone fireplace near Etienne's table and crouched next to the stack of wood near it. *Now I just have to think what to say to get him to help me and Adriana.*

From there he had a better view of the other man, whose fancy clothes were embroidered in golden thread to match the braid in his beard. *Huh, he's a dwarf,* Manny thought. His booted feet didn't quite reach the floor, but his powerful build suggested that he would be a fearsome opponent in any battle. Manny wondered if he was a Chevalier, since he didn't wear a tabard. He was saying to Etienne, "Is Captain Corvus certain, then? I can't believe even Magneric would go against the King's will in such a blatant fashion. It's a disgrace!"

"The old King, yes, the new one, no," Etienne said. "With Clovis a sickly child and the queen occupied with caring for him, Magneric is seizing more and more power for himself."

The dwarf shook his head. "Still... Disbanding the Chevaliers is a drastic step, and likely to cause even more unrest. Is Corvus certain?"

Disbanding the Chevaliers? Manny thought, shocked. No wonder Etienne looked so worried and preoccupied.

"Unfortunately, he is, Gaudulfus." Etienne sat back and poured himself some more wine.

Gaudulfus sighed. "It's none of it good, Etienne. Though my late lady wife was as rich as the day is long, our neighbors still see me as Sidhe dirt because I have no title. And I've no hope of becoming a baron now. It wasn't that way when you and I fought side by side against the soldiers of Albion. Ah, but those were the glory days."

"Those days are many years gone, my friend." Etienne frowned, turning his wine cup around on the table. "Something or someone has been encouraging this divide between Sidhe and Men. It's not good for the Men, but it's a horror for the Sidhe. Everywhere I go, I see Unseelie, and goblins where there were once elves."

"It's the same in every city across Aquitania. This kingdom is sliding into darkness," Gaudulfus said, the craggy lines of his face etched with worry. "And damn me if there's a thing to be done about it."

Manny swallowed in a dry throat. He hadn't realized things were that bad here.

It suddenly occurred to Manny that he had been trying to think up a good lie to make Etienne help him, just by habit. *Dummy,* he told himself. He didn't need a lie; the truth would do, even though the truth meant admitting that he was a thief. *I just hope he doesn't decide to throw me in jail. Or the Foundry.* Manny steeled himself, took a deep breath, and walked up to the table.

Etienne glanced up, then his expression turned grim with annoyance. "You again!"

Gaudulfus looked Manny over with a smile. "What's this? You know this child?"

"No, despite his protestations to the contrary." Etienne sounded exasperated. "Look, boy, you must—"

Manny held up his hands and said quickly, "I'm sorry to bother you, but you're the only Chevalier I know, and I'm not here to say anything crazy. I need to tell somebody about Morrigan."

That stopped them both. Gaudulfus glanced sharply at Etienne, then lowered his voice. "Morrigan the Sidhe hag?"

Manny nodded, relieved they were listening to him. "Yes. She has a gang, the Hands of Shadow. I know where her hide-out is. And she's got some kind of big plan, I'm not sure what that is yet. But she needs a lot of money to pay for it and she's getting people to steal for her."

Etienne eyed him, caught between interest and skepticism. "And why do you want to betray her, little goblin?"

"To lure Chevaliers into a trap, no doubt," Gaudulfus suggested, tugging thoughtfully at his beard.

"Because I'm not a goblin," Manny said. This was going to be the hard part. "I'm a human kid, from another world. I got brought here by a magic coin, and stuck in the body of this elf kid who's turning into a goblin. His name is Remy, mine is Manny. I don't want to be a thief, I don't want to steal, and I especially don't want anything to do with Morrigan. And she said she's going to kill me. And I think she knows I'm not really Remy," he added, remembering the warning in his dream again.

Etienne sat back, disgruntled, and folded his arms. "This is even more mad than your previous tale."

"And what was that?" Gaudulfus asked with interest.

"That I was his father," Etienne told him.

"Is that so?" said Gaudulfus, looking at Manny. "Well, if I squint and cock my head so, I suppose I could see some resemblance..."

Etienne turned a scowl on his companion.

Manny was getting annoyed, too. "Hey, I said that because you look just like my dad, and I was confused. Sometimes people here look the same as people back in my world, but I hadn't figured that out yet when I saw you. And..." The words caught in Manny's throat, but it was important that he get them out. *He's not going to believe anything but the truth, the real truth.* "Back in my world, my mom and dad are dead." Manny swallowed hard. He hated to say those words out loud. "So when I saw you looked like him, I got...startled."

Etienne frowned at him, but the expression was more thoughtful than angry. "It can't be true."

"Yet it makes a damn good tale, true or not. Sit down, lad, and tell us more." Gaudulfus waved toward a serving man. "You, bring drink and food for our storyteller here!"

"Wait, what's this?" Etienne muttered.

Manny looked around to see three of the human swordsmen in the black tabards approaching their table. He grimaced at the interruption; he could tell Etienne and Gaudulfus were beginning to believe him. If they had to stop and fight a duel or whatever, he might have a hard time getting their attention again.

But the swordsman in the lead, a tall man with a pointed beard, said, "We'll take the thief."

CHAPTER 15

Thief? Oh no, Manny thought, his eyes widening. They were here for him. *Do they know we robbed that house?*

"You're interrupting a private conversation." Gaudulfus dismissed them with a gesture. "If he is a thief, we're perfectly capable of dealing with him ourselves. Away with you!"

The man ignored him, reaching for Manny's arm. Manny pulled away, hurriedly taking cover behind Gaudulfus' chair.

Etienne stood, hand going to his swordhilt. "He said you're interrupting us. Did you not hear?"

"This is none of your concern." The human swordsman eyed Manny, but seemed reluctant to get within arm's reach of Gaudulfus. "We're here for the goblin boy. Hand him over."

The dwarf leaned back and stuck his boots out to block the way, watching the swordsmen with lazy amusement. He said, "What has the boy stolen? Who has ordered his arrest? Is the Chief Minister sending his Guards after child sneak-thieves now? Is there some affair of state jeopardized by boys who steal apples in the street?"

The guard gritted his teeth. "And I said this was none of your concern."

More Minister's Guards appeared in the archway

and started across the room toward them. *Oh, this is bad,* Manny thought. He didn't know where they wanted to take him, but it couldn't be anyplace good. The other men in the tavern, Sidhe and human alike, looked up, frowning and wary.

Watching the new arrivals approach, Etienne said, "Such a lot of interest in a little thief, for reasons no one will say." He glanced down at Gaudulfus, who slanted an inquiring look up at him. "It makes one wonder. The timing is rather suspicious."

"Aye," Gaudulfus agreed. "As if they don't want us to hear his foolish, although admittedly quite intriguing, tales."

Etienne added grimly, "As if at least some of them aren't so foolish."

"Thus making them even more intriguing," replied Gaudulfus.

"Even so," Etienne said, his eyes on the guards.

Manny's heart pounded in relief and excitement. *He believes me! Sort of, a little. At least enough to listen more. If I can get away from these guards...*

With a frustrated grimace, the lead guard drew his sword and advanced around the table toward Manny. "You'll surrender the thief—"

Gaudulfus kicked the guard in the kneecap and as he doubled over, picked up the pottery jug and smashed him over the head with it. The man dropped like an unstrung puppet. Gaudulfus leapt to his feet, telling Etienne, "Sorry, it was the word 'surrender.' It always sent me into an uncontrollable rage." He didn't sound sorry.

The fallen guard rolled across the floor, groaning. As the other Minister's Guards shouted in fury and charged, Etienne shouted, "Then I hope you haven't lost your edge!" and drew his sword.

Gaudulfus upended the table, temporarily blocking the guards. The other men in the tavern surged to their feet, shouting angrily, and the fight was on.

Manny dodged, ducked, and tried to stay out of the way. Some of the tavern's patrons attacked the guards, helping Gaudulfus and Etienne, others joined the guards against them, and others just randomly attacked each other. Etienne took the guards on with his sword, agilely avoiding thrown bottles and punches and other hazards; Gaudulfus seized a chair and beat at all the attackers with it until it fell apart, then drew his sword, which was much broader and heavier than Etienne's rapier.

Manny saw a guard shove the overturned table aside to come up behind Etienne. He yelled a warning, but everybody was shouting, drowning his voice out. Desperate, he grabbed up a pottery goblet, aimed at the guard's head, and threw it. To his surprise, it hit the guard right in the temple, sending the man staggering backward and crashing to the ground. *Yes!* Manny had forgotten that he was Remy, that he could do things like this. He ducked around another knot of fighting men, looking for something else to throw.

He took out two more guards with thrown goblets and pottery cups, plus an elf soldier who blundered into the way at the wrong moment. Then an arm wrapped around his neck from behind and dragged him away from the fight. Manny clawed at it and kicked hard, but he couldn't break the grip and he couldn't get any air to yell for help. Etienne was halfway across the room, sword fighting with two guards, and he could barely see Gaudulfus through the crowd.

Then suddenly the man holding him staggered and his grip loosened. Manny ripped away and whipped around to see a Minister's Guard collapse. Standing behind him was Adriana, holding her staff. Manny gasped in relief. "Adriana!"

She stepped over the guard's body, grabbed Manny's arm, and hauled him toward a doorway in the back wall of the tavern. It led to a narrow passage, empty and quiet after the din in the other room. The door at the far end was open to a little courtyard and Manny realized Adriana meant to haul him all the way out and away.

Manny dragged his feet. "Adriana, we can't go! Etienne—"

Adriana pulled him through the door into a courtyard with vine-covered walls and a big square well. "We have to get out of here, Manny. How do you think I found you? You were spotted by one of Morrigan's Redcaps and they've been searching the streets for you. The word has spread so far even the Pixies were speaking of it!"

"But he believes me! He'll help us!" Manny let himself be towed unwillingly along, figuring if he struggled too much she would be even less inclined to listen to him. "He was already sort of listening to me, then when the guards came and wouldn't tell him why they wanted me, that made him really suspicious!" That was weird, the way the guards had shown up. The ones Manny had seen in the tavern must have recognized him and sent for the reinforcements, but how had they known who he was? Unless they were connected to Morrigan somehow, like the Redcaps. "Hey, do you think—"

Adriana banged open the wooden gate into a small street. "Manny, a King's Chevalier is not going to stir himself to help—" She halted abruptly.

"But he—" Manny bumped into her, his heart freezing as he saw why they had stopped. *Uh oh.*

Lothair the troll stood at the end of the alley, his bulk almost concealing the scatter of Redcaps behind him. Adriana fell back a step, pushing Manny behind her. Tense with fear, Manny saw another five Redcaps stood at the other end of the alley, armed with a variety of wicked looking knives. He said quietly, "Adriana, they're behind us."

She squeezed his arm.

Lothair stalked toward them, saying, "Now then, did you really think we wouldn't find you? You can't fight Morrigan, darlin', she's too powerful."

Adriana backed away another step, throwing a look over her shoulder at the Redcaps that who blocked the other end of the alley. She whispered, "Manny, I'll distract them. You get over the wall—"

Manny's throat was so dry it hurt. "I won't leave you." Remembering the knife tucked in his belt, he drew the blade and prepared to throw it.

"Oh, don't think the little goblin can get away from us." Lothair grinned. "That runt's the one Morrigan wants. A shame, really, since I was looking forward to eating him. Ah well, I suppose you'll have to do."

Adriana held her staff at ready, and said with chilling conviction, "I can't fight you all, but I swear on all that's holy, Lothair, it won't be you who takes him to Morrigan. The others may kill me, but I'll split your skull first. You're out in the sun, Lothair. You're not as tough as you think."

Lothair hesitated, squinting up at the sky. "Brave words," he sneered, then drew a pair of huge curved daggers. "You always were the feisty one. I'm betting that fire gives your flesh a smoky flavor. Mmm..." He licked his tusks and advanced, raising his blades.

Etienne vaulted over the wall and landed in front of them, facing Lothair. The deadly crystal needle of his sword gleamed in the sunlight. Manny gasped, his heart thumping in relief.

Lothair jerked back in surprise, then growled, "This is none of your business, elf!"

"Every time someone says that, I believe it less." Etienne's sword point drew a circle in the air. "Run now, brute, and you may survive."

Lothair laughed, low and vicious. "You think you can take on all of us—"

The gate banged open and Gaudulfus charged out, wielding his heavy sword, and he looked mad. He roared and charged the Redcaps at the other end of the alley. They screeched and charged him.

Manny saw enough to realize that Gaudulfus had been holding back in the tavern fight. He plowed into the Redcaps and knocked them aside, hewing left and right, sending them sprawling in bloody heaps. Some bolted away without even trying to fight.

"I see your friends have never faced a dwarf in a battle frenzy before," Etienne said, casting a quick glance at the melee.

Then Lothair lunged at Etienne, swinging one of his daggers. Manny yelled in alarm but Etienne ducked smoothly under it and slashed at Lothair's chest, his sword slicing a bloody path through the troll's heavy armor and the scaly skin beneath. Lothair growled and jerked back, clearly not used to being wounded so easily. He eyed Etienne's glittering sword warily.

Etienne said, "Amechanteur is the sword's name. And a deadlier blade you will never face." He brought the sword *en garde* again. "Especially in my hands."

The troll snarled, grabbed the nearest Redcap, and threw it at Etienne. The Redcap slammed into the Chevalier and knocked him flat.

Adriana leapt into the battle and swung her staff to thunk the struggling Redcap in the head. Etienne pushed it off and rolled to his feet, just as the other Redcaps rushed them, knives flashing and teeth snapping.

Etienne and Adriana fought back to back, his sword and her staff parrying blows and slicing and smashing Redcaps, while keeping Lothair at bay. Manny ducked and dodged and slashed with his knife at the Redcaps' legs, but mostly tried to stay alive and out of arm's reach of the goblins. Twice he managed to grab up a stone and bounce it off a Redcap's skull.

Then suddenly Lothair turned and ran away down the alley. The few Redcaps who were left limped or bolted after him.

"Why are they leaving?" Manny gasped, but then he heard men shouting and horses clattering on the cobbles of the main street.

"It must be the Minister's Guards or the city watch," Etienne said. He glanced at Adriana. "We have to get out of here before we're surrounded."

Behind them, Gaudulfus shouted, "This way, to my coach!"

Breathing hard, Manny looked around. Gaudulfus stood at the end of the alley, surrounded by the limp sprawled bodies of Redcaps, waving at them to follow him. Manny yelled, "Come on, we have to run!" and tugged on the back of Adriana's tunic.

"Manny, no! Wait!" She grimaced, frustrated, then followed Manny and Etienne.

They ran down the alley and around the corner. At the end of the cross street stood a square boxy coach, painted black, with four gray horses, their silver manes braided and their coats so shiny they had to be faerie horses. The driver was a portly, older spriggan with a waxed mustache and a pointy beard, dressed like Gaudulfus in a gold-embroidered doublet. He looked up, startled, as they all pelted toward him.

"Othon, we depart at once with great haste!" Gaudulfus called out to the driver.

"Where to, sir?" said the bewildered driver.

"To the Stone and Ivy," Gaudulfus replied. He flung the door open and Manny scrambled into the coach, falling onto a padded leather bench then scooting over hastily as Adriana and Gaudulfus followed him. But Etienne shut the door. The windows were covered with sliding wooden shutters, so Manny couldn't see what he was doing.

"He's not staying behind?" Manny asked anxiously.

Gaudulfus reached down beside his seat and scooped up a huge pistol. "No, lad, he's going to sit up on the box with Othon, the better to watch our backs. One can never be too careful." The dwarf cocked the pistol and laid it across his lap.

The coach's springs squeaked and the wood creaked as Etienne climbed up the side. The coach jolted into motion, moving rapidly away down the street.

"Where are we going?" Adriana asked, her voice tense and wary.

"To an inn I own, my dear," Gaudulfus told her. "It's safe from prying eyes and ears, and will give us a chance to talk in private. It also happens to serve the best mutton and wild mushroom stew in all of Aquitania." He grinned and stroked his beard. "Fighting always gives me such an appetite."

Manny sat back against the cushions, relieved but amazed that Gaudulfus could be thinking of food after their harrowing encounter. "Whatever gets us away from here sounds good to me."

The look Adriana gave him was not pleased.

CHAPTER 16

They drove what felt like a long distance. It wasn't very comfortable; the coach had springs, because Manny could hear them squeak, but they weren't anywhere as good as a car's shock absorbers and the ride was bouncy and jolting. Gaudulfus didn't let Manny peek out the windows until he said they were past the city gates.

The houses were bigger out here, with more trees and gardens, and the rutted dirt road was much wider. Other coaches passed them, as well as wagons and people on horseback. Manny glimpsed something that looked like a horse with wings and feathers, and a head like an eagle's, walking along beside a couple of brownies, and almost fell out the window trying to get a better look, until Gaudulfus and Adriana made him sit down again.

Finally the coach turned into the courtyard of a big, two-story rambling stone building. As the coach drew to a halt, Gaudulfus gave a gusty sigh and swung the door open. "Here we are."

Manny jumped down first. The inn had big multi-paned glass windows, the shutters open to the late afternoon sun. A big tree shaded the courtyard and vines climbed the walls to the slate-shingled roof. More spriggans hurried from the stables to unhitch the horses. Manny said, "Wow, this place looks really cool."

"It's the tree, lad," said Gaudulfus, gallantly helping Adriana out of the coach, though it really didn't look like she wanted the help. "Its shade keeps the sun off the inn while the spacious windows allow the evening breeze to flow through the interior."

Manny smiled. "No, I meant it's really nice. That's what 'cool' means where I come from. It's a big compliment."

"Ah, I see. Well, thank you. You're certainly the most well-mannered goblin I've ever met."

"That's because I'm not really a goblin," Manny said.

Etienne swung down from the driver's box. "So you said." He gave the wary Adriana a cautious nod. "Let's go inside and discuss it."

They ended up sitting around a table in one of the inn's private dining rooms, with a fire in the small hearth and wine, bread, and cheese on the table. They had all been served large bowls of really good lamb stew, though it wasn't as spicy as the one Tia Licha liked to make. Adriana had barely touched hers. It didn't go to waste, however, as Gaudulfus politely finished it off for her, taking his personal tally of bowls devoured to an even half a dozen. Manny had asked for a cup of water instead of wine, which Gaudulfus and Etienne seemed to find really odd. But Manny didn't want to take a chance on getting drunk, not when he still had to convince them he was telling the truth, and there was a possibility they would be attacked by trolls and Redcaps again.

As the light outside the windows dimmed to early evening, Manny told them the whole story from the beginning, from when he had found the book in the bookstore. Etienne listened intently, frowning in thought. Gaudulfus smiled occasionally, but Manny still got the feeling that the dwarf believed him. Adriana sat back in her chair, arms folded, her expression set in angry lines. She got really angry when Manny got to the part about Morrigan. She leaned forward, her boots thumping on the wood floor. "Manny, you can't—"

"I have to," Manny told her. He had had time to think all this out on the coach ride. "She's not going to let us go, no matter how far or how fast we run, you know that. And now that Lothair's seen us with the Chevaliers, there's no way she's going to believe we haven't told them everything. So we might as well tell them everything." He had seen enough TV detective shows to know this was true.

Adriana blew out an exasperated puff of air and turned away, rocking her chair back and forth. By the time Manny had finished, Adriana was pacing the floor, refusing to meet his gaze.

Etienne and Gaudulfus shared a long look. "What do you think, Gaudulfus?"

The dwarf barked out a booming laugh, slapping the table with his meaty hand. "Oberon's blood! I think that's the most amazing story I've ever heard, and I've heard some truly astounding tales in my time."

"But you believe me, right?" said Manny, watching them anxiously.

Gaudulfus got to his feet and clapped him on the back. "Every word, my boy, every word."

Manny turned hopefully to Etienne. "What about you?"

He leaned forward, fixing Manny with his gaze, chewing thoughtfully at his lower lip. Manny couldn't believe it. In that moment, Etienne looked exactly like his dad; those intense blue eyes searched for some hidden answer in Manny's expression, his mouth twisted. Manny fought an urge to reach out and touch Etienne's arm.

Finally, Etienne leaned back and nodded. "Aye, I believe you are telling the truth."

Gaudulfus moved around the room, lighting the candles with a spill of twisted paper. Manny smiled at Adriana, who had stopped pacing and was now gnawing her thumbnail. "See? I told you they'd believe me. And they'll help us." He glanced back at Etienne. "Uh, you will help us, right?"

Etienne took his empty mug and poured himself more wine. "That is another matter entirely. I'm not sure if we can help you. We're not magicians." When he saw Manny's crestfallen look, he added, "But we'll certainly do what we can. At the very least, I intend to find out why the Minister's Guards were so eager to arrest you."

"Indeed," added Gaudulfus, tossing the spill into the fire and coming back to sit down. "Magneric's interest can only mean that he is somehow aware of this boy's amazing story. Could he be behind the magic that brought him here?"

Looking over at Adriana, Etienne said, "Tell us what you know about Morrigan's scheme. What does she intend to do?"

Crossing her arms, Adriana shrugged. "I don't know. She didn't share her secrets with me."

"Could her darkling sorcery be responsible for bringing Manny here?" asked Gaudulfus, watching her thoughtfully.

Adriana shook her head. "I don't think she knew what had happened to Remy—" She frowned and rubbed her forehead. "I mean, Manny."

"But I think she knew I wasn't Remy," added Manny. "I got that feeling from her somehow."

"Could she be in league with Magneric?" Gaudulfus said, his eyes gleaming as if the notion was exciting instead of frightening.

"It's a distinct possibility." Etienne sounded considerably more worried. "We must find a way to discover Morrigan's plot. Whatever it is, it's no doubt sinister. It could also be the key to helping Manny return to his own realm."

Etienne stood and faced Adriana. "You must tell us what you know of Morrigan and the Hands of Shadow." His tone was insistent and Manny could see that it just made Adriana angrier.

Exasperated, she shook her head and took a step back, holding up her hands. "I've already said too much. I should never have come here. Our lives are in danger and if we don't—"

Etienne grabbed her wrist. "If you don't tell us everything you know, then we will not be able to protect you."

She jerked her hand free, her voice tightening. "You can't protect us! You have no notion what Morrigan is capable of. She's an ancient, eldritch creature, as old as the Undercity."

"We're quite familiar with Morrigan's reputation, my dear," said Gaudulfus, leaning back in his chair as he watched the confrontation. "The Hands of Shadow are well known in Lutetia."

"And until today," Etienne said, "I'd never heard of a human member of their ranks. The Unseelie do not mingle with your kind willingly. So forgive me if I suspect you possess far more knowledge than you've shared."

"And forgive me," Adriana snapped, "if I am less than confident in the protection of a bravo who wastes his time fighting pointless duels or carousing like a drunkard in taverns. You admitted yourself that you are no magician."

Manny winced. He could tell from the tension in Etienne's shoulders that that shot had hit home. Etienne's expression hardened and he stepped closer to Adriana. "Answer my questions."

Adriana didn't back down. "Show some courtesy like a proper gentleman and perhaps I will."

Etienne's eyes narrowed. "You are a member of a notorious gang of thieves and murderers and should face the king's justice for your crimes. Given that, I'd say my manner is more than courteous."

Adriana was clearly furious, and looked ready to punch Etienne. Manny knew he had to do something. If a fight started, they would never figure out what to do. "What about that secret meeting, Adriana?" He pushed to his feet. "I remember you said something about that." Adriana ignored the question, glaring at Etienne.

"Come, come," said Gaudulfus, his deep voice surprisingly soothing. "Let's allow both our meals and this information to settle a bit before continuing. Besides, I want the lad to try my inn's renowned apple and almond tart." He grinned at Manny. "The best in all of Aquitania."

Reluctantly, Etienne turned away from Adriana and sat down at the table. He picked up his mug and took a deep drink, clearly just as angry with Adriana as she was with him.

Feeling guilty for causing the argument, Manny went to Adriana and stood by her side, mimicking her stance and crossing his arms. She gave him a slight smile, and lightly patted his arm.

"Are you okay?" he asked.

Adriana nodded. "I just need to feel a cool breeze on my face." She cast a pointed glance at Etienne. "The air in here has become sour and unpleasant."

"Can I come with you?" asked Manny, a little worried she'd say no.

Adriana cocked an eyebrow at him. "I think it would be for the best." She turned and strode out of the room.

Manny smiled half-heartedly at Etienne and Gaudulfus. "Uh, we'll be right back. I'll talk to her. Just wait right here."

"Where would we go, lad?" asked Gaudulfus.

"Oh, right." Manny hurried after Adriana.

Outside the inn, Manny found Adriana leaning on the big tree in the courtyard, staring up at the sky. It was darkening to purple as the sun sank past the trees, the first stars just starting to come out. *Don't say the wrong thing, you big dummy,* he thought. He took a deep breath. "I'm sorry Etienne called you a thief."

Adriana glanced down at him. Her expression was very unhappy. "But that's what I am, Manny. A thief. And a very good one."

"Well, yeah, technically. I guess what I meant was that I wish he hadn't said it to you that way."

She sighed. "The Sidhe who live in the streets receive far worse than that. You've witnessed and suffered it yourself. The Chevaliers talk about the cities slipping into darkness, but it's not hard to see why. And yet they would never acknowledge that they have had a hand in it." She kicked a tree root, frowning. "Remy wasn't turning into a goblin as a result of an abundance of kindness and charity."

Manny didn't want to believe that the Chevaliers were part of it. He wanted to see them as heroes, even though he knew nobody was perfect. "But it's the humans who mistreat the Sidhe. I didn't see any Sidhe beating up others."

"The Seelie hate the Unseelie more than the humans, even though they are kin. Two sides of the same coin." She shook her head and looked away. "You are living proof of that."

Manny turned that thought over. He was both an elf and a goblin. Maybe that was why Etienne had treated him badly when he first encountered him. But Gaudulfus had taken an instant liking to him. Though even on short acquaintance it wasn't hard to see that Gaudulfus did and said pretty much whatever he wanted. *Adriana has to be wrong,* he thought. *If the Seelie hate the Unseelie it's only because they do bad things, like Morrigan and her thieves.*

He rubbed his eyes, suddenly realizing that he was still very tired. "So you're not going to help Etienne and Gaudulfus?"

Adriana looked up at the sky again, but gave him no answer.

Manny fidgeted uncomfortably, wondering if he should just give in. Adriana didn't have a lot of reason to listen to him, anyway, just a kid from another world inhabiting the body of her friend. Remy probably hadn't given her very good advice lately either, what with the goblin transformation going on. Finally, he said, "I don't think they can stop Morrigan without you. But I guess you know that." When Adriana didn't answer, he turned to go back inside.

She said suddenly, "I made a vow long ago to protect and aid Remy."

Her voice stopped Manny. He slowly turned to face her again.

"For better or worse, you are Remy now," she said, her face serious. In the dim light, she didn't look as much like his mother. This woman had had a much harder life than anyone Manny knew at home, and he had the feeling she had done things that she now regretted. "And that means my vow extends to you. But I fear this fight will not end well for me, Manny." She grimaced and shrugged. "Perhaps that can't be helped."

She pushed away from the tree and walked past Manny. "I'd better go answer your Chevalier's questions before he decides to put me on the rack."

Manny watched her disappear back into the inn. Adriana's decision to help Etienne should have filled him with relief. But what they might have to do scared him as well, and he found himself wishing that he and Adriana had been able to escape on that skyship after all.

CHAPTER 17

When Manny returned to the private room, Adriana was already talking to Etienne, who sat opposite her. Gaudulfus was listening intently between huge bites of pastry. Manny took a seat near Adriana. Gaudulfus slid a small wooden plate over to him with a piece of the pastry on it. It smelled of spiced apples and almonds.

Manny reluctantly tore off a small piece with his fingers.

Gaudulfus was watching him closely, his bushy eyebrows raised in anticipation. Manny chewed on the bit of pastry and managed a smile and a nod at the dwarf. Satisfied, Gaudulfus returned his attention to Adriana.

Etienne's questions focused mainly on Morrigan herself and not on Adriana's part in past crimes, which was a relief. Adriana had been part of the Hands of Shadow for many years. Morrigan employed Unseelie spies all throughout Lutetia, especially goblin pickpockets and cutpurses, but she also had far more fearsome Unseelie at her disposal, like Lothair and the Redcaps. Although Adriana had never seen Morrigan cast any spells, she was certain that the witch wielded great magical power. She had a way of knowing what you had done even if you told no one, and her enemies had a way of disappearing in the night.

Manny felt a chill, remembering the hag's eyes and

her terrible smile. It was weird that she seemed only interested in thieving. She looked like she should be doing something way worse than that.

As the interrogation continued, Adriana refused to answer any questions regarding Remy. She declared that topic forbidden and would not budge.

"But there may be a connection between Remy and Morrigan," insisted Etienne. "It may be the key to why Manny is here now."

"There is no connection beyond the fact that Remy was another one of her pickpockets," Adriana said. "And if you continue to question me about him, I will leave."

Etienne glanced at Gaudulfus, who shrugged and said, "Fair enough. Everyone is entitled to their secrets, after all."

"Very well." Etienne didn't look happy. "Tell us about this secret meeting, then."

Adriana made an impatient gesture. "All I know is that it's happening at Gassot's place at midnight."

Etienne frowned. "I haven't heard of that establishment."

"I'm not surprised." Adriana smiled tightly. "It's a private tavern frequented by Unseelie. It's also reserved for very important meetings between the Hands of Shadow and... others in the trade. Whatever will be discussed there should no doubt be of great interest to you."

"How many hours before midnight?" Etienne asked Gaudulfus.

"I'd say three, at the most," Gaudulfus said.

"Then we should waste no more time." Etienne got to his feet.

Manny sat up straight. "You're going back into the city? What about us?"

"You're welcome to stay here." Gaudulfus waved a hand, indicating they had the freedom of the inn. "You should be safe enough. I'll have Othon and my men stand guard outside."

"That's a fine idea." Adriana glanced at Remy. "We'll stay here."

"Oh, not you," Etienne said. It was clear he didn't entirely believe everything Adriana had told him. "We need you to lead us to Gassot's and to act as a witness against Morrigan. I want you close at hand for now."

"You mean to say you don't trust me?" Adriana pressed her hand to her chest, her tone mocking.

Etienne snorted and headed for the door.

"Wait, no! I'm not going to stay here," Manny said. "Not if all of you are going back. I'm a witness, too."

"But you are the one Morrigan wants," Etienne told him patiently. "And Chief Minister Magneric is after you as well. It seems wise to keep you out of their reach."

"I don't care about that. I'm coming with you," Manny insisted. "Nothing against Gaudulfus' men, but I'm not sure they'd be able to protect me from Lothair or Morrigan's Redcaps."

"Othon is quite handy with a musket, lad," said Gaudulfus. "I trained him myself."

Manny shook his head. "I'm not staying behind. And if you leave me here, I'll sneak out and follow you."

Etienne looked at Adriana. "He can be very stubborn," she admitted. "I certainly couldn't get him to stay put."

"As you wish," Etienne agreed, still reluctant. "But you accompany us against my better judgment."

"Isn't it always so?" Gaudulfus laughed.

They reentered Lutetia through one of the least trafficked gates in a large wagon drawn by two draft horses. The back of the wagon was laden with casks of wine, covered by a dirty canvas tarp. Manny and

Adriana hid among the casks, bracing themselves as the wagon bumped over the cobblestones. Gaudulfus drove with Etienne on the driver's bench beside him. They had swapped out of their rich silk and linen clothes for rough homespun wool, disguising themselves as country tradesmen. Wide-brimmed hats were pulled low to conceal their faces. Their swords, several muskets, and a brace of pistols lay wrapped in blankets between them, easily accessible should the need arise.

Suspecting that the Minister's Guards would be on the lookout for Gaudulfus' coach, the dwarf had Othon drive it through one of the main gates into the walled city. The spriggan was to act as a diversion and lead any potential pursuers on a distracting chase before attempting to once again flee the city.

"What if Othon is caught?" Manny had asked with concern.

"He's a wily rascal," Gaudulfus had replied. "No doubt he will elude Magneric's halfwits. And if he is caught and imprisoned, I'll stand bail for him after we've settled matters with Morrigan."

Although that plan had not sounded all that good to Manny, it certainly seemed perfectly acceptable to both Gaudulfus and Etienne. As Manny and Adriana lay down in the back of the wagon, she whispered, "Spriggans are quite clever creatures. I think Othon will be just fine. It's our fates that worry me."

Adriana hadn't spoken another word throughout their journey, but she spent quite a bit of time peeking out from under the tarp. At one point, she signaled Manny to join her.

The street they were driving along was wide, lit by torches, but the tall rickety buildings lining it seemed to lean in, as if they were driving into a dark cavern. In the flickering firelight, Manny could see surreptitious movement, as people, creatures, darted in and out of dark doorways, the gaping upper floor windows, and rickety balconies. Manny said, "This street is kind of creepy." And that was an understatement.

Adriana whispered, "Gassot's tavern is deep in an old area of Lutetia that's claimed by the Unseelie. It's called the Phantom Quarter."

The buildings were crammed close together, some seeming as if they were held up only by scaffolding, and there were piles of rubble everywhere. Manny didn't want to see the kind of things that lived atop these roofs. He was pretty sure it wouldn't be pixies.

They turned into another street. This one was the same, except that dark shapes huddled on the promenade or slouched against doorways and sagged out of windows.

"Are all those people—" he whispered to Adriana. He broke off when a group of goblins dressed in rags tumbled out of a doorway, fighting viciously in the street.

"Unseelie?" Adriana whispered in reply. "Yes, most of them are Dark Fae, or on their way to becoming so."

From above them, Etienne leaned down, and said, low-voiced, "Are we near Gassot's? Which street are we looking for?"

Adriana shuffled closer to the driver's seat and pulled the edge of the tarp back, whispering through the gap, "Turn left at the corner and stop before you get to the old bridge. It's just across it, on the right. There's a sign with a dog's head impaled on a lance."

"Charming," Etienne muttered.

The wagon continued to trundle along, squeaking and creaking for several more minutes until Gaudulfus reined in the horses. Manny peeked up from the tarp behind Etienne, studying the scene.

Not far ahead a ramshackle bridge crossed a dark gap in the street, and Manny could hear the water rushing below it. The bridge led into a small plaza, and the tavern loomed over the open space like a big crouching monster. It was made of grimy stone, and stood at least three stories tall, maybe more, with lots of gables and little balconies sticking out at odd angles. Big statues of crouching animals with horns and fangs stood to either side of the wide arched doorway. In the flickering light of basket torches, he saw the sign that Adriana had mentioned. *Ugh, that's nasty,* Manny thought with a grimace. Most of the windows were dark, but a few glowed and flickered behind their filthy drapes.

"There are plenty of eyes on the streets," Gaudulfus said. "We'll never be able to approach without being seen."

There was a raised stone hearth in the center of the plaza with a fire burning in it, and by its light Manny could see the shapes of many Unseelie loitering around in the plaza. Manny also spotted some movement in the deep shadows outside the tavern, and across the street near a dark rambling building that appeared to be an old stable.

"They're lookouts," whispered Adriana, squinting into the darkness. "Many more than usual. Someone values secrecy quite highly this night."

"What now?" said Gaudulfus, leaning close to Etienne. "Shall we risk a frontal assault?"

Etienne had been studying the tavern. He shook his head. "That would not get us the information we need. One of us will have to enter by stealth."

Adriana groaned under her breath, but said, "I'll do it." She began to slide out from under the tarp, but Manny grabbed her arm.

"No," he whispered urgently. "If anyone can sneak up there, it's me. I can ghost, you can't."

"Ghost?" Gaudulfus said in surprise. "What the devil is that?"

Adriana shook her head. "No, Manny, it's too dangerous. I won't allow it."

"What is he talking about?" said Etienne.

"I can disappear if I want to," Manny whispered hurriedly. "I call it ghosting. I don't know what it's really called, but I know I can do it."

"You have the gift of glamour?" asked Gaudulfus, sounding intrigued. "Well, that's most fortuitous."

"Is that what it's called?" asked Manny. "But that's not a big deal, right? I thought all Sidhe could do that."

Etienne shook his head. "We all possess magical gifts, but not all Sidhe can employ glamour. It seems to manifest mostly among those who have a need to remain unseen or to trick humans, usually more diminutive, vulnerable Fae... or certain Unseelie."

"It doesn't make a difference who has it," interrupted Adriana, "since Manny will not be the one sneaking in." She tried again to slide out from under the tarp, but this time it was Etienne who put his hand on her shoulder.

"Adriana, Manny speaks true," he said. "If he can use glamour to make himself unseen, that is our best chance of getting a pair of eyes and ears into that tavern."

"Aye, my dear," added Gaudulfus. "As gifted as you might be in the arts of stealth, there are goblin eyes out there. They will see you no matter how impenetrable the darkness may seem. Fae glamour is needed."

Settling back into the wagon with a scowl, Adriana said, "What if he's detected?"

"Then we shall arm ourselves and rush to his defense," said Etienne.

"We won't let any harm come to the lad," Gaudulfus assured her with a determined nod.

Adriana glanced down at Manny, then reached out and wiped some dirt from his cheek. "If anyone could do this, it would be Remy."

"Then that means I can do it, too," Manny said, smiling at her. He hoped he could do it. But he had snuck into the big mansion they had robbed, and that gave him some confidence.

Nodding, Adriana squeezed his arm. "Go slowly, Manny. If you rush, your glamour may fail."

Gaudulfus added reassuringly, "Be cautious and trust your instincts. I have faith in you."

Manny smiled; the words reminded him of his shadow voice's encouragement.

The dwarf is right. You can do this, his shadow voice whispered in his head. *You and the darkness are friends. She will shield and protect you.*

Taking a deep breath, Manny slid over the side of the wagon and crouched by the wheel. He closed his eyes for a moment, trying to get his heartbeat to slow down and his excited breathing under control.

Don't see me... don't see me... The thought echoed over and over in his mind.

Opening his eyes, Manny crept to the bridge, sticking close to the stone railing and the shadows gathered there. The water rushed through the dark channel below. Manny expected it to have a bad odor, like a sewer, but it didn't. It smelled like a wild mountain river, dark and deep and dangerous. As if he was crossing out of this world and into some place even stranger.

He reached the end of the bridge, took another deep breath, and started toward Gassot's tavern, as silent as a living shadow.

CHAPTER 18

Manny knew trying to go in the front door would be a bad idea, even ghosting. The goblins would be watching the archway for anyone trying to sneak in, and he had the feeling that concentrated attention might let them see through the glamour. Also, the thought of passing between those two statues gave him an uneasy itch between his shoulder blades, like they might come alive and grab him. He made for the alley beside the tavern, a narrow space between the weird angles and projections of the tavern's side wall and the crumbing stone of the ruin next to it.

He ghosted along the side of the plaza, keeping as much distance as possible between the dark shapes of the goblins and other creatures skulking just outside the circle of light from the hearth. He couldn't see much detail, just an occasional horn or high pointed ear outlined by the firelight. It reminded him unpleasantly of Morrigan's cavern, as if this might be a similar kind of meeting place. Then two shapes stepped out of the shadows near the doorway and started toward him.

Manny froze, panic closing his throat. But he fought the impulse to run, and instead just thought harder: *Don't see me, Don't see me.* The two big figures passed within three feet of him, close enough for him to hear the leather in their boots creak and the faint jangle of chain.

As they moved on across the plaza, Manny let out a long slow breath, feeling a flush of cold in his veins. He remembered health class and wondered if that was unused adrenaline. He wished he was back in health class right now.

He heard a shout from across the bridge, and looked back. Etienne and Gaudulfus were trying to turn the wagon in the narrow street, making it into an awkward process with a lot of noise and recriminations.

Good, Manny thought in relief. The goblins would be distracted, and they would hopefully think the wagon was driven by two lost farmers.

Manny reached the alley without anybody shouting an alarm. The space was a narrow cave, with openings into the ruin next door that was perched on the edge of the channel. It seemed filled with stealthy movement and rustling. He crept along it, trying not to think about what he might be stepping on or what rats or spiders might be hiding in the crevices in the walls. It was hard to see the windows and balconies above, because the angles were so odd, but he spotted a lit window up on the third floor, tucked under a balcony. That looked like a good place to start the eavesdropping.

Manny climbed the wall, finding lots of hand and footholds in the chinks and gaps of the damp mossy stone. Climbing around a gable that stuck out from the side of the tavern, he started to put his hand into a gap and heard a low growl. He jerked his hand back, almost swinging right off the wall, biting his lip to hold in a yell.

Huddled in the gap, something small and furry muttered, "Watch it."

"Sorry," Manny whispered automatically. He rubbed his hand on his shirt, suppressed a shudder, and quickly climbed on.

He reached the window. The glass was broken out and the ragged remains of rich velvet curtains hung just inside. Manny pulled himself up and cautiously peered over the sill. Inside was a dark corridor lined with closed doors, lit only by a couple of guttering candles in wall sconces. At the far end he could make out a stairwell, and he could hear a low grumble of voices, and an occasional low-pitched laugh.

I've got to get down there, Manny thought. He couldn't stop now, no matter how much he wanted to.

The alley was silent, nobody was conveniently having their secret meeting near a window. His glamour might not help him at close range, so he had to move fast, before somebody stepped out of one of those doors.

Manny climbed over the sill before he could change his mind. Concentrating on stepping lightly and his *don't see me* refrain, he hurried down the hall. The wooden planks didn't creak under his feet, so he hoped that meant the glamour was working.

He reached the stairwell. It was musty and dark, with the remnants of rich gold curtains hanging like shrouds from the upper floor, and two crooked passageways leading off into the depths of the tavern. A small balcony projected out over the stairs and he stepped cautiously onto it, peering down over the railing.

There was a big firelit room on the floor below. He could just make out some Redcaps seated at a round table, and some other smaller goblins moving around, barely visible in the bad light. The low rumble of voices was louder, but he still couldn't make out words.

Manny bit his lip. Going down there would be tricky, but he had to hear what they were saying.

Footsteps from above froze him. Two, no, three sets of boots, coming down from the upper landing. Manny stepped quietly into the nearest corner, sank down and went still as two Redcaps and something big and scary with a lot of hair came down the stairs. They turned off at the landing, and clattered right past Manny and off down the passage across the way.

Holding his breath, Manny waited for their footsteps to fade. His legs a little shaky, he pushed to his feet and went to the head of the stairs. And stopped, cocking his head to listen.

"Let's be done with this bloody mess. Keep a sharp eye out, we still—"

That was Lothair. The voice had risen and then been cut off, like it had come from a room where the door had opened and closed. But he was sure it was the troll. He wasn't likely to forget that voice. And he was sure it had come from upstairs.

So maybe that room below was the actual tavern room, where the drinks were served, and the secret meeting was on the floor above. Manny cautiously started up. He made it to the next turn, to where he had a view of part of the landing, a doorway, and a big black dog sitting beside the doorway as if standing guard.

Not a dog, his shadow voice whispered. *A Fae taking on a dog's shape.* Manny had no trouble believing it. The dog was huge, wearing a collar set with polished white stones, and it had strange light-colored eyes that almost glowed.

There had to be something worth guarding in that room. But how to get closer?

The dog turned his head, staring down toward the stairs. It bared its fangs and sniffed the air suspiciously.

Yikes, not this way, Manny thought, and eased back down the steps. But now he knew where the room was, he might be able to get to it from outside.

He ghosted back down the passage to the broken window, climbed out again, and continued up the outside wall. He made it to the roof, scrambling up over the extended eave with only a little scrabbling over the rotted wood and loose shingles. There was nothing alive up there that he could see in the dark, but with all the peaks and valleys formed by the uneven roof, it was hard to tell.

He made his way carefully toward the gable near the front of the tavern where the meeting room was. The window wasn't tightly fitted. Manny was able to work his fingers into a crack and open the catch. He swung the window open and heard voices, but still couldn't make out the words.

A big heavy beam right below the window stretched over the dark expanse of the room below. He could see someone lighting a candle to the right. Manny stepped onto the dusty surface of the beam and crouched, edging out along it, trying to get a better view. Then Lothair's voice said, "Took you bloody long enough."

Manny froze for an instant of heart-stopping terror, before he heard someone else reply, "Still your warty tongue, you stinking brute. I'm not your lackey."

Manny let out his breath slowly. Lothair hadn't been talking to him. He eased out farther along the beam. The troll, stood beside an empty stone hearth, holding a large wooden goblet loosely in his clawed hand.

Two figures faced him: one a tall man, a human, wearing a dark cloak concealing his clothes. He had long dark hair, and a wide scar running down the left side of his face from the corner of his eye to his chin. The other figure was a tall, willowy goblin man, with hair like a drift of white cornsilk, sharp handsome features, and very pale unmarked skin. He was dressed in a leather doublet over gleaming dark silk, and the sword hilt at his side was iridescent black, like the shell of a beetle. He looked delicate, almost ethereal, but there was something eerie about him, something dangerous. It was like looking at a very prettily colored snake.

The human continued, "You will enter from the

gardens. The way to the royal apartments will be unguarded." He tossed a piece of parchment on the table. "Leave the palace using the route indicated on that map. Otherwise, you run the risk of being shot."

Lothair glanced at the map. "I know the bloody plan. You just do your part. You know what's in it for you if this fails." He bared his tusks. "Morrigan ain't exactly the forgiving kind." Despite the growl in Lothair's voice, Manny thought there was an uneasy undertone to the words. As if Lothair was nervous.

Sounding disgusted and angry, the human said, "Treason, even against a boy, means a traitor's death. Far more ignoble an end than to die by a Fae hag's sorcery."

Lothair snorted. "But nowhere near as excruciating." He set his goblet down with a thump, spilling wine onto the table. "Even being hanged, drawn and quartered would be merciful, compared to what she'll do."

The human threw a wary look at the silent goblin. He said, "You trust this animal with such an important task? How can we be certain the king will not be harmed?"

Oh no, Manny thought, cold prickles creeping over his skin. *It's not just a big robbery.* They were going to do something to the king. He wasn't a very good student in history, but he knew you didn't do things to kings unless you were planning to take over the whole country.

The goblin said, "He will do what must be done. I will make sure of that." His voice was light, barely audible to Manny, but the tone sent a cold spike down his spine.

The troll shifted restlessly and growled, "Oi! I'm in the bloody room! And I ain't the one you should be worried about."

The human looked warily from one to the other. "The troll is right on one account. Failure on anyone's part is sure to be punished severely. So make certain your men are prepared for tomorrow evening..."

Manny lost the rest. The goblin man turned his head, staring straight up at Manny's hiding place. His gaze was cold and opaque, like looking into a shark's eyes. *Don't see me, don't see me, don't see me,* Manny thought, trying for calm as his heart pounded like a drum. He was deep in the shadows; the goblin couldn't possibly see him. But he felt like he was wearing a neon sign on his head.

Finally the goblin turned back to Lothair and the human. He didn't give the alarm, and the others were still talking, but Manny figured he had used up all his luck.

He eased back along the beam, silent and slow, and out the window. He carefully pushed it closed again, though he couldn't reach the catch, and started his climb back down. His hands were shaking just a little, but he made it.

CHAPTER 19

When Manny got through the alley and back to the plaza, he saw the wagon had been turned to face back down the street. Gaudulfus and Etienne stood beside it staging a rambling drunken argument that had the attention of all the Sidhe in the plaza and in the crooks and crannies of the surrounding buildings.

"Oberon's bones!" Etienne shouted. "May I be cursed with a pox if I ever take one of your blasted shortcuts again. Always we are late! It's a miracle we still have patrons in Lutetia."

"At least I'm not the one who can't stop sampling the bloody wares," Gaudulfus shouted back.

"No? Then how do you think you've arrived at your current state?"

The dwarf hiccupped loudly. "It's the only way to tolerate your incessant nagging. You're more of a tormenting harpy even than my shrew of a wife!"

Manny ghosted across the bridge, and slipped past a couple of bogles laughing at Etienne and Gaudulfus.

Moving slowly, Manny climbed onto the bed of the wagon and slipped under the tarp. "Are you all right?" Adriana whispered immediately.

He crawled up to where she was crouched just behind the wagon bench. "Yeah. We need to go." He could see Etienne and Gaudulfus jabbing fingers at each other as they continued to argue.

Adriana reached up to gently tug on one of the reins, just enough to make the harness jingle. One of the horses snorted and stamped restlessly.

In the middle of the argument, Etienne suddenly flung his arms wide to Gaudulfus. "But what does any of this matter? Always have you been as a brother to me."

The dwarf followed suit and gave Etienne an enthusiastic bear hug, causing the elf to grunt. "Aye! Surely our mothers were sisters." He kissed Etienne's cheek. "Or at the very least, close second cousins." He released Etienne and slapped him on the back. "Shall we, brother?"

"Aye," said Etienne, rolling his shoulder. "Let us complete our worthy quest."

They climbed unsteadily onto the wagon bench and urged the horses into motion, heading away from the tavern.

Gaudulfus reeled on the bench, leaning over the bed, and whispered, "Wait until we're out of the quarter."

They drove more quickly as Etienne retraced their route out of the Phantom Quarter. They turned onto a street where the buildings were less shabby and rundown, and the torches and the candlelit windows seemed brighter. "We're well out of there now," Etienne said.

Gaudulfus lifted the tarp a little. "You weren't in there very long. Did you find anything, lad?"

Manny was about to burst with the news. "They're going to do something to the king. Tomorrow night!"

"What?" Etienne jerked the reins and the horses danced in protest.

Gaudulfus muttered a curse. "That they would dare! It's madness!"

Adriana gripped Manny's arm, just as startled as Etienne and Gaudulfus. "Are you certain?"

"I'm positive," he told her. "At least that's what I

heard. Lothair was there, talking to two others."

Etienne worked the reins, easing the horses to a halt. He twisted around on the bench to face Manny and said grimly, "Tell us everything."

Manny quickly told them all he had heard, and at Etienne's prompting he described the human and the goblin who had been with Lothair. When he was finished, Etienne said thoughtfully, "The human sounds like Vasseur. He's the Captain of the Minister's Guards, and one of Magneric's chief spies."

"This is dire indeed, Etienne." Gaudulfus sounded more serious than Manny had ever heard him. "If Vasseur is involved, surely Magneric is complicit in the plot. But what does he intend? According to Manny, Vasseur seemed concerned about the king being harmed."

"I don't know..." Etienne just shook his head. "Why would Magneric give Unseelie thieves access to the king? Adriana, do you recognize the description of this goblin?"

"No." She sounded as if she was racking her memory. "It's like no one I've seen at Morrigan's lair. But if Lothair fears him, he must be a powerful Unseelie."

Gaudulfus sat back on the bench. "We had best go to Captain Corvus. We'll need the King's Chevaliers to thwart this fiendish plot."

"Yes, we'll go at once," Etienne said, and shook the reins, urging the horses into motion again.

Manny was so anxious he thought the ride across the city to the Chevalier's hotel would feel like an eternity. But despite the jouncing of the wagon, he actually fell asleep leaning against Adriana and didn't wake up until she shook him to tell him they were there. Apparently all the running and climbing and fear really wore you out.

Manny cautiously poked his head out from under the tarp as the wagon rolled to a halt. The street was still very dark, and he could just make out a gate in a tall stone wall surrounding a big house. The back gate of the Chevalier's mansion? Candlelight glowed in windows on the second floor, visible above the wall and the trees shading the courtyard. The air had a cool early morning feel to it, and Manny thought it might not be too long before dawn.

Etienne jumped down from the wagon bench and exchanged a few whispered words with the brownies guarding the gate. One of the brownies hurriedly unlocked it and swung it open, the other coming out to take the horses.

Gaudulfus climbed down from the wagon, saying, "Come on, quickly now," and gestured urgently to Manny.

Manny climbed over the side and dropped to the ground, Adriana right behind him. They followed Etienne and Gaudulfus through the gate and the dark courtyard beyond. Leaves crunched underfoot as he stumbled a little. He hoped they would have a chance to rest soon. Gaudulfus had fed them so well he wasn't too hungry, but he was beginning to feel like a sleepwalker.

Gaudulfus muttered, "Seems oddly quiet."

"It does," Etienne answered, sounding worried. "If the garrison's been called out—"

A door swung open in the house ahead, light spilling out, and Manny recognized Etienne's friend Rabican the faun. Keeping his voice cautiously low, Rabican said, "Come in, come in. Gaudulfus! By Pan's beard, it is you. I thought the gate guards must have mistaken you for someone else!"

"I retired to the country, not the grave, you impertinent goat," Gaudulfus grumbled as they followed a grinning Rabican down a short hall and into a big room.

Manny stared in awe; it was like the great hall of a castle. A stone stairway curved up to a gallery running along the second floor hung with shields and banners, and a giant hearth in one wall was almost big enough to park their wagon in. Benches and chairs and tables lined the walls, but the hall looked like it might be used for sword fighting practice by the way the wooden floor was scarred and scuffed. It was meant to hold dozens of people, but the only ones who were there now were a few older elves and brownies, sitting near the fire and sharing a bottle of wine. They looked up, startled, as Rabican led Manny and the others into the room.

"What's happened?" Rabican asked Etienne. "By these disguises you wear and your companions—not to mention the mighty Gaudulfus bestirring himself—there must be something strange afoot."

"Strange and deadly," Etienne agreed. "We need to speak to Captain Corvus immediately."

Rabican said, "He isn't here, my friend. He was called to the palace a few hours ago."

Uh oh, Manny thought. Corvus's absence might be a coincidence, or it might be part of the plot against the king.

Clearly thinking along the same lines, Etienne exchanged a worried look with Gaudulfus, and said, "Did the message explain why? Or who summoned him?"

The few other Chevaliers in the room got to their feet, drawing near to listen. Rabican made a helpless gesture. "I wasn't told the why of it, and being a good soldier I didn't question. And I assumed it was Magneric who had called for him."

It had to be part of the plot. Somebody was making sure Corvus wasn't around to help the king. "That's not good," Manny whispered to Adriana, and she squeezed his hand.

Rabican's brow furrowed with worry. "Is this to do with the regiment's orders? I thought there was something odd about them, and Corvus was none too pleased." He turned to Etienne. "The Chevaliers have been ordered to muster at dawn to journey to the Northern Garrisons."

Etienne stared. "What? When did these orders arrive?"

"This morning, not long after you left." Rabican waved a hand at the empty hall. "That's where everyone's gone, to settle their affairs in the city and make ready to depart."

Gaudulfus snorted. "Well, isn't that just a timely coincidence. It's Magneric at the center of this web, sure enough."

Maybe, Manny thought. But he figured that Morrigan wasn't the type to share the center of the web with anybody, even a Chief Minister.

"What web?" Rabican demanded. "If there's trouble afoot with Magneric—"

Etienne drew Rabican aside, speaking rapidly, "Listen to me. I must get a message to Corvus. We have reason to know there is a plot against the king—"

Manny jumped as a clatter and a bang sounded from the front of the house. Everyone in the room whipped around and drew their swords.

"The front entrance," Gaudulfus said grimly.

Adriana clutched Manny's shoulder, murmuring, "I knew it would come to this. Our luck's run out."

A spriggan ran in from the front passage, calling out, "Rabican! Minister's Guards! They attack!"

Behind him more than a dozen Minister's Guards burst into the hall. They charged the small group of Chevaliers, who surged to meet them. In the lead was Vasseur, the scarred man who had been at the meeting with Lothair and the strange goblin.

That goblin did see me after all, Manny thought, his

heart pounding as he and Adriana backed away.

Etienne shouted to Gaudulfus, "Get our friends to safety!"

Rabican wheeled around, telling Gaudulfus. "Out the back! We'll delay pursuit!"

Gaudulfus growled under his breath but said, "Save some of Magneric's men for me!" He turned, urging Manny and Adriana to the passage.

Adriana grabbed Manny's hand and they ran, Gaudulfus knocking away two of the Guards who had gotten past the Chevaliers. But just as they reached the passage two loud bangs sounded from ahead. Adriana slid to a halt, pushing Manny behind her. "That was musket fire," she said. "The house must be—"

"Surrounded!" Manny finished, as more Minister's Guards charged up the passage. He turned back, shouting, "Gaudulfus, there's more of them!"

"Get back, behind me!" Gaudulfus shouted, raising his heavy sword.

Manny and Adriana huddled together, as the fighting raged around them, swords clashing, men shouting. Adriana drew her knife, but without her staff there wasn't much she could do against the swords. Three of the Minister's Guards went down but so did one of the brownies, and the Chevaliers were still outnumbered.

Then more Minister's Guards ran in from the front of the house, carrying muskets. Manny yelled, "Look out, Etienne, they have guns!"

The Guards stopped, aiming their weapons at the knot of Chevaliers. Standing back from the fighting, Vasseur shouted, "Stop or I will order my men to fire! Lower your swords!"

The Guards drew back, and the Chevaliers backed away, but didn't lower their swords. Manny and Adriana stood behind Gaudulfus, but Manny felt as if every eye in the room was on them. This was the second time the Minister's Guards had come for him. Morrigan had to be behind this somehow.

Rabican and Etienne faced Vasseur. Rabican demanded, "Vasseur, what is the meaning of this outrage? Have you gone mad?"

Etienne said, "Perhaps he's at the wrong house. The Minister's Guards are not known for their sense of direction."

"Particularly in war," Gaudulfus contributed. "They tend to run the wrong way, toward the baggage train rather than the line of battle. I am sure it is unintentional."

"And Chevaliers are known for their unbefitting humor, even at the darkest hour," Vasseur said, unmoved by the comments. "I have warrants for the arrest of the Chevalier Etienne, and the former Chevalier known as Gaudulfus."

"On what grounds?" Gaudulfus said.

"You are accused of aiding members of the notorious gang of thieves known as the Hands of Shadow." Vasseur smiled, and gestured to Manny and Adriana. "The proof stands there."

"And if we refuse to surrender ourselves?" asked Etienne.

Vasseur raised his hand. The guards raised their muskets and taking careful aim at Etienne and his friends. Vasseur pulled a pistol, cocked it, and aimed it at Manny. Adriana pulled Manny behind her, shielding him with her body. But Vasseur moved his pistol to aim at her face. "Then you make matters far more simple for me, for which I would be most appreciative."

Etienne snarled and sheathed his crystalline blade. Slowly, the other Chevaliers followed suit.

As Gaudulfus grudgingly slammed his blade back into its scabbard, he growled, "You are a coward and a villain, Vasseur."

Vasseur smiled but lowered his pistol. "There are,

no doubt, those who think so."

CHAPTER 20

First the Minister's Guards searched Manny, Adriana, Etienne, and Gaudulfus, taking away all their weapons. Manny was the only one who didn't have extra knives hidden all through his clothing, which seemed to puzzle the guards.

Then they were escorted at gunpoint outside to a heavy wagon with a cage mounted on it. Just looking at it made Manny's skin creep; it was like something out of a horror movie.

No one spoke a word as they were made to climb in and the cage was locked. The driver urged the horses forward, and a mounted and armed escort of guards, led by Vasseur, paced the wagon as it trundled through the cobblestone streets.

Manny held onto the bars to stay on his feet as the wagon swayed back and forth. Adriana stood behind him, her hand gripping the bar just above his. Manny exchanged a gloomy glance with her and she slid her arm across his chest and hugged him close. It was still early dawn, the sun's light just touching the rooftops, and the few people in the streets stared as the wagon trundled by.

"No need to be so glum," said Gaudulfus. The dwarf sat leaning against the bars of the cage, his back to the driver, apparently completely at ease. "Etienne and I have gotten out of far more dire situations than this, lad. Why I remember one time, there was this lady of the court who Etienne had taken quite a fancy to, a buxom young nymph—"

"Gaudulfus," said Etienne, cutting him off. He looked far more grim. "Let's focus on our current dilemma." He was standing near Gaudulfus, his fingers looped over the bars at the top of the cage. He cast a glance at Manny. "He speaks true, boy. It's clear that Magneric wants us alive or else Vasseur and his men would have shot us all where we stood. Now we just need to discover why and what he intends to do with us."

Manny wished some human guy was all they had to worry about. "I think Morrigan is the one who wants us, not the Minister. Adriana's right, she's way more dangerous." He glanced up Adriana, who gave him a tight worried nod.

"But it makes no sense, lad," Gaudulfus leaned forward, sounding as if he was at least giving the idea serious consideration. "Why would an Unseelie hag with a taste for stolen jewels and gold be involving herself with the Chief Minister of Aquitania? She's the pawn, I tell you, a pawn of Magneric's. He's a wily one, that scheming old goat. He's had his eye on the throne for some time now."

"Enough talk," said Adriana, jerking her chin toward the driver. "There are others who listen."

Manny was beginning to get the shivers. "Where are they taking us?" he asked in a low voice.

Etienne pointed to a big fortress-like structure with eight towers looming in the distance. "To the Foundry, boy. Where else?"

Manny studied the intimidating towers with a growing sense of dread. "You mentioned the Foundry before. Is it a prison?"

Gaudulfus snorted. "It's *the* prison, lad. Built by my own people to contain the realm's most dangerous criminals. It's where prisoners are sent to be forgotten by the world."

Manny swallowed. "That doesn't sound good."

"Indeed," replied Gaudulfus. "It's an impregnable fortress filled with granite cells overrun by rats and guarded by cruel jailors trained in the distasteful and gruesome arts of torture."

Etienne shot a scowl at Gaudulfus, and Manny suspected his expression had just gone from worry to terror. "But not to worry lad," Gaudulfus quickly added, "for if anyone can escape from the Foundry, it will most definitely be a dwarf."

The wagon rattled across the bridge over the Foundry's moat and through the imposing gates. They passed through an outer courtyard, where there seemed to be lots of people loitering and staring, and then through a second well-guarded gate protected by a portcullis of heavy iron bars. In the big courtyard the wagon stopped, the door of the cage was unlocked, and the guards ordered them out.

As Manny climbed down he looked furtively around, curious despite the hard knot of fear in his stomach. At first glance it looked more like the inside of a castle than a prison, with stone or timbered three story buildings tucked against the walls, some opening onto a gallery that looked down on the courtyard. Manny caught the smell of cooking, and heard chickens cackling somewhere nearby.

But the guards made them walk across the court toward the base of the nearest tower, toward a big double wooden door with heavy locks, and there was no mistaking that this place was a prison.

Many of the Foundry's turnkeys seemed to be spriggans. Two hurried to open the door for the Minister's Guards, and Gaudulfus said, "It's to be the dungeons, then. How thorough of Magneric."

Manny felt even more sick. He hoped they weren't separated. He hoped nobody would try to torture him. And he knew he needed to be the streetwise elf kid right now, not the ordinary human kid from Austin, but it was hard.

The heavy door swung open and they were conducted through a guard room and down a dark torch-lit spiral staircase. A lump of fear stuck in Manny's throat. The air was dank and smelled of foul water and rot.

He wasn't sure how far underground they were when they turned down a corridor, and then were prodded through another doorway into a cell.

The door to their cell closed with a loud, permanent-sounding clank. Manny had never heard such a depressing sound before. The cell itself was roughly octagonal in shape, with dirty straw, caked in mud and other substances Manny didn't even want to guess at, covering the floor in stinking patches. The smell of dirty water was stronger, and Manny heard frogs croaking somewhere nearby, though it was too dark to see if there were any in the cell. A narrow iron bed was fixed against one of the walls. Stools, which seemed to be held together with mold and grime, sat at the base of the wall. A little light came in through the small grill in the cell door, and weak dust-filled sunlight trickled in through a tall, barred slit at the very top of the wall.

Gaudulfus lay down on the metal bed, which creaked in protest under his weight. "I still say we could have taken them, Etienne. Vasseur only had about a dozen of his men. A bare dozen! An insult, if you ask me."

Etienne paced in front of the cell door like a trapped tiger. "If it were just you and I, my friend, I might agree. But I saw the look in that assassin's eyes. Vasseur would not have hesitated to shoot the boy."

He cast a quick glance in Manny and Adriana's direction. "Or Adriana."

"I'm touched that you care." Adriana rolled her eyes, and took a seat on one of the battered stools.

"So what do we do now?" asked Manny, still standing in the middle of the room. There was nothing in here he wanted to touch.

"I'm thinking," replied Etienne, still pacing.

"Don't you have any kind of Sidhe ability?" Manny asked, even though he knew he sounded a little desperate. "Something that can help us escape?"

"Yes, now, wouldn't that be rather convenient," said Gaudulfus, his hands behind his head, his eyes closed. "Maybe you can produce a lock pick out of your nose, or a goodly amount of black powder out of your bum so we can blow the door to splinters."

Adriana chuckled, which earned her a frown from Etienne. "You're a thief," he said. "Do you have any lock picks secreted somewhere on your person?"

She patted her clothing. "Sorry, I seem to have put all my secret lock picks in my other vest. And that search was rather thorough."

Manny shifted uneasily, certain he saw something moving stealthily under the straw. To distract himself, he said to Etienne, "If only you had your crystal sword."

"Hah!" Gaudulfus waved a hand dismissively. "For all the good that fancy bit of Fae glass would do us."

"What do you mean?" Manny said, startled. "I thought it was magic." He was pretty sure it was magic, at least from the way it looked when he had watched Etienne fight the duel.

Etienne stopped pacing and turned to face him. As if reluctant to explain, he said, "Amechanteur is an enchanted blade, but it wouldn't help us escape, no more so than an ordinary sword."

Manny could tell Etienne didn't want to talk about it, but he had to ask. "What does it do? Besides skewer people, I mean."

Etienne said, "It's an ancient Fae weapon, said to have great power—"

"Don't fill the lad's head with such nonsense," Gaudulfus grumbled.

"Do me the courtesy of remaining silent, Gaudulfus," snapped Etienne.

The dwarf shrugged, then crossed his hands over his chest and pretended to settle in to sleep.

Etienne took a deep breath before continuing. "It was forged over a thousand years ago by King Oberon himself, and was given to King Childeric IX as part of the treaty that ended the Hundred Year War and brought peace to Albion and Aquitania. It was a mighty gift and proof that Oberon truly wanted friendship between his subjects and the people of Aquitania, Sidhe and human alike."

Manny frowned, confused. "Okay, so what great power does it have?"

"In a time of great need, it awakens and sings." Etienne's gaze was on the far wall of the cell, his expression distracted, as if he saw something else past the dirty stone. "But only when wielded by a swordsman whose cause is just and whose heart is true. The spirit of the blade bonds with the soul of that swordsman and he becomes a Blade Singer, a champion without equal."

Gaudulfus cleared his throat loudly and rolled onto his side, his back to the room.

"Why do you have it?" Manny asked, then thought, *Okay, that didn't come out right.* "Not that you aren't a champion without equal, I mean, but..."

Etienne straightened, his chin lifting. "It was a reward from His Majesty, a gift for saving his life during the War of Supremacy."

"This king? The one that's in danger?" asked Manny.

"No, his father, Clovis VI," replied Etienne. "After

King Oberon's assassination, King Clovis threw his support behind Queen Gloriana during her struggle against her sister Mab for the throne of Albion. The violent civil war that followed almost tore Albion apart. Mab would have won the crown had we not mustered to the defense of the fair Gloriana." Etienne folded his arms and leaned on the cell door. "But those were different times."

Manny glanced over at Adriana and found her studying Etienne carefully. Turning his attention back to the Chevalier, Manny said, "But still, why would the king have given away such an amazing sword? Didn't he want it for himself?"

"Because," said Gaudulfus, suddenly sitting up on the cot. "The damn thing doesn't work. It's just a story, lad. It's not really magic. Which was why the king didn't hesitate to part with it. He had enough pretty baubles, and a pretty bauble that doesn't do what legend said it should is an embarrassment." He eyed Etienne. "Such a gift is no mark of favor."

Etienne gave Gaudulfus a hard look but kept silent.

Gaudulfus sighed. "Although it's still a very fine blade," he added.

Manny knew he should probably stop prodding this sore point, but he couldn't help it. "Has it ever worked?"

Etienne looked down, tapping his boot against the wall to dislodge some mud. "Not for me. Not yet, at least."

Manny could hear the self-reproach in the elf's voice, and recognized it in his downcast eyes. His father had had the same telltale signs when he had been guilty about something he had done. Or in this case, not done. *But it's not his fault,* Manny thought. *It can't be.*

Manny was about to say that when approaching footsteps caused them to face the cell's door.

Through the small grill, Manny saw the jailor, a

nervous spriggan with few teeth, unlocking the door. Behind him stood Vasseur and several Minister's Guards armed with muskets. The jailor yanked the cell door open and four of the guards moved in and fanned out, aiming their weapons. Etienne and Gaudulfus stepped in front of Manny and Adriana.

Smiling as if he was enjoying this situation far too much, Vasseur stepped into the cell. "I do hope I'm not interrupting anything."

"What do you want, Vasseur?" said Etienne.

"His Eminence, the Chief Minister, wants a word with one of you," Vasseur said.

Etienne and Gaudulfus exchanged a look, then Etienne stepped forward.

"Oh, the audience is not with you, Chevalier." Vasseur held up his hand. Then he pointed at Manny. "It's with the little goblin pickpocket."

Manny's heart sunk.

"No!" Adriana snapped, grabbing Manny's shoulder. "He's not going anywhere with you."

"I'm afraid he doesn't have a choice," said Vasseur, his smile vanishing. He drew a pistol, cocked it, and aimed at Etienne. "I can see what you're thinking, Chevalier. You and that fat dwarf think you can rush us."

Etienne and Gaudulfus hadn't moved, but something in their stance had turned predatory.

The guards in the cell knelt and cocked their muskets.

"The boy is not to be harmed," Vasseur said, watching them carefully. "But if you resist, I have orders to shoot all of you."

"Contemptible coward," Gaudulfus growled, scowling fiercely at Vasseur. "Take one of us, not the boy."

"What good is the word of an assassin like you?" Etienne said, his voice tight with tension.

Manny could see that the Minister's Guards were

nervous. Some of them looked ready to fire at any moment. He bet that Vasseur wanted an excuse to shoot, he wanted to be able to say that Etienne and Gaudulfus had forced his hand. *It's me, or we all get killed.*

He didn't want to do it, but he made himself step forward, pulling away from Adriana. "I'll come with you. Just don't shoot them."

"Manny, don't!" Adriana lunged, reaching for him, but Manny ducked past her hands. Vasseur grabbed him by the shoulder and spun him around, pressing the barrel of his pistol to his ear.

"There's a sharp lad," Vasseur said easily, his eyes still on Etienne. "It's not surprising the wisest of your number is a street urchin."

Gaudulfus started forward, but Etienne caught his shoulder. "Be still, Gaudulfus," said Etienne. "And you." He moved to block Adriana as she tried to shoulder past him.

"No! They'll kill him! I know they will!" Adriana sounded furious, but there was real fear in her eyes.

"Don't worry, Adriana," said Manny, swallowing the lump in his throat. "I'll be okay. You'll see." He tried to sound brave but he knew he mostly sounded sick.

Manny lost sight of his friends as Vasseur dragged him out of the cell. The Minister's Guards backed out after them, their weapons still trained on the prisoners.

As the jailor locked the door, Etienne looked through the barred window. "If you harm him in any way, Vasseur, I swear on my life that I shall kill you."

The level of menace in the Chevalier's voice startled Manny. Behind him, he could feel Vasseur stiffen. Even the Minister's Guards backed away.

Etienne's expression was tight with anger. "I will come for you, Manny. You have my word. I will come for you."

As Manny was taken away, he couldn't tear his gaze

away from those blue eyes. He could no longer see Etienne, the King's Chevalier, or even an elf from a magical realm. All he could see was his father.

CHAPTER 21

Holding Manny by the scruff of his shirt, Vasseur hauled him up the stairs, angrily knocking him into stone corners. They took Manny out through the tower door, into the inner courtyard, and Manny winced at the suddenly too-bright cloudy morning light.

Vasseur hauled Manny toward the gate to the outer courtyard, the spriggans and other workers staring. Manny tried to pull free of Vasseur. "You don't have to drag me!" Vasseur just tightened his grip and gave Manny a violent shake.

"Keep still, you Unseelie rat!" Vasseur snapped.

An immense black carriage with thick drapes pulled tight across the windows sat in the now deserted outer courtyard. Vasseur headed straight for it and pulled open the door.

"Where are you taking me?" Manny demanded, still struggling.

Vasseur lifted him by his scruff and the seat of his pants and tossed him into the carriage. Manny landed hard on the wooden floor, and the door slammed shut behind him.

The rank odor inside hit Manny immediately. He scrambled to his feet and pressed himself back against the cushioned seat closest to the driver.

Opposite him, a big shape loomed in the darkness, but Manny didn't need to see it to know who it was.

Lothair leaned forward into the dim light falling through the gaps in the curtains. He smiled, his lips pulling back to show his sharp tusks. "Well, ain't you the slippery one. We've been looking all over Lutetia for you, runt."

Manny glanced at the doors of the carriage.

"Oh, you're fast," said Lothair, reading his intention. "But you ain't that fast. Just try and make a run for it. I'll bite your fingers off." He licked his lips with his warty purple tongue.

Manny swallowed, and managed to find his voice. "Vasseur said I was going to see Minister Magneric." *Didn't he?*

The troll laughed. "Now what would a minister want with an insignificant lump of dung like you? No, runt, you've got another audience in your future. Morrigan misses you so. She's eager to see you again."

Fighting off a shiver, Manny pushed himself up into the seat and took a deep breath. "So Morrigan is interested in lumps of dung?" He eyed Lothair from head to foot. "I guess that makes sense."

Lothair's expression went flat with anger. His clawed hands balled into fists, his knuckles popping.

Uh oh, thought Manny in a panic. *Yeah, that was probably a mistake.*

Lothair grabbed Manny's arm, his sudden movement causing the carriage to rock violently back and forth. Manny was stunned. He had no idea something that big could move so fast.

"Have a care," Lothair snarled, "how you talk to me, rat!" Manny cried out as the troll squeezed his arm. It felt like it was going to break.

The door opened and a tall, slender figure slid into the carriage.

"Drop him."

Lothair turned to the cloaked and hooded figure, squinting at the light. "This runt can't mouth off like that—"

"You heard me," the voice said.

With a growl, Lothair released Manny, who dropped to the seat and huddled in the corner. Lothair eased back, watching the figure warily.

The figure closed the door, shrouding the interior of the carriage once more in shadows. He took a seat next to Manny.

It took several moments of deep breathing and rubbing his arm for Manny to get the pain to subside and some feeling back into his fingers. The carriage jolted and started to move. He could hear the driver's whip and muffled voice spurring the horses forward.

The figure slipped off the hood. It was the tall pale goblin Manny had seen in Gassot's.

"It's not wise to taunt a troll," he said, studying Manny with those opaque eyes. His expression was so cold and neutral, as if nothing that happened here was his concern.

Manny rolled his shoulder and flexed his elbow. "Tell me about it." His voice sounded hoarse and strained.

"I understand you are quite an interesting creature," the goblin said. "Why is that?"

"You got me." Manny shrugged, trying to sound tough and brave. "Maybe it's my sparkling personality."

The goblin smiled. "You speak in a strange manner. I cannot place the land of your birth. I have traveled extensively and am familiar with many languages and many modes of speech. But yours... Most peculiar. Tell me, who are you and where do you come from?"

Manny's mouth clamped shut. *You idiot. Stop talking. He'll know something's wrong with you.*

"I suggest you answer my questions," said the goblin. "Or I may allow Lothair to persuade you."

The troll snarled, leaning forward. Manny shrank back.

"Who are you and where do you come from?" the

goblin repeated.

"My name is Remy. I'm from Lutetia," said Manny. "Where else would I be from?"

"You are most definitely not Remy. Although I must confess both of you have a similar spirit."

Manny frowned, looking up into those cold yellow eyes. "Have we met before?"

The eyes widened in surprise. "You don't recall?"

Stop talking! Stop talking! You're making things worse! Manny squirmed. "Uh, sure. Of course I remember."

"Then describe it to me."

Manny chewed his lip. "Uhm, I met you... in Morrigan's lair." He held his breath and hoped that hadn't sounded too much like a question.

The goblin tilted his head thoughtfully. "We've never met before today."

Manny slowly released his breath, his shoulders slumping. *Crud...* He couldn't believe he had fallen for the oldest trick on TV.

The goblin said, "So allow me to introduce myself. I am Thomas Grim." He inclined his head. "Formerly of Albion."

Manny blinked. *Albion?* He had managed to piece together enough from Etienne's story to know that Albion was a land inhabited mostly by Sidhe. That was the kingdom that Oberon once ruled, and it was also the enemy of Aquitania.

Grim arched his brow. "And you are?"

Manny just stared. He had done a bad job of lying to Grim so far, and he didn't think continuing to try would do him any good. And he had no intention of telling him the truth.

The goblin studied him. "Very well, keep your secrets for now. But allow me to offer a little counsel. When you are brought before Lady Morrigan, I suggest you loosen your tongue and tell her everything she wishes to know. She is neither as patient nor as kind as Lothair."

The troll snapped his teeth and snarled.

Manny drew his legs up underneath him. *Why did he call her "Lady" Morrigan?* He couldn't imagine such a hideous hag being called a "lady" by anyone, even a creepy goblin like Grim. He knew that there was much more to that Unseelie witch than met the eye; maybe she had been the one responsible for bringing him to this world.

And that thought scared him more than anything.

The journey down to the sewers and into the depths of the Undercity was even more oppressive in the company of Grim and Lothair. Manny couldn't stop thinking of the story in his mythology book of Orpheus and his descent into Hades, the Greek Underworld. He wished now that he'd read that story much more carefully because he couldn't remember how Orpheus had escaped that gloomy place.

He knew that he had no chance of eluding both Lothair and Grim, even if he tried to ghost. The goblin especially gave off vibes that he would not only be able to see through his glamour, but could easily catch him. Whenever Manny dared a peek, the goblin had been watching him, his strange eyes unblinking.

The vast subterranean chamber appeared abandoned and was no longer lit by a fire. Instead, shafts of sunlight shown in from several barred grilles high overhead. Manny was surprised to realize that the chamber actually had openings to the surface, though the bright bands of light made the shadows at the edges of the room darker. He knew that Lothair had no love of the sun and wondered if the troll found that annoying. He hoped so.

Morrigan, her winged figure a series of shadowy

coils in the dark, reclined on her fur-covered throne on the raised dais. Her owlish eyes followed Manny as he made himself cross the chamber toward her.

Manny could sense her smiling, could feel it raising gooseflesh on his arms. He froze about fifteen feet from the dais. Grim pushed him closer to the witch. Lothair hung back in the darkness, growling.

Morrigan leaned forward, her wings creaking like an old leather jacket. "My dear boy, why have you been such a bother to your old Auntie Morrigan? I was starting to think you were avoiding me on purpose." She sniffed, her lips set in a mocking pout. "And that hurt your Auntie's feelings."

Manny's throat closed and his legs shook. *Don't be scared. Stay calm. She'll use your fear to control you,* his shadow voice urged.

"There's no need to be afraid of me." Morrigan easily read his terror. "I only want to have a few words with you. That's all. Just a pleasant little chat."

Grim put his hand on Manny's shoulder, making him jump. Manny managed to croak, "I—I don't have anything t—to say."

"You'll have to speak up," said Morrigan. "I'm afraid I'm not as young as I once was. They say your hearing is always the first sense to go."

Manny braced himself and tried to speak again. "There's nothing to talk about." Although his voice quavered, he was pretty sure she had heard him that time.

"Quite the contrary," she corrected. "Your presence here is certainly portentous, and, in my learned opinion, no mere coincidence."

Manny looked down at his feet. "I don't know what you're talking about." He really didn't.

Morrigan rose from her throne. Manny stepped back in alarm and bumped into Grim. With delicate grace, the hag stepped down from the dais and stood towering over Manny. "Oh no, we shall not begin like this," she hissed. "If we are to proceed, and I assure you we will, then we must be completely honest with one another."

Manny could only stare into her eyes, his breath caught in his throat.

Morrigan tapped her clawed finger on her chin. "I shall make you a generous offer. I vow to be truthful with you, on any topic you might choose to discuss, if in exchange you vow to be truthful with me. What do you say? Do we have an arrangement?"

Managing a quick shake of his head, Manny muttered, "I can't answer any of your questions. I don't know anything."

Another exaggerated pout pinched Morrigan's features. "Oh, is that because you want to guard your secrets from me? What if I told you I already knew most of them?"

Manny's eyes widened in surprise. "I... don't believe you. I don't have any secrets."

Morrigan glanced at Grim. "Where has trust gone in this world, Lord Grim?"

"It is certainly a rare commodity these days, my lady," he replied.

Morrigan regarded Manny. "Your name is Manny. Your spirit has come from another realm and it currently occupies the body of one of my pickpockets, a budding goblin known as Remy. The world you hail from possesses a strange and potent magic and devices of such cunning and such destructive power that men use them to dominate and rule over vast and mighty nations. An enchanted coin brought you here, a relic whose secrets I am quite eager to learn."

Manny just stared, stunned and horrified.. "How how do you—?"

"Know all of this?" she finished his question. "My dear boy, do not fret, for I have every intention of showing you."

CHAPTER 22

The crystal glowed with an eerie purple light. It was shaped roughly like a jagged teardrop, with angular facets that glittered and sparkled. It floated, spinning like a top, above a golden brazier with struts that supported a ring in the center. It was obviously intended to cradle the crystal when it wasn't suspended in the air.

"Isn't it beautiful? It's a scrying crystal. This is how I see the truth." Morrigan's voice was a gentle purr.

Manny stared deep into the crystal's mesmerizing light. It was beautiful. So much so that it even banished some of his terror. And given the fact that he was kneeling across from a nightmarish Unseelie hag, terror was a natural emotion.

Morrigan had awakened the crystal with a few waves of her spidery fingers. After forcing Manny to kneel in front of the table, Grim had gone to stand in the shadows. Lothair had disappeared.

Morrigan studied the scrying crystal. "It shows me almost anything I ask, even the most secret desires locked in a man's heart. And when I grew curious about you, dear Manny, oh, the things it revealed to me." She looked up at Manny with a smile.

Manny settled back. "If you have this, what do you need me for?"

"As I said, it shows me *almost* anything I ask. There

are still some unanswered questions. Some force seems to be shielding you, you lucky boy. A powerful force. Don't you find that intriguing?"

Manny did find that intriguing. *What could be protecting me?* He hadn't made any other allies besides Adriana, Etienne, and Gaudulfus, and he didn't think any of them did that sort of magical stuff. He needed answers of his own.

"You said you would be honest with me if I was honest with you," he said. "Did you mean that?"

"Of course! I never break a vow. Ask me anything."

"Okay, who are you?"

Morrigan lifted her brows. "My sweetest Manny, surely you know who I am."

"I mean, who are you, really? Everyone believes you're a dangerous witch, a thief, and the leader of the Hands of Shadow. But you're more than that, right? Grim called you a 'lady' and you're involved with really important people like Minister Magneric."

He could tell Morrigan wasn't displeased by the question, as if he was a student she was trying to teach. "True."

"So who are you, really?"

Morrigan stood and slowly spread her wings. Up close Manny found them both intimidating and fascinating. The maze of wrinkles and veins that covered the leathery membranes looked almost like some sort of archaic script. The rest of her body was covered in layers of flowing black rags of tattered silk. Her gray hair was a rat's nest atop her elongated head, the tips of her long, pointed ears poking out like two reeds. Her glowing eyes and her wide mouth, filled with those sharp teeth, were her most disturbing features.

"What you see is Morrigan, the creature you have described so eloquently, my boy," she said. "My countenance is hideous, befitting that of a monstrous hag that haunts the sewers of Lutetia and steals for a living."

Manny couldn't argue with that.

"That is who I am now," she said, her voice low. "But that is not who I have always been."

In a quick motion, she wrapped her wings about herself, her form shuddering and undulating. A bitterly cold wind suddenly blew in from the surrounding darkness and buffeted Manny, nearly knocking him over backward.

In the midst of this tempest, Morrigan's form shifted and transformed. Her wings melted into a black cloak of shining silk, whipping around her body until the wind died down. The cloak lowered and parted as her arms came to rest at her sides.

Manny gaped at her.

Where the hag had once been there now stood an elegant, beautiful woman whose pale skin glowed with a ghostly light. Her eyes were oval pools of darkest night and her lips were as red as a rose. Her hair cascaded down her shoulders in rivers of shimmering ebony. A long, silk gown of the deepest red covered her shapely form, as snug and sinuous as snake's skin.

"This," she said, her voice like a chill evening breeze, "Is who I truly am. I am Queen Mab, monarch of Albion."

"Whoa," Manny gasped. "You— you're Queen Gloriana's sister? The one who tried to take the throne from her?"

"Silence!" snapped Mab, her angelic face contorting and briefly transforming back into its demonic visage.

Manny winced away, covering his ears.

With a great effort, Mab relaxed, taking a deep breath. Her features smoothed out into angelic beauty again. "You must forgive me, dear boy, but that name is not to be spoken in my presence. Do you understand?"

Swallowing nervously, Manny removed his hands from his ears. "Sorry..."

"No harm done. Now it's my turn. Where did you get the enchanted coin that brought you here?"

Manny's mouth clamped shut. *I can't tell her that. She might find a way to get to my world and hurt Tia Licha. I've got to lie to her.*

"Now, now, dearest Manny," Mab said, "don't back out on our arrangement now. That would vex me quite terribly." She leaned forward, her smile sweet and chill.

"I borrowed it," Manny stammered. "From a friend."

"Does this friend have a name?" asked Mab.

"Yeah," he replied, his mind racing. *Who can I blame? Will she know it's a lie? What will she do if I don't tell her the truth?* "His name is Gregory Salazar," he blurted out, then bit his lip. "And I didn't borrow it. I stole it from him."

Mab studied his face for a long time. Manny hoped the mix of truth and lie was convincing. "I see. And do you know where Gregory acquired it?"

Manny shrugged. "I'm not sure, but I think it might have been in a book."

"Excellent, now we're getting somewhere."

"Now it's my turn!"

Mab inclined her head. "So it is."

"What are you going to do to the king?"

Mab looked up at Grim. "Should I tell him that, Lord Grim?"

"You know best, my lady," the goblin replied. "But I would advise caution. At least until after the deed is done."

Mab reached down and caressed Manny's cheek with a slender finger. "Do you hear, sweetest Manny? You've made Lord Grim nervous. And that is something very few people can do to the legendary Bloody-Bones, or as I prefer to call him, Tommy Rawhead."

Glancing at Grim, Manny frowned. Those names sounded awful, but they seemed to suit the cold-eyed, willowy goblin. "Uh, okay."

"But in the spirit of our arrangement," Mab said, "I shall answer your question. I intend to send Lord Grim and Lothair into the palace tonight to murder the young King Clovis and his mother, Giselle."

"That's terrible!" Manny said, but he wasn't surprised. "Why would you do that?"

"Because the deaths of human royalty at the hands of Sidhe assassins is precisely the fuel that is needed for the cauldron that is Aquitania. You've seen the situation in the streets, my clever boy. A civil war between the humans and the Sidhe bubbles just beneath the surface, and I've done everything I can to stoke the flames. All it needs now is just a little more heat in order to boil over and consume this kingdom and her people."

Manny shoved to his feet. "No! I won't let you do that! I'll warn Etienne and Gaudulfus and they'll stop you."

Mab laughed. "Foolish child, Etienne is to blame for all of this. If he and his accursed king had not meddled in my affairs, it would be my hated sister rotting in this stinking sewer now instead of me. I have a score to settle with him and I intend to do just that."

Taking a deep breath, Manny bolted into the darkness, making for the cover of some crumbling pillars. *Don't see me! Don't see me!* he chanted to himself.

He sensed more than saw Grim behind him. Manny ran in a zigzag pattern, trying his best to elude capture. There was a blur of motion just at the edge of his vision moments before a searing pain hit Manny in the back of his head. His legs went wobbly and his vision dimmed.

He felt himself falling and a roaring sounded in his ears. Monstrous faces with viper eyes and needle-like teeth swam before his vision.

The last sensation Manny felt before darkness

claimed him was of being lifted by icy cold hands, the last thing he heard was a hiss, "Stupid boy!"

Manny came to with a terrible, pounding headache, and a bright light in his eyes. Wincing, he reached up and touched the back of his head. It was wet and sticky. His bloody fingers confirmed he had been hit by something hard enough to break the skin.

He lay on filthy animal skins covering the bottom of a circular metal cage. It hung in one of the shafts of sunlight that fell through the barred openings high above. He sat up, and the cage swung slightly, setting off a sympathetic lurch in his stomach. The bottom was a few feet above the floor. A quick glance up at the top of the cage revealed the thick rope tied around the uppermost bars, suspending it from a beam stretching between two of the stone pillars.

"Welcome back," a voice said.

Manny twisted around and focused on Morrigan. And it was definitely the witch Morrigan who was speaking to him, and not her alter-ego Mab. The bat-winged hag reclined once again on her throne, only a short distance away. The scrying stone sat on its tripod at her feet, glimmering in the faint light.

"Your rude gesture has forced me to rescind our arrangement," she said. "A shame, as I was so enjoying our discourse."

Grim stood a few feet away from Morrigan, giving Manny a cold unblinking stare.

"But it seems Lord Grim was correct," continued Morrigan. "We should attend to the matter at hand. Then, afterwards, as Lutetia burns, you and I can spend as much time as we wish together."

Manny got painfully to his knees, holding onto the bars to keep from falling over. "Etienne... will stop you," he said. "You'll see."

Morrigan chuckled. "You are very fond of this Chevalier, aren't you? I must admit, he does have an annoying habit of appearing where he is not wanted." She got to her feet. "I have decided to take Grim's advice and make sure he will never be a thorn in my side again."

She held out her clawed hand and closed her eyes. A strange chanting began deep in her throat, a droning, disturbing sound. Her lips did not move but the bizarre sound grew in volume and intensity, reminding Manny of the cicadas that hid in the trees of his yard on the hottest summers.

Morrigan opened her eyes, her impossibly wide mouth parted with a wet gasp. A sickly, luminescent blood-red vapor oozed out from behind her sharp teeth and slithered down her torso, pooling on the floor in front of the dais.

The vapor started to coalesce and take shape in the bloody pool. A tiny, red and black lizard-like shape began to squirm in the center, slowly absorbing more and more of the vapor. The creature's tiny mouth parted and it shrieked like a banshee.

CHAPTER 23

Disgusted, Manny winced as he studied the tiny creature. "What is that thing?"

"Just a little newt to make certain your friends in the Foundry don't talk to anyone likely to listen." Morrigan made a sharp gesture, and the creature leapt out of the mist and whipped across the room, glowing red in the shadows. Quicker than thought, it shot up the long stairway, around the upper part of the room and vanished out through the doorway into the sewers. "Once it arrives, it will assume its true form." She added, "I told Adriana the consequences of betrayal."

Manny stared after the creature, horrified. *She's sending it to kill them.* Trapped in the cell, unarmed, they would have little chance against whatever that thing was.

Morrigan swept to her feet and stepped down off the dais. "And when I return from my work at the palace, you will tell me what I want to know, dear boy. Make no mistake. If you defy me, you'll envy your friends their quick deaths."

Manny sat silently, watching Morrigan and Lord Grim leave the lair. Once they were gone, he let out his breath in relief. The good thing was, he didn't think there were any guards left behind, at least in this room. It was difficult to see into the darkness past the circle of sunlight, but he couldn't hear anyone, or sense any movement. Morrigan must have needed all the members of the Hands of Shadow to attack the palace. *I've got to get out of here, and fast, before that newt thing gets to the Foundry.*

He pulled at the lock, wrenched it back and forth, putting all his weight and strength into it. He used a lot of swear words that Tia Licha liked to pretend he didn't know, but it wouldn't give way.

Remy could pick this lock, he thought in frustration. He sort of knew how himself, fragments of knowledge that popped into his head out of nowhere, out of that part of him that was somehow still tied to Remy. Except he needed some metal picks to try it, and he had nothing but his clothes.

Okay, okay. Be calm and think. He looked up. *Maybe I could untie the rope, then at least I'd be on the ground.* He stood, wavering a little as his head swam, then climbed the bars to reach the top of the cage.

He dug at the rope with his fingers, then tried to gnaw on it. But it was so big and solid it was like concrete, and even his half-goblin teeth didn't put a dent in it. Clinging to the top of the cage, Manny looked around again.

A few feet away, there was a pillar, one of the supports for the beam the cage hung from. An old rusted torch bracket was attached to it. If he could get his hands on it, he might be able to take it apart to get some pieces of metal he could use to pick the lock. Manny strained to reach for it but it was just too far. He dropped to the floor of the cage, making the whole thing sway. He eyed the bracket again. *Okay, let's try this.*

He pulled his shirt off, twisting and knotting it until he had a short rope with a loop on the end. Climbing to the top of the cage, he worked his arm out through the bars and tried to lasso the bracket.

After a moment, Manny had to give up. The rope was just too short. He dropped to the floor of the cage again, feeling it jerk a little under his weight. Now there was a possibility. He flung himself forward into the bars, then back as hard as he could, and was rewarded with a sway from the heavy cage.

Manny kept at it, though his head hurt. He hit the bars so hard he was bruising himself, making himself dizzy, but soon he had the cage swinging back and forth. When it was going as far as he could make it, he swung up to the top again, reached out, and slung his rope toward the bracket. The loop caught.

Manny's gasp of triumph cut off as the cage swung back and the rope yanked hard at his arm. With a snap, the bracket broke right off the pillar, taking a large chunk of stone with it. The rope jerked out of Manny's grip, banging his elbow painfully against the bars.

Manny dropped to the floor of the cage again, sitting in a dejected slump and holding his aching head. The cage swung back and forth, finally slowing to a halt. *Augh, that was a waste of time...*

He looked down. The bracket had bounced out of reach, but the stone chunk had broken apart and now lay in scattered fragments below the cage. Pulling the animal skins aside, he flattened himself against the bottom of the cage and tried to reach the fragments. The ground was just a little too far so he worked a leg through the bars and managed to pick up a few good chunks with his toes.

That minor triumph didn't last long. Now he had some rocks, but bashing the lock with them didn't work, and the stone wasn't sharp enough to cut the rope. Manny looked around again, frustrated, biting his lip. And his gaze fell on Morrigan's scrying crystal, still sitting on its tripod.

The edge of the crystal itself might be sharp, and if he could get a hold of the tripod, that was metal. It was definitely worth a shot. Manny took a piece of stone and scooted forward, working his arm through the bars, and threw the stone at the base of the tripod.

It took a few tries, and he was down to his last good-sized rock, but he finally hit the leg of the tripod. It fell, sending the crystal rolling toward the cage. Manny retrieved it with the help of his toes.

He could already tell this wasn't going to work, because the edge didn't feel nearly as sharp as he had expected. But as soon as he pulled the crystal into the full sunlight, it sparked like a spotlight.

Manny winced away from it, black spots dancing in his vision. It was like looking into the sun. *Maybe because it's an Unseelie thing, and it's not supposed to be out in the sun.*

Wishing he had a pair of dark sunglasses, he angled the crystal back and forth, trying to figure out what he could do with it. At least it was letting him see more of the room, reflecting the sunlight into a laser-like beam.

Like a magnifying glass in the sun, only much stronger, Manny thought, inspired.

Magnifying glasses or lenses could be used to start a campfire, like that kid lost in the mountains had done in the book they had read a couple of years ago in English class. Squinting his eyes, he angled the crystal around, trying to aim it up at the rope holding the cage.

Soon he was rewarded with the smell of burning rope, like a weird combination of burning hay and hair. The crystal was getting warm in his hands, too warm. He wished he had thought to use his knotted shirt to protect his skin, but he didn't dare move the crystal.

The cage jerked suddenly, knocking Manny painfully against the bars. It hung for a heartbeat, then the rest of the rope gave way. The cage hit the floor with a clang, fell over, and rolled across the room.

It bumped against something and came to a stop. Manny groaned, holding his aching head, and managed to sit up. The cage rocked with his movement, grinding against the stones around the fire pit that had halted its progress across the room.

At least I've got plenty of rocks now, he thought woozily. Then he focused on what else lay at the edge of the fire pit, just within reach.

Metal skewers.

Hah! Manny's thought blended with a triumphant echo from his inner voice. He grabbed two of the skewers and within minutes managed to pick the lock.

He shoved the door open, climbed out, and staggered a little. "I did it," he said aloud. "I really did it." Now he needed to get back out through the sewer...

A sudden noise made him freeze in fear. Voices and footsteps echoed from above. Somebody was coming.

Morrigan did leave guards! They must have been in the passage just above the lair, and heard the bang when the cage fell.

Manny grabbed his knotted-up shirt and sprinted across the room, to the base of the stairs. There he huddled back into the shadows and ghosted.

Two goblins clattered down the steps, their weapons and the chains on their shabby leather armor rattling like bones. They saw the fallen cage and growled in alarm, running to it.

Manny didn't stay to watch. He hurried up the stairs, ghosting as hard as he could. He reached the top and slipped through the big doorway and into the tunnel. The sewer stink was almost a relief. He knew the way back to the surface, or at least Remy did.

Now he just had to find a way to save Adriana and the others.

Manny took a direct route across the rooftops, glad

he could see the Foundry in the distance. He had to detour to the street at one point to bypass a multi-roof pixie city. But he caught a ride on the back of a big wagon stacked high with barrels, without the driver seeing him.

As Manny neared the Foundry, he ghosted to blend with the Sidhe and humans on the street, just one more kid nobody looked twice at. This time as he approached the high walls and towers of the prison, he was too impatient and worried to feel intimidated. Sneaking up on the place to try to get inside was a lot less nerve-racking than being carted there as an inmate.

A few men were crossing the bridge over the moat when Manny got there, and he ghosted along right behind them. The first gate still stood open and he slipped past the guards, holding his breath.

The only people in the first courtyard were the human and spriggan workers. Everyone looked normal as they went back and forth, and some spriggans stopped beside a doorway to talk casually. It was a good sign. Morrigan's creature must not have reached the prison yet.

But the heavy inner gates were tightly closed. *Okay, this could be tough,* Manny thought.

He crouched next to a water barrel, so no one would blunder into him and break his glamour. He might be able to climb the wall to the top, since the stone was old and pitted, but he would have to ghost the whole way; if he slipped for even a second, the whole courtyard would see him. But he couldn't spot any other way to get in.

Manny sat up as a well-dressed man on horseback rode in. He reined up before the inner gates, waiting impatiently as, with a creak, the portcullis slowly rose.

Manny stood. The man on the horse must be important, because everyone in the courtyard had turned to watch him. It was broad daylight and this was going to be tricky.

Wrapping his sense of "you don't see me" around him like a cloak, Manny moved toward the gate. He kept his pace even, unhurried, his gaze on the ground. The glamour didn't make him invisible, it just made people less inclined to notice him; he knew instinctively that it wouldn't hold if he did anything that made people look at him.

As the gate swung open, the man urged his horse through, and Manny followed right behind him. Once through the big gates, a spriggan hurried to take the horse's bridle, and two others approached to talk to the man as he dismounted.

Manny carefully didn't look at anyone, just kept walking at a normal pace. Out of the corner of his eye he saw the horse turn its head to look at him as he went by, but the spriggans were talking to the rider and didn't notice.

He walked all the way across the big courtyard, fetching up against the corner of one of the houses built against the wall, then leaned against the damp stones to take a deep breath. Cold sweat ran down his back. He was tired, and his temples ached. Ghosting at night and in shadow had been much easier.

He needed to get into the tower above the dungeons, where the others were being held, but its heavy ironbound doors were still securely shut. Manny could try pickpocketing the keys, if he could figure out which spriggan had them, but he would have to open the door in full view of the court.

Or I could get in from above, Manny thought, craning his neck to study the tower. Above the second floor there were barred windows, and one was near the partially enclosed gallery running along the third floor of the house behind him. *Right.*

Manny worked his way along the front of the building, and found an open archway with steps leading up to an unlocked door. He slipped into a stone-floored hall with more doorways opening off it. Voices echoed from the back. Some quick frantic searching and Manny found the stairwell, hurried up it to the third floor and then found a door out onto the gallery. It was wooden, partly enclosed, with open sections looking down onto the court below. He reached the end nearest the tower just as someone, a woman spriggan, came out another doorway. Manny froze, but she just shook out a blanket over the railing, then turned to go back inside.

Breathing again, Manny climbed up onto the railing of the last open section, and eased along it until he could grab one of the bars across the tower's window. He hauled himself up for a peek, and found the window was in a corridor. *Good, 'cause you'd feel pretty stupid sneaking in to find yourself locked in another cell,* Manny thought. He pulled himself up onto the ledge and wiggled through the gap between the bars.

The corridor wasn't well-lit, just the light coming through this window and one further down, so it was better for ghosting. Manny hurried, hearing faint noises of movement and voices from behind the locked doorways.

He reached a narrow spiral stairway lit by a couple of oil lamps and hurried down it, successfully ghosting past two spriggan guards who were having a conversation in the stairwell.

On the first floor landing he recognized the foyer area he and the others had been taken through that morning. Across it was the doorway that led down to the dungeons. Through one more doorway he could hear a distant mutter of voices, as if the speakers were one or two rooms away.

Manny made to dart across to the stairs, then hesitated. *Can I pick the lock on the cell door?* he thought, directing the question toward the part of himself that was Remy. It had looked a lot more complicated than the simple padlock on Morrigan's cage.

The sense he got from Remy was doubtful. Manny decided he had better try to get the keys, and only attempt picking the lock as a last resort. He was pretty certain the spriggan with the keys had come out of that other room as they had been led to the stairs. He edged along the wall, and took a quick peek inside.

It was a guard room, with racks along one wall for muskets and swords. A doorway in the far wall led to another room, the source of the muted voices. But the thing that caught Manny's attention was the big wooden table in the middle of the room littered with a pile of weapons and sword belts.

On top of the pile was Etienne's sword Amechanteur.

The sword was sheathed, but Manny recognized the silver design guarding the hilt. He stepped forward, thinking that this was great. Adriana's short barreled pistol lay near the table's edge. He meant to grab as many weapons as he could and keep moving, but instead he found himself taking hold of Amechanteur's hilt and drawing it.

Even in the dim lamplight, the crystal caught and captured the light, trapping the fire in the long narrow blade.

That's weird, Manny thought, a little dazed.

It was like the sword had just called him over here and told him to draw it. Even now, with guards in the next room, a monster on its way, and his friends to rescue, he couldn't put it down.

That's really, really weird. And I really wish whatever was doing this would stop.

Then a spriggan turnkey stepped into the doorway from the foyer. Manny met his gaze, startled. He'd forgotten to ghost. The turnkey blinked, equally startled, and said, "Curse my teeth! Who the blazes are you?"

A huge crash echoed from somewhere below their

feet, followed by an animal roar that shook the tower's foundations.

Oh no, Manny thought, horrified. Aloud, he said, "It's here!"

CHAPTER 24

After the clatter of overturned chairs from the guardroom, three more spriggans rushed in. They stared at Manny, and one demanded, "What was that?"

Another roar split the air. Someone shouted, "It's coming from the dungeons!" and the spriggans ran for the stairs, ignoring Manny.

His heart pounding, Manny shoved Amechanteur back into its scabbard and slung the belt over his shoulder. He grabbed one of the flintlock pistols as well as Adriana's smaller gun, stuffing that into his belt. Remembering that they needed a lot more stuff to load them than regular guns, he grabbed the other belt that had the pouches for balls and powder. He then raced down the stairs after the turnkeys.

They reached the dungeon corridor just as another ear-shattering roar echoed off the stone. The spriggan in front of Manny stopped so abruptly that Manny slammed into his back. Manny ducked around him, then froze.

The door to the cell where the others were held stood open, wrenched partly off its hinges, the ironbound metal singed and blackened, still steaming with heat. One spriggan turnkey and a human guard lay crumpled in the corridor nearby, their flesh singed and their clothes smoking. Manny swallowed down bile, trying not to look at them, forcing himself to move closer to the cell. If his friends were already dead...

Then he heard Gaudulfus curse loudly, followed by a crash like a chair striking stone. *They're alive!* He darted to the cell doorway.

The first thing he saw was Morrigan's newt grown to the size of one of those giant twelve-foot salt water crocodiles from Australia. It perched on the wall of the cell, its barbed tail whipping back and forth. The long fanged jaw gaped, making the creature look as if it was mostly teeth and gullet.

Manny gasped, and almost strangled on the breath. The air stank with the reek of burning, and something acrid like oil fumes.

Then he saw Etienne, Gaudulfus, and Adriana had backed into the far corner, armed only with the broken stools from the cell.

Etienne said, "Be ready, wait— Now!" Just then the dragon hissed out a stream of fire. The three barely moved in time, ducking away from the flames.

Etienne darted in and cracked the creature across its jaws with the stool, trying to distract it as Adriana lunged for the doorway. But the creature moved too fast and leapt to the opposite wall, and slapped at Adriana with its tail. She fell, but rolled away, cursing, and came to her feet.

Gaudulfus ran at the creature, swinging his stool, but it hissed another breath of fire. To Manny's complete surprise, Gaudulfus simply turned his face away as Etienne and Adriana shouted in alarm. The flames engulfed the dwarf, igniting his doublet. Gaudulfus stumbled back against the wall, shaking his head and beating at his flaming clothes. Although his hair and beard were smoking and glowing in patches like smoldering embers, Gaudulfus seemed mostly unfazed by the attack.

He's fireproof? thought Manny, gaping in surprise. Then he abruptly remembered he was holding their weapons. "Here!" he shouted hoarsely.

As Etienne looked up, Manny ran through the doorway and tossed Amechanteur's scabbard to him. The elf caught it and Manny ducked back as the dragon rounded on him. Its roar blasted Manny and the sound actually staggered him. Then it took a hissing breath and whipped back around as Etienne slashed it across the back.

His ears ringing from that last roar, Manny stumbled sideways, trying to see.

Etienne stood, holding Amechanteur. The dragon seemed to watch him warily, and Manny realized the crystal sword had split a long gash in the creature's rough hide. Black blood from the dragon's wound dripped like acid on the stone floor.

Gaudulfus and Adriana shouted at Manny; he couldn't make out the words past the ringing in his ears but he knew what they wanted. He pitched the flintlock toward Gaudulfus, then slung the belt with the ball and powder pouches after it.

Etienne had the dragon's full attention. He stood back against the far wall of the cell, moving Amechanteur's point in slow hypnotic circles. The dragon angled its huge head to follow the movement, tail lashing back and forth. Manny saw the wary expression in its heavy-lidded eyes; it knew Amechanteur could hurt it, and it knew it could kill Etienne, if it timed its next fiery breath just right.

Then Gaudulfus dropped the flintlock and fumbled with the powder pouches, while Adriana stood guard over him, the last leg of a broken stool her only weapon. Manny remembered the spriggan guards and turned to shout for help.

They had all vanished.

Manny figured it would be a little too much to hope they had all run to get their big muskets. He looked back to see the dragon's spine ripple as it surged forward.

Etienne lunged to meet it and sliced it across the face, but the armored skin deflected the blow away from the dragon's eye. A swipe from its leg slammed Etienne down and stunned him. The creature's chest swelled as it drew a hissing breath, ready to loose a stream of fire.

Manny didn't think, he just charged in, yelling. He almost collided with Adriana, who leapt forward and flung a broken stool at the dragon's head.

The dragon whipped toward Manny and Adriana, eyes blazing, jaws open. From behind them Gaudulfus shouted, "Get down!"

Adriana pulled Manny to the floor, shielding him with her body.

Gaudulfus rushed forward and flung a bulging pouch at the dragon's mouth. The creature jerked its head aside at the last moment and the pouch bounced off its lip.

Gaudulfus cursed and leapt at the monster, his powerful arms outstretched. The dwarf collided with the dragon and locked his arms and short legs around the creature's head and neck. The dragon thrashed around, shaking its head violently and trying to dislodge the growling dwarf.

"The pouch!" Gaudulfus yelled. "Get the pouch!"

Adriana scooped up the pouch and ducked as the dragon's tail lashed the air above her.

Etienne regained his feet and lunged, his crystal sword glittering. He slashed and thrust, scoring several hits on the monster while keeping out of range of its claws and tail.

Gaudulfus had managed to get one of his arms over the dragon's snout. Using his legs to keep himself firmly in place, the dwarf wedged his thick fingers into the dragon's mouth and began to pull the monster's jaws open.

"Throw it!" bellowed Gaudulfus.

Adriana leapt up and threw the pouch right down

the dragon's gullet.

The creature reared back, startled, then made a funny gulping noise. Gaudulfus released the monster, dropped to the floor and rolled to his feet. A thud, like a small muted firework, sounded from inside its stomach. Almost matter-of-factly, Gaudulfus turned to Manny and said, "Now run, lad. Very fast."

Adriana grabbed Manny's arm and they bolted past the dragon into the corridor. "What about Gaudulfus and Etie—" Manny started to say, then both men came barreling out.

Etienne shouted, "Get down!" and Gaudulfus slammed the cell door. Manny flung himself on the dirty stone flags, Adriana landing next to him a second later.

The cell's window flashed a blinding white and heat washed over Manny. A tremor passed through the stone floor and dust rained down from the beams overhead, and it smelled like a gas station had exploded. Then the heat died away with a whump, like a gas furnace going out.

Manny sat up on one elbow, cautiously, and looked at what remained of the door. The splintered wood was singed and smoking.

"Was that the newt?" Manny realized he was shouting to hear himself. He shook his head, but it felt like there was cotton stuffed in his ears.

"That was a wyrm, boy," Etienne shouted back. "And yes, it blew like a powder keg." He sat up and gave Gaudulfus a slap on the back. Large pieces of the dwarf's scorched clothing fell off in tatters. "Thanks to your quick thinking!"

Gaudulfus shook his head, thumping one ear with the heel of his hand. "I'd heard rumors that wyrms were vulnerable to their own fire. An overstuffed pouch of black powder down the gullet seemed the most opportune way to test it."

Manny blinked at Gaudulfus. "You're immune to

fire?"

Gaudulfus shrugged. "To a degree, lad. Most dwarves have that talent." He glanced down at his ruined doublet. "Although as you can see my clothing does not share my gift."

Adriana grabbed Manny in a hard hug. "Lady of the light, you're alive! I thought they'd taken you away to kill you."

"Me, too," Manny gasped, so relieved that she was okay.

Etienne asked, "Manny, where were you, and how did you escape Magneric?"

Manny pulled away from Adriana. "It wasn't Magneric, it was Morrigan, she had me taken to her hideout in the sewers. I escaped, but Morrigan is really Queen Mab! And it's not Magneric doing this at all, it's her, and she's going to kill the king—"

"Morrigan is Queen Mab?" Etienne looked more horrified by this than he had the wyrm's attack. "It can't be true!"

"Manny, are you certain?" Adriana demanded. "She would have been lying to confuse you."

Manny shook his head furiously. "No, I saw her. She turned into Queen Mab. The Morrigan thing is like a magical disguise. She only showed me because she was going to kill me. And there's something important she thought I knew, but I didn't. I think it's got to do with the magic that brought me here, like she wanted to know what it was, or wanted it, or something. I didn't understand everything she said," Manny admitted, "but I know she and Lord Grim were going to the palace to kill the king."

"Lord Grim?" Gaudulfus and Etienne spoke in chorus. Their expressions were incredulous and deeply worried at the same time. Etienne added, "Are you certain?"

"Yes! Morrigan said that was his name. She called him Bloody Bones and Tommy Rawhead. He's helping her."

"Oberon's teeth," muttered Gaudulfus. "That fiend is here? In Lutetia? Then Morrigan must be Queen Mab as Manny claims."

Given that Gaudulfus had just wrestled with a small dragon, Manny found it deeply disturbing that Grim's presence in the city unnerved him. "Who is he?"

Etienne got to his feet. "He's Queen Mab's assassin, the deadliest blade in all of Albion."

Adriana said, "This Lord Grim was the goblin you saw at the tavern?"

Manny nodded. "It was him all right. And he's a lot more creepy close up."

"We can waste no more time," Etienne said, his face hard as he sheathed his sword. "We must get to the palace now."

CHAPTER 25

Manny followed Etienne and the others back up the spiral stairs to the tower's main floor. It was empty except for two nervous spriggan guards, armed with muskets. The spriggans exchanged confused looks, maybe because they were surprised to see that anybody was still alive down in the lower level. With Manny's ears still ringing from the wyrm's stone-shattering roars and the final explosion, he couldn't blame the spriggans for thinking there would be no survivors.

"Where is it?" demanded the larger spriggan, his musket still aimed at the stairwell. "That monstrous creature—"

Gaudulfus stepped forward, scowling ferociously. "The Foundry has just been attacked by a wyrm sent by Queen Mab! We're headed to the palace to save the king's life. Stop gawking and give us those muskets!"

The two spriggans stared, astonished. One automatically handed his weapon to Etienne while Gaudulfus snatched the other out of its bewildered owner's hands.

Adriana headed for the guard room and the racks of weapons. She took a stout quarterstaff leaning against the wall and a slender dagger in a leather sheath.

Manny followed, remembering her pistol tucked in his belt. "Oh, Adriana, I found this." He handed her the weapon.

She checked it. "Thank you, Manny." She handed him the dagger. "Don't throw that unless you have no other choice or you'll disarm yourself."

Manny slid the dagger into his belt. "Got it."

Out in the foyer, Etienne told the larger spriggan, "The two of you must hurry to the Hôtel Corvus and rally the Chevaliers who are still there. They must head to the palace at once. Do you understand?"

The craggy-faced spriggan started to shake his bulbous head. "A plot against the king? But Queen Mab is surely dead! How can—?"

Etienne seized him by the shoulders and shook him. "Listen to me! The king's life is in grave danger. This attack on the Foundry is only the beginning! Enemies of Aquitania prepare to attack the palace. It may already be too late!"

The spriggan hesitated, but then gave Etienne a firm nod. "Yes, yes, of course. Yes, sir!"

Gaudulfus clapped the other spriggan on the shoulder. "We're counting on you, lad. You'll be a hero to the people of Aquitania."

The spriggans exchanged dubious glances but hurried out of the tower.

"Will they really bring help?" Manny asked. He had seen enough of this place to know that a couple of spriggans running around telling people that a strange elf said there was an attack on the palace probably wouldn't be listened to.

Adriana snorted. "No."

Etienne gave her an exasperated look. "They will rouse the other guards who saw and heard evidence of the wyrm for themselves, and give them a task besides rounding up escaped prisoners."

Adriana inclined her head to him, conceding the point. "True enough."

Etienne started to follow the spriggans but Gaudulfus called, "A moment!" He had gone to the weapons rack, rummaging through it like it was the discount table at the department store. He discarded several rapiers that looked fine to Manny, then took up a stout axe. "There we are," he murmured. Flashing a grin at his companions, he cried, "Let's fly like the wind, my friends!"

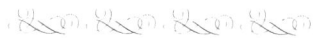

As Manny and the others left the tower, the sun was just setting. It was much darker inside the high walls and the inner courtyard was all torchlit confusion, with the spriggan and human guards and workers nowhere to be seen, though Manny heard voices and shouts from other parts of the fortress. The wyrm's attack had toppled the slate shingles from the roofs of the towers and collapsed a wooden shed. Manny followed Etienne and the others across the courtyard and through the open gate.

The confusion was worse in the outer courtyard where some of the guards and people from the street gathered in a loud, frightened group. There was a lot of shouting and running. Etienne scanned the area, spotting two saddled horses near the wall, their reins held by a very small spriggan.

Etienne took the reins from the confused spriggan. "My thanks, lad," he said, as if the spriggan had brought these horses specifically for him.

Gaudulfus took the reins of the second horse, adding a cheery, "Well done!" to the spriggan, who still seemed doubtful but didn't object.

Etienne handed his musket to Manny and swung up onto the first horse, then stretched his hand down. "Come on, boy."

Manny caught his hand and was lifted easily onto the saddle in front of Etienne, still clutching the musket.

"Hold tight, Manny," Etienne told him. The horse shifted impatiently under him, eager to leave the noise and confusion of the courtyard.

Manny wrapped an arm around the musket, tucking it against his stomach, and grabbed the saddle horn to steady himself. "Got it!"

Adriana took Gaudulfus' musket and stood back as the dwarf clambered into the other horse's saddle, not nearly as gracefully as Etienne had.

"Hurry, my dear," Gaudulfus said to Adriana once he was mounted. She took his hand and vaulted into the saddle behind the dwarf, tucking her quarterstaff and the musket against her body.

Manny felt a rush of excitement when Etienne spurred his horse forward with a "Hah!"

The horse raced through the massive gates, hooves clattering on the stone bridge. They shot into the dark street, scattering passers-by. Manny gasped, clutching the heavy musket to his chest and holding on to the saddle horn in a death grip. This was bumpier and faster than any rollercoaster he had ever been on.

The torchlit streets sped by in a dark blur. Manny had never been on a horse before and had no idea how hard it was to control one, but Etienne made it look effortless. The horse flew through the streets, dodging past barrels and crates and startled pedestrians. Manny was certain that had he wanted to, Etienne could have urged the horse to sail into the clouds.

I hope we're not too late, Manny thought, his excitement dulled by this sudden worry. *If Morrigan and Grim haven't already killed the king.* Remembering the king was just a kid like him made it all the worse.

By the time Manny and the others reached the

Royal Palace, night had fallen and the sky glittered with stars. The moon, a scythe-like crescent, was poised ominously over their heads.

The torches in tall metal stands flickered on an imposing building of white stone on three sides of the square, with elegant columns like a Greek temple.

Etienne spurred his horse toward the guards posted near the arched entrance. They wore striped uniforms of blue and gold and shiny metal helmets that reminded Manny of conquistadors. Some were armed with swords and some with elaborate pole arms Manny recognized as halberds. There was not a single Sidhe among them, which couldn't be a good sign. *I hope they believe us,* Manny thought.

The guards readied their pole arms as Etienne reined in his horse before them and leapt off the saddle. Manny wasn't sure how it had happened, but he suddenly found himself on the ground next to the Chevalier, his legs still a bit unsteady after the dizzying ride.

"I am Etienne, Lieutenant in the King's Chevaliers," Etienne said, loud enough for everyone in the courtyard to hear. From the looks on the guards' faces, Manny could see that several of them must recognize Etienne. Now all of them stood frozen, watching the Chevalier intently. "Assassins mean to take the lives of Their Majesties this very night!"

Gaudulfus stepped up beside Etienne. "We've no time, noble soldiers of Aquitania! Come with us to the royal apartments so that we may defend our liege."

The palace guards exchanged incredulous but alarmed glances. One said, "But all's been quiet—"

"Because they are entering the palace by stealth," Etienne said. "Every second we hesitate they draw closer to the royal apartments!"

The palace guards started to lower their halberds when dozens of Minister's Guards poured through the arches.

"Stay where you are!" barked Vasseur. "Etienne has been placed under arrest as an enemy of the state." He drew his pistol and stopped a few yards from the Chevalier. "Surrender, Etienne. Or I'll order my men to open fire." The Minister's Guards knelt and raised their muskets to their shoulders.

Etienne swung the barrel of his musket to aim at Vasseur. "I should shoot you where you stand, you traitor! We know you've conspired with Queen Mab to have the king assassinated."

The palace guards all stared suspiciously at Vasseur. Manny got the distinct impression that the idea of a conspiracy didn't sound all that unlikely to them. Vasseur ignored the guards, still aiming his pistol at Etienne. "That *elf* is nothing but a liar, like all his kind."

Gaudulfus' expression went cold. He stepped forward, his musket aimed. "Speak the word, Etienne," he said, "and I'll give that coward a third eye."

"Worthless as your lives may be," said Vasseur, "why throw them away? You cannot prevail here. You are outnumbered. Drop your weapons and perhaps we can arrive at some understanding."

Manny could see Etienne weighing his options. The Chevalier cast a glance in his direction, his eyes full of concern and indecision. Manny knew that if Etienne attacked, they would all be fired upon. Out in the open like this, with absolutely no cover, it would be a massacre.

"Captain Corvus is inside," added Vasseur, as if he sensed the Chevalier's hesitation. "He can shed some light on this situation."

"It's a trap," Manny whispered. If Corvus was inside, he was probably a prisoner.

Adriana nudged him. "He knows."

Etienne frowned. "You are the liar, Vasseur. Captain Corvus is not here."

"Oh but he is," insisted Vasseur, lowering his pistol,

his voice now taking on a conciliatory tone. "If you like, I'll fetch him. I'm sure he can explain. There is no need for anyone to die tonight."

"Don't trust that viper," Gaudulfus said, still aiming his musket at Vasseur. "He wants to join the conspirators already inside the palace."

Vasseur took a step back, his pistol now at his side, his other hand raised. "Don't do anything rash," he said. "Corvus is just inside with His Eminence. Wait a moment, and I'll call for him."

"Stay where you are, Vasseur." Etienne moved forward, watching Vasseur warily.

Vasseur lowered his hand. Manny couldn't be sure in the low light but he could have sworn the Minister's Guard smiled ever so slightly.

Diving for cover behind a large stone column, Vasseur yelled, "Fire! Kill them all!"

CHAPTER 26

Manny hit the cobblestones face first as someone tackled him from behind. Musket shots rang out all around him, thundering just over his head. The courtyard filled with smoke and the cries of wounded men.

Disoriented, Manny looked up into Adriana's face, inches from his. Etienne had dropped to his knee and had fired his musket into the ranks of the Minister's Guards. Next to the elf, Gaudulfus still stood, holding his own smoking musket.

Several of the Minister's Guards had been hit. Too many, in fact, given that their side only had two muskets.

A great cheer erupted from the courtyard as about a dozen Chevaliers, led by Rabican, charged forward from across the plaza. A few of the Minister's Guards hastily returned fire then drew their swords to meet the charge. Startled, the palace guards also drew their swords or readied their halberds, prepared to repel the invading force of Sidhe Chevaliers.

Etienne drew Amechanteur and charged the Minister's Guards, his blade flashing in the torchlight as it struck here and there.

Adriana got to her knees, her gaze on the fighting. "Are you hit?"

Manny patted himself automatically, even though

he was pretty certain he'd know it by now if he had been shot. "No, I'm fine."

"Good." She hauled him to his feet and pulled him away from the battle.

Gaudulfus dropped his empty musket and unslung his axe, then charged, hewing right and left, parrying sword strikes with the haft of his weapon and delivering heavy blows to any guard who drew near. Shocked, Manny saw the shoulder and side of Gaudulfus' doublet stained with blood. Apparently some of the enemy's muskets had found their target.

Rabican the faun, armed with a slender rapier and a long dagger, engaged two guards who sought to flank the dwarf. "You're bleeding!" Rabican said to Gaudulfus as he parried sword strikes and knocked aside halberd slashes. "Has the mighty Gaudulfus forgotten how to duck?"

Gaudulfus barked out a laugh. "You randy goat! You should know that the mighty Gaudulfus never ducks!" He bashed a Minister's Guard across the jaw with the haft of his axe, felling him like a tree. Toward Etienne, Gaudulfus yelled, "We'll deal with these scoundrels! Get to the king, quickly!"

Etienne dispatched another guard with a quick thrust, then nodded at Gaudulfus. "Hold the line, my friend," he called before dashing under the colonnade toward the palace doors.

"Just like the old days!" bellowed Gaudulfus, rushing into a knot of palace guards with his axe raised.

Manny took off at a run, circling the melee and following Etienne.

"Manny, come back!" Adriana cried.

As Etienne neared the open double doors of the palace, Vasseur stepped out from behind a column, his pistol leveled at Etienne.

"Etienne, look out!" Manny yelled.

In one graceful move, Etienne spun and ducked low

as Vasseur's pistol discharged. The ball punched a hole in one of the flaps of the elf's tabard. Manny gasped, horrified. But Etienne straightened, seemingly unhurt, his hard gaze on Vasseur. He leapt to the attack.

Vasseur dropped the pistol and barely drew his sword in time to meet Etienne's downward cut. Blades clashed with a hard ring of steel on Fae glass. They traded vicious cuts and thrusts, the sword points stabbing perilously close to each other's chest and face.

Adriana reached Manny's side. Manny stared in awe at how fast Etienne spun and lunged. The white sleeves of Vasseur's shirt betrayed small dark blotches—the blood from little wounds, received despite his best efforts to match his opponent. The Minister's Guard fought desperately for his life.

"You don't understand," Vasseur said, backpedaling as he parried a flurry of strikes. "The king is not in danger! Stop this foolish attack!"

Etienne halted, breathing hard but perfectly in control, his sword's point making small menacing circles in the air. "You're a liar and you shall pay for your treachery."

"No, listen to me!" Vasseur's voice grated. Blood stained his doublet as he backed toward the open doors. "I don't know what you've heard, but the only intrigue here is controlled by His Eminence. That Unseelie witch and her footpads are Magneric's creatures."

Etienne didn't look convinced. "She's Queen Mab, you fool. Don't you know what that means?"

"I know who she is, elf! The minister knows what he's about. You are meddling in affairs of state beyond your understanding."

Etienne lowered his blade, his expression turning incredulous. "Oberon's blood! She's tricked all of you. Magneric doesn't know she intends to murder the king, does he?"

"Of course she will not murder the king," Vasseur

said through gritted teeth. "She wouldn't dare oppose His Eminence. Not if she wants his help in reclaiming her throne."

Maybe it's true, Manny thought. Maybe Morrigan had fooled Magneric, tricked him into going along with her, not knowing her real intention was to kill the king. As if he was thinking along the same lines, Etienne asked, "So that was the bargain Magneric struck with that demon? In exchange for what? What does Magneric get in return?"

Vasseur's jaw clenched. "This is your final warning, Chevalier. I'll give you one last chance. Turn and run."

"You are a gullible fool," Etienne told him. "Mab means to murder Queen Giselle and the king, whatever her arrangement with Magneric. She intends to ignite an Aquitanian civil war, a struggle between humans and Sidhe. It's her revenge for our part in thwarting her designs on the throne of Albion."

It was Vasseur's turn to hesitate. He shot a quick glance at the doors into the palace, his brow furrowed. "No, you're wrong. His Eminence is in control. The king is perfectly safe."

Etienne took a step closer, his voice urgent. "This is your final warning, Vasseur. Step aside and let me go to the king. Or come with me if you wish. Together we stand a better chance of stopping Mab and her assassins. But whether you come or not, I'm going to the king. If that means killing you, then so be it." He raised the point of his blade and waited.

The two swordsmen stared at each other for several tense moments. Manny held his breath. Then Vasseur lowered his sword and stepped aside, leaving open the path to the open doors. Etienne stepped forward, his attention never leaving Vasseur. The Minister's Guard had turned away, his gaze cast down to the paving.

Etienne ran toward the doors as Vasseur reached down to the cuff of his boot. At the brief flash of luminous silver, Manny and Adriana yelled a warning. Vasseur pulled out a dagger, whipped around, and raised his arm to hurl it at Etienne.

Manny flinched as a shot rang out. Vasseur hunched, the silver dagger slipping from his fingers. He clutched his chest, then sank down to a sitting position. His gaze locking on Etienne, he gasped a final time, then slumped over on his side.

Gaudulfus stood a few yards away, holding a smoking musket. The dwarf's usual ruddy complexion had blanched to a deathly pallor. "Coward," he muttered, then collapsed to his knees.

Etienne ran to his friend's side, catching him before he fell. The dwarf's eyes were half-closed.

"Gaudulfus! Gaudulfus!"

Manny flung himself down beside the dwarf, who didn't appear to be breathing. "Is he dead?" Manny asked, suddenly very afraid, a painful lump rising in his throat.

Adriana touched Gaudulfus' face, then put her hand just over his nose and mouth. Her expression grim, she said, "He's still alive. Barely. He's lost a great deal of blood." She stripped off her sleeves and used them to staunch the flow from his abdomen. She glanced at Etienne. "What are you waiting for? Go! I'll look after him."

Etienne got to his feet, his gaze still on Gaudulfus.

"Go!" said Adriana. "Save the king!"

He turned and raced through the doorway into the palace.

Manny jumped to his feet, but Adriana seized his wrist with a bloody hand. "Not you! Stay here."

"But Etienne needs me! He can't face all those Unseelie alone." He tried to pull free.

"Manny! You must listen to me for once!" The desperate look in her eyes made Manny stop struggling. "If Morrigan and Grim and Lothair are in there, there's nothing you can do to stop them. I only pray there's something Etienne can do."

"Please, Adriana." Manny knelt next to her. "I have to try to help him. I know you love Remy and want to protect his body, but I can't just sit here and do nothing. You've got to let me go."

She shook her head; there were tears in her eyes. In the bad light, she didn't look like his mother at all; she looked thin, harsh-featured, and desperate. "You don't understand, Manny. If you were Remy, I would likely let you go. But Remy never needed me like you do." She touched his face. "You two are alike in many ways, yet so different. You are more kind, gentle, generous. And far more fragile."

Manny put his hand over Adriana's where it rested on his cheek. "So you like me, too, it's not just Remy?"

She shook her head. "No, you little idiot. It's not just Remy." She pulled him into a tight hug.

Closing his eyes, Manny held on. He had stopped thinking of Adriana as a substitute for his mother, but maybe the feelings he had been wrestling with were genuine. Adriana had protected him, taken care of him, been his friend when there was no one else. The knowledge that she didn't just see him as some stranger in Remy's body made Manny feel much better.

"Help... Etienne..." The low voice was barely a whisper.

Startled, they both looked down at Gaudulfus. His eyes were open but bleary and unfocused. "You're not dead!" Manny said. "Thank God! I mean, thank Oberon!"

"A few musket shots... and sword thrusts... and halberd slashes... cannot fell the mighty Gaudulfus," he wheezed. He clutched Adriana's hand. "I'll be fine, my dear. Hurry... aid Etienne. He is not... as formidable as I."

Adriana kissed Gaudulfus on the cheek, an act that brought a smile to the dwarf's face and even a brief flush of color. Then she got to her feet.

The palace doors opened into a long dark hall. It was ominously silent. Surely someone inside had heard the musket fire and the fighting, but no one had come out to help the palace guards, or even to see what was happening. That had to be a bad sign. "We've got to hurry," he said.

"Yes," Adriana said, sounding resigned. As they neared the open doors, a glint of metal caught Manny's attention.

It was Vasseur's dagger. The handle was made of polished wood, the guard and pommel of steel. Only the long silver blade shone with an unnatural luminescence: Fae silver. Manny reached for the handle.

"Manny, don't!" said Adriana. "It'll make you weak and sick. I told you that." She bent down and picked up the dagger and tucked it into her boot. "But it might come in handy. Come on!" With that, she and Manny raced into the palace.

CHAPTER 27

Manny and Adriana ran through a dark high-ceilinged hall lined with gilded tables and vases. The place reminded Manny of the Texas governor's mansion that his class had visited on a field trip a couple of years ago. *Except this place looks a lot more expensive,* he thought. The only light was moonlight through the tall windows, the air filled with the familiar waxy-smoky scent, like birthday candles right after you blew them out. The lights in the sconces and chandeliers had all been extinguished at once. That couldn't be normal.

The corridor ended in a big hall with a grand staircase that branched in two, both sides curving up to a gallery along the second floor. It was like an empty cavern. In the movies, palaces had always been filled with servants and pages and guards, but there was no one in sight. "Where is everybody?" Manny said, keeping his voice low.

"Magneric must have sent the servants and guards away." Adriana stopped at the base of the staircase. "He doesn't want any witnesses."

Manny could hear the faint tinkling of crystal pendants, stirring in the breeze through open doors and windows. "Where now?" he asked. Doors and smaller hallways led off the hall, but from the big house they had burgled, he knew the living quarters and public rooms would be upstairs. He couldn't hear anything, no fighting, no shouting.

"Up here." Adriana started up the stairs. At the top they found another large corridor, also dark, the faint breeze stirring the flowers in the vases. With a frustrated expression, Adriana looked down the hallway to her right and left. "The royal apartments should be in one wing, the minister's in the other, but I don't know which."

"Let's go this way," said Manny, indicating the right hallway with his thumb.

Adriana nodded and strode down the hallway, Manny right on her heels. A woman's scream broke the silence and Manny nearly jumped out of his skin. "Wrong way!" he gasped, and they bolted down the hallway in the other direction.

Manny couldn't tell which room the scream had come from. Adriana threw open the first door she came to. It was a big salon. She dashed to a second door, threw it open, then raced into a small bedroom.

Taking her lead, Manny threw open the next door and froze.

Lothair hunched over a big polished sideboard with all the drawers open, a bulging sack hung over his shoulder. The troll seemed as surprised as Manny. "You!" he roared and advanced. Manny yelled a warning to Adriana and retreated to the landing. The troll lumbered after him, growling like a grizzly.

Manny leapt up on the balcony's railing and balanced for a precarious instant. He thought, *Oh crap*, even as Remy's voice in his head said, *Trust me!* He jumped. A second later Manny knew he had made the right decision when he felt Lothair's claws brush against his back.

Manny landed, tucked into a roll, and came up into a crouch. He jerked sideways to avoid the sack that came flying at him. The bag crashed on the marble floor, spilling silver boxes, mirrors, brushes, and perfume bottles.

Manny blinked at the dazzling treasures on the floor. "You miserable thief!" He glared up at Lothair. To his horror, Lothair smashed through the railing as he launched himself off the balcony, his powerful arms outstretched.

Rolling clear of the falling troll, Manny yanked the dagger out of his belt and spun to face him. Lothair crashed so hard the marble cracked beneath him, and shoved to his feet.

"You're dead, runt!" Lothair roared. "Dead!"

Adriana leapt down and landed on Lothair's shoulders. She held her quarterstaff in one hand, but Manny saw her lift the Fae silver dagger and stab it deep into the troll's thick neck. Lothair bellowed, the sound vibrating the chandeliers overhead. He reached back for Adriana but she somersaulted off his shoulders to land in front of Manny, her quarterstaff held at the ready. "Run, Manny!"

But Manny stood his ground, gripping his dagger tightly. "I won't leave you!"

Lothair's piggish eyes squeezed shut and he grabbed the handle of the dagger sticking out of his neck. He made a choking noise. "You... miserable...."

Adriana darted in and smashed Lothair's hand with her staff. Lothair staggered back, grabbing at Adriana's quarterstaff with his free hand. Adriana danced back out of range.

With an agonized groan, Lothair pulled the knife from his neck. The wound smoked and hissed like acid had been splashed on it. Lothair hurled the silver knife aside and drew his two huge, curved daggers. Still reeling, he shook his head repeatedly, blinking his eyes to clear his vision. His arms dropped, and he listed a few steps to the side.

Adriana lunged again, aiming a blow at Lothair's face. But the troll snapped back into motion, bringing his dagger up to parry the blow.

Furious, Manny yelled, "He's faking!"

Lothair attacked, his daggers flashing in the dim light. Adriana tried desperately to parry the deadly blades. The powerful blows made short work of Adriana's quarterstaff, chopping chunks of it away with each impact. The last blow turned it into a short, splintered piece of wood; she threw it aside and turned to run. Lothair struck out, slashing viciously. Adriana made a strangled cry as his dagger blade bit into her back. She staggered and fell to the floor.

"No!" Manny threw his dagger, aiming for the troll's face. He was rewarded with a surprised grunt from Lothair. But as the monster turned to snarl at him, Manny saw his dagger had bounced off Lothair's tusk, doing little more than chipping a piece off the top.

Ignoring Manny, Lothair turned his baleful gaze back to Adriana. She tried to crawl away. Blood stained the back of her shirt and she grimaced with every movement. Lothair sheathed one of his daggers, licked his chops with his warty tongue, then started forward. "I'm going to enjoy this bit."

"You stinking monster!" yelled Manny, taking a few steps forward. "You keep threatening to eat me and yet here I am, uneaten! You're such a pathetic jerk! You can't even beat a skinny half-goblin! I'm amazed Morrigan puts up with someone worthless and incompetent like you!"

Lothair stopped to stare at Manny. Even Adriana stared at him over her shoulder. Lothair smiled and chuckled, then bellowed with laughter. "Oi, runt! That was pretty good. You always could get a rise out of me, you scrawny little cuss. But I'll deal with you after I've bitten off this pretty lady's head."

The troll turned back to Adriana and grabbed hold of one of her ankles. He dragged her nearer, flipped her over, then scooped her up by her neck. "Hello again, darlin'. I thought I'd never see you again."

Lothair brought Adriana close to his hideous face. "Then again I was thinking you were the smart one. Morrigan always thought so. But coming here was foolish, really foolish."

"That's funny... coming from a buffoon like you," Adriana gasped. One of her arms hung immobile, and she struggled to lift the other.

Think of something, Manny told himself. He saw the glint of silver on the floor near a large vase. *The Fae silver dagger!* He darted for it, his heart racing. Behind him, Lothair chuckled, "Your face is quite lovely when it's that shade of purple." He heard Adriana making a horrible gurgling sound.

Manny snatched up the dagger, turned, and took careful aim. Even with the wooden handle to protect him from the Fae silver, he felt weakness wash over him. It was like he couldn't get enough air, a sick sensation like the aftermath of a hard punch in the stomach.

He wanted to drop the dagger, but Lothair opened his huge mouth, bringing Adriana close to those awful yellow teeth. Adriana managed to lift her one working arm to fumble weakly in her vest, as if searching for a weapon. She was on the verge of passing out, her face a frightening shade of blue.

Manny took a deep breath, ran a few steps, then hurled the Fae silver dagger. The blade glittered as it spun across the room. It seemed to move in slow motion.

Lothair bellowed and jerked his head back in a spray of dark blood. The hilt of the dagger sprouted from the troll's eye. Then Adriana pulled the short-barreled pistol from her vest, cocked it by sliding the hammer along Lothair's hand, still wrapped tightly around her throat.

Lothair blinked his one remaining eye and stared down the barrel of the gun.

BLAM! The troll's other eye vanished in a gout of

flame and a puff of smoke. Lothair dropped Adriana and staggered backward, his shocked look slowly melting into a slack-jawed expression. Falling to his knees, he groped blindly in the air. With a thump that echoed down the marble corridors, Lothair fell on his face. He groaned and shuddered, then lay still.

Still weak-kneed from the effect of the Fae silver, Manny flung himself to his knees beside Adriana. "Are you okay? Please say you're okay." She gasped and coughed violently, but her face didn't look blue anymore. Manny winced when he saw her back. Her shirt was completely soaked in blood.

"I'm... fine..." said Adriana, still trying to catch her breath. "Hurry..." Another coughing fit wracked her body and she pushed weakly at Manny. "Etienne... the king..."

Manny got his feet. He didn't want to leave her, but they hadn't seen Grim or Morrigan yet, and Etienne was all alone. Adriana wheezed "Dagger," pointing at Lothair.

Right, I need a weapon, Manny thought. He told her, "I'll get it, don't try to talk." He circled the troll's body until he saw the handle of Vasseur's dagger sticking out of Lothair's eye socket. Steeling himself, he grabbed hold of it, closed his eyes, and pulled. To his surprise, it slid out easily, leaving behind smoking flesh that smelled vaguely of rotten eggs. The sick feeling washed over his again, and Manny blinked and shook his head. He wasn't going to be able to carry this thing for too long.

With a final worried look at Adriana, Manny ran up the stairs to the second floor and into the upstairs hallway. That was when he heard the sound of sword play.

He ran down the dark hall, following the sound to a door on the left. It was ajar and Manny pushed it open.

CHAPTER 28

Inside the big room, by the light of a couple of guttering candle stands, Etienne fought Lord Grim, Amechanteur ringing against the goblin's blood red blade. Murky spirals swirled along Grim's sword and it gave off an unnatural light. *Oh no,* thought Manny, *he has a magic sword, too!* The thrust and parry of the blades was almost a blur, Etienne breathing hard as the two Sidhe moved back and forth across the floor, kicking a small table aside, slamming into an upholstered chair.

Manny gripped the Fae dagger, wondering if he could dart in and try to stab Grim, but they moved so fast, blades whirling like propellers. *Okay, maybe not that bad, but close,* Manny thought in awe. And the Fae silver was making him woozy and unsteady on his feet.

He saw movement in the shadows at the far end of the room, near a big curtained bed that stood on a dais. Squinting, Manny spotted a woman in a blue gown clutching a scared-looking little boy. Three men sprawled dead on the floor in front of the bed's dais, two in palace guard livery and one in shirtsleeves and vest. The silk and tasseled bed curtains had been torn aside, the covers tumbled.

Manny swallowed in a dry throat. *That's the king, those are his guards and a servant, and that's the queen.* Etienne must have been just barely in time.

He took a step toward the bed and the queen gasped and pulled the boy king closer, shielding him with her body. "Stay away!" she screamed.

Uh oh, she thinks I'm a bad guy too. Manny said, "No, it's okay, ma'am—I mean Your Majesty! I'm with Etienne! I'm here to help you!"

Etienne heard the queen's scream. "Manny, get them to safety!" His hair was plastered to his head with sweat, and flecks of blood from small wounds stained his shirt and doublet, while Lord Grim didn't even seem to be winded. Manny's insides went cold. Etienne looked like Vasseur had, just before he had lost his fight.

Grim paused to cast a quick glance at Manny and the queen. "Stay where you are, boy!" he snarled, baring his needle-sharp teeth.

Etienne suddenly launched into a vicious attack and backed Grim up against a long upholstered couch that stood near the wall. "Manny! Get them out! Be quick!"

Manny raced to the queen. As he drew close, he could see the young king's terror-stricken face. *He's younger than I am,* thought Manny. The king clutched his mother close, squeezing his eyes shut. "Mama, I'm frightened!"

"It's all right," said Manny, trying to sound reassuring but feeling anything but confident. "Just follow me."

Grim leapt up and backward, landing on the wall near the door. He clung to the striped silk wallpaper like a big spider. *Holy—* Manny thought, stepping back with a gasp. *You've got to be kidding me!*

Etienne fell back a wary step. Grim scuttled across the wall toward the door, his teeth bared in a grimace.

He's cutting off our escape, Manny thought in panic.

Etienne circled his enemy, keeping Manny, the queen, and king at his back. "You can't succeed," he said. "Sooner or later help will arrive. The palace will be swarming with Chevaliers."

Grim kept his terrible gaze locked on Etienne. Then he leapt off the wall, slashed at the Chevalier, and cut him across the chest. Etienne staggered and Grim rushed toward him, but then jerked back, snarling. Dark blood sprayed from Grim's wrist, a deep cut across the vein.

Etienne lunged. It happened almost too fast for Manny to register, but Grim switched the sword to his unwounded hand, bashed Amechanteur aside and slammed his bleeding arm into Etienne's face.

Etienne fell back, stunned and half-blinded by Grim's blood, slashing wildly to hold the goblin back. Grim leapt away, bounced off the wall to land behind Etienne.

"Behind you!" Manny cried, and Etienne whipped around and stabbed Grim through the shoulder, Amechanteur's crystal point sliding all the way through the goblin's flesh.

Manny gasped in relief but then Etienne let go of the sword and staggered back. He half-fell, going to one knee, blood spreading across his doublet from where Grim's blade had bitten deep.

Grim pulled Amechanteur out of his shoulder and looked at it with disgust. "This sword once belonged to the Sidhe. Now it is dishonored in the hands of an elf who swears fealty to a human." He tossed it contemptuously aside and the blade hit the wooden floor with a faint crystal ring. He stalked toward Etienne, who was struggling to stand. "Queen Mab was right to oppose her father. There can never be peace between our peoples. Oberon was a fool to think so."

"It is you who shame our people, assassin," Etienne said. "There is no greater treachery than to turn against your sovereign."

Grim laughed, a bitter sound. "Humans are no better. It is only due to Magneric that I am here."

Manny saw the queen flinch. Grim continued, "I recognize no sovereign but Queen Mab. It is for her glory that I take your lives now."

Manny lifted the Fae silver dagger, wincing as it made his head swim. He drew on Remy's skills, took aim, and threw it at Grim's chest. He stared, shocked, as Grim just batted it away with his sword and the dagger flew across the room to bang harmlessly into the far wall. Adriana had said not to throw the dagger; Manny wished he had taken that advice.

Grim stepped toward Etienne, smiling coldly, and lifted the point of his sword. "So much for the great swordsman Etienne," he said. Manny did the only thing he could: he ran forward, snatched up Amechanteur, and yelled, "Leave him alone!"

In his heart, Manny didn't expect this to work. He hoped it would distract Grim, that Etienne would have time to recover, that some more Chevaliers would rush in and save them. But mostly he thought that Grim would kill everybody in the room, starting with him, and he couldn't just stand here and watch.

Grim cocked his head, his smile still cold but a trace more amused. He advanced on Manny, lifting his blade, the ebony streaks along its edge swirling like oily droplets in water. "Your bravery is admirable, boy, but futile. Prepare to pass from this world."

Manny saw Etienne groping blindly, desperately for a weapon. Cold with fear, Manny lifted Amechanteur.

Then Manny heard the whisper. Grim must have heard it, too. He stilled, staring. "Manny," Etienne gasped. "It's the sword. Call on its power, boy!"

Confused, Manny looked at the sword that was suddenly warm in his hands. It was like the first time he touched it, when it pulled him into the guard room to pick it up. "I don't know how—"

Etienne grasped at the air, trying to locate Grim. "Manny, let the sword act through you!"

Manny focused on Grim, who weaved back and forth

like a snake. Then the images flooded into his mind. Everything around Manny faded: Grim, Etienne, the queen and her son, even the room itself.

Manny lay in his bed in his parent's house, his father sitting at his bedside. His dad was smiling, his expression full of tenderness. "You're the only one who can solve your problems, son. I can show you the way, but only you can walk there."

Then he was in his kitchen, watching his mother cook breakfast. "Always try to shine, Manny," she said, nodding at him, her eyebrows raised, as if what she was saying was as obvious as the nose on her face. "The world is brightest when people shine."

Then he rode in the truck with Beto, who was slipping on his favorite pair of sunglasses. "No one tells you when you're a man, jefe. That's up to you."

Then he was on his aunt's front porch watching his Tia Licha water her garden. "I love you, mijo, the way my roses love the rain and the sun."

Then he was back in the royal bedchamber holding onto Amechanteur and facing Lord Grim. The crystal sword hummed. A powerful compulsion gripped Manny, like the sword was suddenly in charge of his body.

Grim's expression had lost the cruel amusement and turned wary. The sword glowed, the fire inside the crystal calling light out of the dying candles, the gold and glass bowls and porcelain vases, the polished wood tables, illuminating the room.

Grim bared his teeth and lunged, the blood red blade of his sword coming straight for Manny's face. And Amechanteur parried it, effortlessly flicking upward to deflect the metal blade. Grim snarled and attacked, coming at Manny with a flurry of cuts. In Manny's hands, Amechanteur parried them all, and didn't even seem to be moving fast. The crystal sword was just there to block Grim's blade, as if it knew where Grim meant to strike long before Grim did.

Manny wasn't wielding the sword; it was wielding him.

Is this the sword or Remy? Manny thought, wide-eyed as the sword fought Grim off as if a much stronger and faster person than Manny held it.

Remy's voice in his head said, *It sure isn't me! I couldn't do this.*

That settled it, *this* was somebody's else's magic, something in the sword itself.

As the sword parried Grim's blade, the clash of Fae crystal against steel grew louder and louder, until it rang in Manny's ears like the roar of the wyrm. It was harder to keep hold of the hilt, as the sword yanked and dragged him back and forward. Sweat ran into his eyes and his arms ached with the strain. Gritting his teeth, Manny held on, knowing if he let go the spell would break and Grim would kill him, Etienne, the king and his mother and everybody else he could catch.

The ringing grew louder, and Manny heard a voice in it, the sound forming words he couldn't understand. But Grim's furious expression said he knew what it meant all too well. He slashed at Manny and leapt toward the wall to repeat his spider trick. But he passed too close to where Etienne slumped on the floor. Etienne lurched upright and grabbed Grim's ankle.

Grim staggered and almost fell, then kicked free, knocking Etienne aside. If Grim climbed across the wall, he could reach the king. Manny darted between Grim and the wall.

Grim turned back toward Manny, his face twisted with fury. Snarling, he lunged. Amechanteur's ringing song hit a pitch that almost split Manny's eardrums as it parried Grim's sword and swung up and around. It moved fast, faster than thought, and Manny saw Grim try to lift his sword to counter. Amechanteur bashed his sword aside and sliced Grim's neck. Manny felt an instant of resistance, then the sword went still.

Grim's body collapsed to the floor and his head landed beside it. His blood, black and steaming, stained the marble floor.

The sudden silence was like a slap. Manny stared, caught between horror and relief. The room seemed to sway and his knees were suddenly weak, as if Amechanteur had leeched all the energy out of him.

He lowered the crystal sword to the floor, and pried his numb hands off the hilt. His head pounded and his ears still rang with Amechanteur's powerful song. He stumbled around what was left of Grim and sank down beside Etienne where the elf lay sprawled on the floor.

Etienne's eyes were barely open, his breathing harsh and strained, but he reached for Manny's hand. Manny held on tightly, dimly aware of shouting in the distance and boots pounding down the corridor outside the room. Then darkness descended and Manny slumped to the floor.

CHAPTER 29

Manny woke slowly, feeling bleary and confused. He lay on something so soft he sank into the mattress, far softer than his bed at home. That was when he remembered he wasn't at home.

He sat up abruptly, then grabbed his aching head, groaning. Blinking, he looked around, wondering where he was.

It was a big room, with blue and gold wallpaper and a marble floor. There was a marble fireplace, blue and white china vases filled with flowers, and the paintings had gold frames. The furniture was richly polished wood with spindly legs and bits painted with gold. Or maybe it was all real gold, because this had to be a room in the palace. Three tall windows in the far wall let in bright morning sunlight.

Manny struggled to the edge of the deep feather bed and clambered to the floor. He was wearing a long nightshirt and all his cuts had been cleaned, though the bruises still ached like crazy. Gingerly he picked his way across the gold marble and the silky rugs to the big windows, and pushed the heavy velvet curtains aside.

Yes, this was definitely the palace. He was looking down from a third floor window on a long garden courtyard with rows of trees, flower beds, and a fountain, surrounded by the light-colored stone wings of the building. A couple of gardeners worked in the flower beds and palace guards walked along the colonnade next to the building. Everything looked calm, nothing was on fire, so Manny guessed everything was okay. But where was everybody?

He turned away from the window to go look for the others, even if he had to do it in his night shirt. Then he saw Adriana, lying asleep on a couch against the far wall.

Relief washed over Manny in a wave. He ran to her side. "Adriana!"

She jerked awake, blinking, and sat up. She was wearing the same clothes, but the shirt under her doublet looked new and clean and a little too big for her, and he could see the edges of the bandages just under her collar. The bruises around her throat looked terrible, like a black and purple ring.

Manny found himself staring at her face. He had noticed before that her features were sharper, her face more angular than his mother's, but now her eyes were lighter then he remembered, her lips not so full. The transformation he had seen in the palace courtyard hadn't been a trick of the light; Adriana didn't look like his mother at all, had never looked like his mother. The whole thing had been in his head.

In a voice that sounded husky and strained, she said, "Manny, it's so good to see you awake. How do you feel?"

Manny tried to stop staring. He wasn't going to tell her; he didn't want to sound crazy. "I'm okay, I guess. What about you? You don't sound very good."

"I sound better than I did yesterday, believe me." She touched her throat.

"What about Etienne and Gaudulfus? They were hurt really bad." He held his breath, waiting for the answer.

"Alive," she said. "Gravely injured, yes, but the palace physicians said they would recover." Her smile was wry. "They are both very stubborn men. Far too stubborn to die."

"Oh. That's good to know." Manny let out his breath and sat down on the rug. He had come to think of Gaudulfus and Etienne as part of his family. He especially liked Gaudulfus and felt the world would have been a much poorer place without him. As for Etienne... *Does he not look like my dad anymore?* If he'd imagined that resemblance too... *Maybe Tia Licha was right and I do need to talk to somebody.*

Adriana watched him worriedly. "Are you sure you're well, Manny?"

He looked up at her. Even though she no longer looked like his mother, she was still Adriana and she was still his best friend. "I'm just really glad to see you. It's like I'm seeing you for the first time."

Adriana smiled and sat beside him. She put her arm around his shoulders and said, "I'm delighted to see you, too."

Glancing around, Manny said, "We're in the palace, so I guess that means everything's okay?"

"Magneric was discovered trying to leave the city disguised as a soldier. He's been arrested and thrown into the Foundry." Adriana shook her head. "He claims that the murder of the king was not part of his plan, that it was only a scheme to unite all of Aquitania, humans and Sidhe alike, against Albion by making it appear that agents of Queen Gloriana had attacked the palace. But one of Vasseur's men revealed that Magneric meant for the king and queen to be kidnapped, to spark a war against Albion. They say Magneric pledged to help Morrigan lead a rebellion against Gloriana. Once Morrigan reclaimed her throne, the royal family would be released and Magneric would be hailed as the hero who secured their rescue and maintained the peace."

"Oh, man," muttered Manny.

Adriana nodded. "He's a wily one, but too clever

again by half. Who will be believed, and if Magneric will rise or fall over this, no one knows yet."

Manny supposed kidnapping was less evil than murder, but it was still pretty evil. There was one thing Adriana hadn't said, and Manny asked worriedly, "Where's Morrigan? In the Foundry, too?"

Adriana sighed. "She escaped, Manny. The Chevaliers and the Minister's Guards have been united under Captain Corvus for the time being, and are searching the city for her. But they think she has fled Aquitania."

Manny took a deep breath, trying to be okay with that. He didn't want to spend the rest of his life looking over his shoulder, expecting Morrigan to be hiding under the bed or in a closet. But if he was trapped in this world, he had the feeling that's what would happen. "So the king and the queen are okay? Grim didn't hurt them?"

"They were unharmed, though several guards and servants gave their lives to slow Grim down until Etienne reached him." Her expression was very serious. "And their sacrifice would have been for nothing, if you hadn't been there, Manny."

"It wasn't me, it was the sword, Amechanteur." Manny had a vivid memory of the sword coming to life under his hands, of the tremor through the hilt when it had sliced Grim's head off. He shuddered and scrubbed his hands on his night shirt. He wasn't sorry about Grim, who had killed who knew how many people. But he wasn't sure how he felt about being the one holding the sword when it had happened. *Not so good, really.* "It just took over. If it hadn't, we'd all be dead, but... It was creepy."

Adriana nodded thoughtfully. "That's what Etienne said." She added, "Not that it was 'creepy,' but that the sword seemed to take you over. As if it responded to something in you."

If there was something in him that made magic

swords cut people's heads off, Manny thought he might want it removed, even if it had come in handy this time.

"And that's not the only thing it did." Adriana patted his cheek.

"What do you mean?"

Adriana stood and walked over to a dressing table. She picked up a hand mirror and held it out. "Take a look." She was smiling.

Puzzled, Manny took the mirror and looked into it. Then he blinked, startled. The face in the mirror was haggard and had the worst case of bedhead he'd ever seen, but it was a young elf boy's reflection. He touched his face. "I'm not—Remy's not—a goblin anymore."

Adriana said, "No, you're not. You're just a simple elf again. Well, maybe not so simple."

"Amechanteur did that, too?" Manny added, "That sword should come with a manual." He glanced up at Adriana's puzzled frown. "That's a set of instructions."

Adriana nodded absently and continued, "The queen has sent for Lord Merlin from Albion to help in the search for Morrigan, and I think Etienne means to ask him about the sword."

"Lord Merlin? Merlin the Magician?" Manny stared. *Okay, that may be cooler than anything else that's happened yet.*

She smiled. "Yes, the greatest wizard of Albion's court. You know of him?"

Manny nodded. "My world has stories about him. It's kind of hard to explain. But I was thinking..." Not only would meeting Merlin be awesome, but a wizard might be just what Manny needed. *This could be it, this could be my chance to go home.* "Could we ask him something else? Since he's going to be here, and everything."

Adriana understood immediately. "You want to ask him how you got here, and if you can return to your place and Remy to his. Yes, I think we should ask him for help." She nodded to herself. "And fortunately, the king owes you a great favor."

Manny sighed in relief. "Where's Etienne? I'd really like to see him."

"That's good," replied Adriana, "because he's eager to see you as well."

Etienne and Gaudulfus were recovering from their wounds in an adjacent palace suite. Adriana and Manny arrived at the doorway as a palace servant backed out with a tray.

Gaudulfus was shouting, "For the last time, I don't need broth! I require something of more substance! Considerably more substance! Bring me a decent meal!"

Etienne was sitting up in bed. He glanced at Manny and smiled. Manny thought, *I was right*. Etienne didn't look like his father anymore.

"Go in, Manny." Adriana gave him a nudge. "The physicians didn't forbid visitors."

Manny stepped into the room. Etienne's hair was dark brown, not blond, and his eyes were hazel, not pale blue. But his features were still strangely familiar, as if Manny had somehow known the Chevalier's true face but only now was able to see it. "Hi," was all Manny could manage as he stopped at Etienne's bedside.

"Hello yourself," Etienne said, reaching out to squeeze Manny's shoulder.

"So good to see you up and around, lad," said Gaudulfus, walking stiffly to scoop Manny up. He gave him a great bear hug, then winced and put him back down.

"Stop that, you great oaf," said Etienne. "You'll open

your wounds again and bleed all over the costly bedding."

Gaudulfus snorted. "You're looking quite handsome these days." He gently thumped Manny's nose.

"Oh, yeah," said Manny. "It was the sword. It changed me."

"No, lad," replied Gaudulfus with a quiet smile, "I don't believe that was the sword at all."

He means I ungoblinated myself—ungoblinated Remy—by being a good person, Manny thought. It was a good thing to hear. He noticed Etienne looking intently at him. "You think it's pretty cool that I'm an elf again, huh?"

Etienne shook his head. "That's not why I'm looking at you."

"It isn't?" Manny reached up to touch his own face. "Is there something wrong with the way I look?"

"No, it's not that at all," replied Etienne, leaning forward as if to whisper. Manny bent close to him.

"It's just that I've never before seen a Blade Singer," Etienne said.

CHAPTER 30

Three days later, Merlin was due to arrive on a special skyship that would dock in the palace courtyard garden. Manny stood outside to wait for it, with Adriana, Etienne, and Gaudulfus. The official greeting party, which included Captain Corvus, the Captain of the Palace Guard, and some other important people, waited a short distance away.

The last few days Manny had been mostly resting, hanging out with Adriana in their rooms or the palace garden, or keeping Etienne and Gaudulfus company. It wasn't boring at all, because he got to hear about past battles and adventures, and he got to talk to Rabican, who had lots of funny stories, and to meet Captain Corvus, and their other visitors.

The palace servants were nice to them, and the food they were served was really good, though it came on very delicate china that Manny was terrified he was going to break. Manny had even gotten presented to the king and his mother, and got called a hero and formally thanked. It was all really neat, except they hadn't caught Morrigan yet, and Manny didn't sleep well at night thinking about that.

Manny wasn't sure what to expect, if the skyship was going to be a blimp like the one that came to football games sometimes, or something far stranger. When it finally appeared, he bounced with excitement.

It looked like a big sailing ship, like one of the galleons in the pirate movies, with the high stern and forecastle. But it didn't have sails, and the rigging suspended the hull from three giant hot air balloons. It drew closer, looming over the palace roof, with that roaring noise that hot air balloons made when the air was heated or released. The prow was carved with the figure of a woman, but instead of a mermaid or something else nautical, she was a winged fairy carrying a spear. People, all Sidhe as far as Manny could see, elves and spriggans and brownies, worked on deck, pulling ropes and adjusting things. Manny stared hard, trying to memorize every detail, wishing more than ever that this world had cameras.

"He's certainly arriving with enough pomp and importance," Gaudulfus muttered into his beard. He was leaning on a cane. "I hope it's worth our time. They've put lunch off for this, you know."

Smiling, Etienne said, "He is one of the world's greatest wizards, Gaudulfus."

Gaudulfus snorted, then winced and rubbed his chest. "And his greatest achievement is in creating troublesome situations in which Chevaliers must risk themselves at great personal cost."

"Are you still on about that?" Etienne looked amused. "It's been years, Gaudulfus, let it go."

"What happened?" Adriana asked before Manny could.

"We had to pull his fat out of the fire," Gaudulfus said. "Literally."

"It was a fire-breathing wyrm," Etienne told her.

"A particularly large and vicious fire-breathing wyrm," Gaudulfus corrected.

"Gaudulfus' beard took some damage," Etienne continued. "It was distressing for him. I know, because he's expressed his distress at length."

Manny bit his lip, trying not to laugh. "So that's the only reason you don't like him?"

"There were other dubious exploits, lad." Gaudulfus sighed. "We were all young and naive, then. But in any case, the fellow just puts me ill at ease. You'll see."

Manny couldn't imagine anyone not liking Merlin. He was one of Manny's favorite characters in movies and books. *But maybe the real thing is different.*

The skyship slowed to a stop over the open middle of the garden court, hanging at about the level of the second story of the palace. When the crew dropped heavy ropes down to the men waiting below, Manny realized it wasn't going to land all the way. The ropes were tied off to heavy stone weights that Manny had thought were garden ornaments.

A group of servants appeared from down the colonnade, pushing a tall wooden structure on wheels—a scaffold with a set of steps attached. They pushed it right up to the skyship. A door opened in the railing and a set of steps dropped out. Spriggan skysailors climbed down to secure the hull to the scaffold, then the passengers began to disembark.

Manny was looking for the guy in the robes and the pointy wizard hat, though he should have known by now that in this place, things were never what you expected. Most of the men climbing down the stairs from the ship were elves or brownies, dressed in richly-colored doublets with formal lace collars, and wearing jeweled swords and with feathers in their hats. He didn't see anybody who looked like a wizard. *Maybe Merlin is too old to climb down from the ship,* Manny wondered. Maybe they would have to go aboard to see him.

A young boy climbed lightly down the steps. Manny wouldn't have noticed him except that he appeared to be a human. He looked about the same age as Manny and was dressed in a doublet and breeches of emerald green, and he wore a tall crowned hat decorated with peacock feathers. His high boots were of soft brown suede. With an infectious grin, the boy adjusted his white ruff collar, then went to join his Albion companions who had stopped to speak to the Aquitanian group.

So who's that, Merlin's assistant? Manny shifted impatiently. Then Captain Corvus motioned to Etienne, who nodded to Manny and Adriana. With Gaudulfus they joined the other group. Manny's stomach fluttered nervously. If these people didn't help him, he didn't know what he was going to do.

As they approached, Corvus said, "Etienne, Gaudulfus. You remember Lord Merlin."

Etienne bowed to the young boy. "It has been a long time, my lord."

Gaudulfus gave the boy a nod. "Not long enough."

That's Merlin? Whoa. Manny's jaw dropped.

From Merlin's grin, he was clearly undisturbed by Gaudulfus' comment. "Well met again, gentlemen." He inspected the dwarf's beard, taking the braided end and rubbing it between his fingers. "Hmm, still singed. Even after all this time? Most unusual."

Gaudulfus pulled his beard away, eyeing Merlin narrowly. "As it so happens, that is from a different wyrm, *my lord.*"

"You do tend to attract the creatures, don't you?" Merlin chuckled and adjusted his lace cuffs.

Etienne gave Gaudulfus an exasperated glance, and said, "This is Adriana, who was also instrumental in foiling Mab's plot."

Manny was still too flabbergasted to react to Adriana's graceful curtsey. Corvus said, "And this is the boy, called Manny Boreaux, a human transported into the body of a street urchin called Remy. At first his story was unbelievable, but events seem to have proven otherwise."

"Yes," Merlin said thoughtfully. He walked right up to Manny and looked straight into his eyes. "Most curious."

Manny stopped doubting this was Merlin. This boy's

gaze had power, and age, and a kind of stillness. He was clearly much older than his face and body appeared, hundreds of years older. Manny felt cold, and a little scared; this wasn't a human, it was a very powerful creature. He wasn't creepy or horrifying, not like Morrigan had been. But he wasn't comfortable to be around, either. He knew exactly what Gaudulfus meant now.

Then Merlin absently straightened his ruff collar again, still looking thoughtfully at Manny. "Yes, I see. There's certainly two of you in there." His grin returned.

"You believe me," Manny said in a rush of relief. Adriana nudged him, and he added belatedly, "Sir. Sir, can you help me get home?"

Merlin said, "It may be possible. But I will need you to tell me everything, every detail you recall, from how you found yourself in this Remy's body to when you wielded Amechanteur and slew the terrible Lord Grim."

Manny glanced away. "Oh, you heard about that."

The peal of delighted laughter startled Manny. Merlin said, "Of course I heard! What a glorious day it was for the world when that fell goblin's spirit was dispatched into the underworld by your stroke. Bloody Bones is no more! And that is reason for celebration." Merlin gave him a little bow. Manny could feel himself blushing and wished he could stop. "I understand that His Majesty will be hosting a banquet this eve in our honor. I would be delighted if you would consent to be seated next to me."

Manny nodded, though he wanted to go to a formal banquet only slightly more than he wanted to fight Lothair again. But if it was the price of getting home, he'd do it.

"Excellent! There is much for us to discuss. And as the good Gaudulfus could tell you, every subject becomes far more interesting when discussed over a fine meal." Merlin winked at the scowling dwarf. "Am I right?"

"In this particular case," Gaudulfus grumbled, "I can find no fault in your thinking, my lord."

CHAPTER 31

"The coin is the key," Merlin told Manny.

After the banquet, they had retired to a small salon on the second floor of the palace, with Etienne, Adriana, and Gaudulfus. The big windows were open to a view of the garden court, letting in a cool night breeze. Manny said, "The coin was definitely magical. Whatever happened, it made it happen, if that makes sense." Talking about it in such detail, answering Merlin's questions, had made Manny remember a lot more. "The sound it made was kind of like when Amechanteur... did that thing to Grim." It was strange that the two sounds should be so similar. Had the coin and Amechanteur been made by the same kind of magic?

Merlin sat back in his chair, tapping the armrest thoughtfully.

"Well? We await your wisdom," Gaudulfus prompted.

"It's Oberon," Merlin said.

"Oberon?" Manny tried to remember the Shakespeare plays his English class had covered. "He used to be the king of Albion, right? You guys sure mention him a lot."

Merlin gave him an odd look—pretty much everybody gave him an odd look—but said, "Oberon was not only a great king, he was also a powerful sorcerer, perhaps the most powerful in all the world. Until he was murdered by his daughter Mab. She sought to take his power but did not succeed. We were never certain what prevented her, but Mab's failure allowed her sister, our beloved Queen Gloriana, time to rally her forces and defeat Mab."

"And send her into exile here," Adriana added wryly.

"Unfortunately we had no idea where she was." Merlin lifted a slender hand in concession. "Certainly not that she was hiding in the sewers of Lutetia disguising herself as a thief called Morrigan." He smiled as if the mental image of Mab skulking in the filth pleased him.

Manny could see Mab/Morrigan murdering her father. He didn't think it would be a stretch for her at all.

"What does this have to do with Manny?" Etienne asked.

"Or Remy, for that matter?" Adriana added.

"I'm not sure." Merlin leaned forward. "Except there is a trace of magic about the boy, a trace that I recognize as Oberon's work."

Etienne and Gaudulfus exchanged a look, startled.

"Lady of light," Adriana muttered. She turned to Manny. "That would explain why Morrigan was suddenly so interested in you, the things she said to you. She must have seen it as well."

"Morrigan seemed to be really interested in where I was from," Manny explained. "She knew my real name."

"I'm not surprised," replied Merlin. "Your world is known to her as it is to me. As it was to Oberon."

"Really?" Manny blinked at the wizard. The others had turned to study him as well.

"You claim there are stories of Sidhe in your world, correct?" Merlin asked. "Stories of Oberon and myself, as well?"

Manny nodded. "People have been writing about you guys for a long time. You make cool characters in comics and books."

"By 'cool' the lad means 'exceptional'," said Gaudulfus.

Merlin smiled, "Yes, I gathered. Well, it so happens our two worlds, Avalon and Terra, are sisters and were once connected. But a terrible conflict forced Oberon to sever that connection, separating the two worlds forever."

"Really? That certainly explains a lot," Manny said.

"Terra? I'm not familiar with this tale," said Etienne.

"This took place thousands of years before you were born, good Etienne," said Merlin. "There are few who remember it. I was but a child when it happened. As was Mab."

"She was there?" Manny gasped.

"Aye, lad," replied Merlin, "she was indeed. She knows of your world, and until recently believed it lost and beyond her grasp."

Manny mulled that over in his head. "So how did Oberon bring me here if our worlds are not connected anymore? Not to mention that he's kind of dead."

"You said the book you stumbled on, and the coin inside it," Merlin told him, "appeared to be artifacts of our world. I believe they were created by Oberon, to store and hide fragments of his power, so that Mab would be unable to take it for her own."

Gaudulfus grunted. "I've never heard of such a thing."

Merlin lifted a brow. "I believe there's a great deal you haven't heard of, Gaudulfus, but that doesn't mean it's not worth knowing."

"So the coin and the book, they're like batteries with magic stored in them, and if Morrigan found them she'd be able to use the magic?" Manny said. "And the coin bringing me here was just an accident?"

"Not quite. Clearly some connection between the worlds remains. Oberon must have wanted it that way. You must have some sort of affinity to our world. Perhaps with the boy Remy." Merlin was watching his expression carefully, as if he was reading Manny's thoughts. "Do you?"

Manny wasn't certain the connection was with Remy. They didn't seem to have a lot in common except that they had both been friends with Adriana. He thought he knew what the connection must be, and Merlin had said he needed to know everything. He said slowly, "It might be because Etienne used to look just like my father. And Adriana used to look like my mother."

"I did?" Adriana stared, surprised. "Truly, Manny?"

"Yeah, you used to look exactly like her."

Adriana sat back in her chair, watching him with a puzzled expression.

"You say 'used to' look," said Merlin. "They don't anymore?"

Manny shook his head. "No, they look different now."

"When did they change?" asked Merlin.

"I think Adriana changed gradually while we were trying to escape from Morrigan, and Etienne changed right after the fight with Grim," Manny admitted. Etienne and Adriana were staring at him, like they weren't sure what he meant or how to react. Even Gaudulfus seemed bemused.

Then Adriana asked softly, "What happened to your parents, Manny?"

Manny let out a breath, bracing himself. "In my world, they...died. Six months ago. In a really bad accident." He had said it earlier to Etienne and Gaudulfus, and this time wasn't any easier. But it hadn't been nearly as hard to get the words out.

Adriana nodded understanding. "I'm so sorry, Manny."

Merlin's face was pensive. He slowly shook his head. "Oberon is clever indeed," he said.

Manny was starting to find Merlin just as annoying as Gaudulfus did. Trying to keep his voice even, he said, "What do you mean?"

"It all makes sense now," answered Merlin. "Oberon hid his artifacts in your world to keep them from Mab. He must have known she was plotting against him and didn't want to leave our world at Mab's mercy. The coin chose you as its champion, Manny. But it could not bring you here physically. That is why it transferred your soul into the body of Remy, knowing you'd have no greater protector than the brave Adriana."

Manny glanced at Adriana. She was looking at Merlin with a brow lifted suspiciously, as if she thought he was kidding her. Manny was glad he wasn't the only one who Merlin had that effect on.

"And it glamoured her to appear like your beloved mother," continued Merlin, "so that you would feel at ease and trust her. It also knew you'd need the services of a hero, a legendary swordsman, especially one who possessed another of Oberon's artifacts, a weapon capable of defeating Mab's terrible minions." Merlin waved a hand at Etienne. "And there is no greater swordsman than the mighty Etienne."

Gaudulfus nudged Etienne's arm. "Did I not say you were the finest swordsman in all the land? Even Oberon knew it."

Etienne frowned. "Gaudulfus, be still."

Manny turned to Etienne. "And so Oberon's magic made him look like my dad."

"Precisely so," said Merlin. "Oberon's artifacts became the keys to Mab's undoing. They called to each other, like seeking like for the purpose of protecting themselves, and us, from her." He chuckled. "Oberon set a trap and Mab fell into it."

"But it didn't work," Manny had to point out. "She

got away."

"Did she?" Merlin's smile was mischievous. "I believe the full extent of Oberon's trap has not yet been revealed."

"But now she knows it's still possible to travel from one world to another," said Manny. He turned to Etienne and Gaudulfus. "What if she finds a way to cross over like I did?" He looked at Merlin. "Everyone I know could be in danger. There are things in my world that are just as bad as her magic. Maybe even worse." The thought of Morrigan using her sorcery to control armies of dragons and armored tanks and goblins armed with machine guns made Manny's skin crawl.

Merlin's brow was furrowed in thought. "I believe she may require Oberon's formidable magic to accomplish that feat. That would explain her interest in the coin and the book. But you are correct, lad. This is a cause for concern and a situation that shall require further study."

Merlin stood and walked over to Manny. "But first things first. Is this what you truly wish, lad? To return home?"

Manny cast a quick glance at Adriana, Etienne and Gaudulfus, then turned back to Merlin and nodded. "Yes, sir. This isn't my real body. I was only borrowing it for a little while. I don't really belong here, and my family is waiting for me back home." He sighed. "Assuming you can send me back home."

Merlin studied Manny with intense concentration, long enough to make Manny shift uneasily. "I said such a feat would require some of Oberon's most potent magic. Fortunately for you, I know exactly where to find some."

Manny shivered a little. They were standing in the nave of the Basilica, darkness turning the soaring arches and stained glass into a big cavern lit only by candlelight. It was late at night and cold and clammy inside the big stone building. And Manny didn't think this cathedral had the same purpose as the ones in his world; it felt strange and alien and full of Sidhe magic. Glowing eyes watched them from the upper parts of the building, and Manny could hear the occasional rustle of a leathery wing. Everyone had said the gargoyles were harmless, but he wasn't sure he believed them.

Merlin had used chalk to draw a circle on the paving stones around Manny with runes or sigils or whatever strange magical characters were called. Etienne, Adriana, and Gaudulfus watched from the shadows, and Manny was glad to have them there. Since the king had said Merlin could have anything he needed, there hadn't been any problem getting permission to use the Basilica, and the guards were all posted outside.

Adriana must have noticed Manny's unease, because she called out, "It's all right, Manny, we're right here."

"Hush," Merlin said, before Manny could answer. He stepped back, looking around the circle one last time. "Now, Etienne. The sword."

Etienne came forward, careful not to step on the drawings. He gave Manny a reassuring look and held out Amechanteur's hilt.

Manny took the sword, and Etienne stepped back. For a moment it was just a heavy blade, then the hilt felt warm under his hand. Manny stared at it, half-hypnotized by the light gleaming inside the crystal.

As if from a long distance, he heard Merlin's voice, "Think about your home. Think about how much you want to return."

Home. Manny visualized his room, with his

computer, his books, the photos of his mom and dad, the house with Licha and Beto at the kitchen table, watching TV late on Saturday night, the school, the playing fields in the morning with wet grass, the way the library smelled of books and air conditioning.

Merlin drew himself up, and suddenly the sorcerer looked different. Darkness gathered around him and he looked taller, older. His face seemed thinner, his nose longer and more pointed, the lines of his mouth harsh. As if his features were more animal and less human. He began to speak, words that washed over Manny, full of meaning even though he couldn't understand them.

I don't want to stay here. I really like Adriana and Etienne and Gaudulfus, but they aren't my family, and this isn't my world. The ache in his heart became overwhelming, so painful it blotted out his vision. He heard the sword begin to hum and felt it vibrate.

Then Manny was moving. Darkness splashed with swirls of light and color flashed around him. Fear stabbed through him. Then he saw a face, a young sharp-featured face, just like the one he had seen in reflections since he arrived here. But this wasn't a mirror image.

Remy? For an instant their eyes met and Remy looked startled, then elated, and he smiled and waved. Then he vanished, whirled away in the darkness. *If that was Remy going back to his world,* Manny thought, *then I'm really going...*

CHAPTER 32

The sound gradually faded, though Manny was still so dizzy his vision was dark and blurred. He realized he was lying in bed. For a moment he thought he was back in his room in the palace. *The sword just knocked me out again,* he thought, and groaned.

"Remy? Remy, can you hear me?" a familiar voice asked. A very familiar voice.

Manny blinked hard and squinted, trying to focus. "Tia Licha?" Abruptly his vision cleared.

He was lying in bed, but it wasn't his palace room. It was a hospital room, with white walls and a blinking machine just like in the movies. Tia Licha was sitting on the side of the bed, watching him anxiously. Beto stood nearby, and behind him was an older woman and a young girl Manny didn't know, though both looked kind of familiar. Then the girl smiled at him and Manny recognized her; she was in his class at school, the granddaughter of the *curandera* from their neighborhood *Botanica*. And the old woman was the *curandera* herself.

The smell of antiseptic and floor cleaner hit him. This wasn't a dream. He lifted his hands, staring at them. His hands, smaller and thicker than Remy's. He sat up, staring down at himself. His body, dressed in a thin hospital gown. "It worked," he gasped. "Tia Licha, it's me, Manny. I'm back."

"Manny? Oh God, Manny!" Tia Licha grabbed him

in a smothering hug and covered his face in kisses, crying from relief.

"Jefe! Welcome back!" Beto patted him on the back in relief and delight. "We were really worried about you."

Licha suddenly stopped kissing Manny and held his face in her hands. "Wait, is it really you? You're not playing another trick on me, are you?"

Manny shook his head. "No, no tricks. It's really me, Tia, honestly."

The *curandera* got up and limped to his bedside. Taking his chin firmly in her bony hand, she fixed him with a milky-eyed stare. After a few moments, she smiled, gold flashing on her teeth. "It's not Remy, Licha. This is Manny."

Licha burst into a new round of tears and hugged Manny tightly again. "Ay, mijo, I love you! I missed you so much!"

Manny closed his eyes and buried his face in the crook of Licha's neck. "I missed you too, Tia Licha," he said. "And I'm really glad to be home."

"Don't hurt me! Please, I don't want any trouble!" Gregory put his hands out and backed away from Manny. The two wide-eyed monkey boys stayed behind their friend, looking at Manny like he might sprout fangs.

Manny continued to hold out the Sony Vita. He had approached the boys at their lockers after the final school bell. Most of the other students in the hall had stopped to stare, but a few of them were smiling and giving Manny enthusiastic thumbs-up.

Tia Licha had told Manny about some of Remy's exploits. Apparently, he had saved a bunch of people from a terrible fire that had engulfed a city block.

That's how he had ended up in a coma at the hospital. After Manny returned to his own body, the police had tried to question him about the fire, but naturally he had no memory of any of those events. The doctors called it "post-traumatic amnesia." But whether he remembered them or not, Remy's actions had made Manny a local celebrity. He'd been invited to appear on several local news stations (and even on a couple of cable networks) to talk about his experience, but so far Manny had refused. Tia Licha had told the reporters that Manny needed to time to heal. Manny just had no intention of trying to make up answers and get himself into trouble. He was done with trouble for a long while.

But judging by the looks Gregory and his monkey boys were giving him now, Remy hadn't spent all his time here being a hero. And not everyone was a fan.

"Hey, take it easy," Manny said, only a little surprised by Gregory's alarm. Since returning to school a couple of days ago, he had quickly realized that Remy had cut a path through the place. Everyone's reactions to him had changed. Before, most of the kids had just ignored him. Now they greeted him with either nervous glances or big smiles. He had even gained a new best friend, a shaggy-haired kid with glasses named Oscar who knew more about comic book characters than anyone else Manny had ever met. He seemed pretty cool and Manny was eager to really get to know him.

Manny glanced around at the sea of faces studying him. *Seems like Remy made quite an impression. At least he didn't hurt anybody.* Manny sighed at Gregory. "Honest, I just want to return your game. I took it and I'm sorry."

"You can keep it." Gregory eyed him like he thought this was an elaborate trick. "I don't want it anymore. It's yours!"

Manny rolled his eyes and walked up to Gregory.

The larger boy actually flinched when Manny took his hand and put the game in it. "It's not mine. And I'm not a thief." Not waiting for a response, he turned and walked away.

The students in the hall parted to let him pass, a few pointing and smiling. One of the ones who smiled at him was Evie, the curandera's granddaughter. She waved at Manny as he went past. Manny gave her a nod, and tried his best to ignore the others, but he couldn't help but walk a bit taller as he pushed the exit doors open.

Oscar waited outside, his brows raised in anticipation. "Well? Feel better now?"

"Actually, I do" said Manny, taking a deep breath.

Oscar fell in beside Manny and the two of them walked down the sidewalk. "Wanna go back to my house? You really gotta check out my X-Men collection. You'll especially love Nightcrawler. He's the coolest."

"That sounds great, but there's something else I have to do first," said Manny. "How about we make it tomorrow?"

"Okay, but you're buying the pizza this time."

Manny grinned. "Deal." The two boys bumped fists.

Oscar trotted down the sidewalk. "See ya tomorrow, Manster," he called over his shoulder. "Try not to fight any supervillains while I'm gone."

Manny watched his new friend until he disappeared around the corner.

The bell above Beltran's Discount Books jingled when Manny gently pushed the glass door shut behind him. It was warmer in the store than usual, but the dusty air was still familiar. Perhaps not quite so comforting, though. Manny had to stop and take a deep breath. It was strange being inside the place where his journey had started. It all seemed like a story now, like it had happened to someone else and he had just been told about it.

There weren't any other customers inside. It was early Sunday morning and lots of folks would still be at church. The store didn't usually start to fill up until after lunch. He couldn't spot Mr. Gray anywhere either. That was who Manny had come to see.

Walking around, Manny scanned the maze of narrow, book-filled corridors. Mr. Gray wasn't at the front counter so he had to be down one of these. *Unless he's in the back storeroom,* Manny thought. Finally, he spotted Mr. Gray's silver hair near the mystery section. Rounding the corner, he found the clerk shelving a box of books.

Mr. Gray turned as Manny approached, his salt-and-pepper goatee lifting in a smile as he regarded Manny through gold-framed glasses perched on the end of his nose. "Well, hello again, Manny," he said.

That was a surprise. "You know my name?"

"Of course I do," replied Mr. Gray. "You've been in the news the past several days. I doubt if there's anyone in the city who doesn't know your name."

"Oh, right," Manny sighed. "I don't remember much about what happened."

"I'm surprised to hear that." Mr. Gray shelved a final book then walked over to Manny. "From everything I've heard and read, you're quite a remarkable young man."

Manny shuffled uncomfortably. "Uh, thanks."

Mr. Gray studied him. "Is there something I can help you with?"

"Yeah, actually there is. I was kind of hoping you could tell me what happened that day. You know, the last time I was here." Manny couldn't bring himself to look Mr. Gray in the eyes.

"Well, let me see," said Mr. Gray, crossing his arms. "The lights went out after that lightning strike. I called out because I heard a thump. When you didn't answer, I looked for you and found you lying on the floor. I couldn't wake you. It was very alarming. I was about to call 911 when you bolted up and scurried out of here faster than a startled rabbit."

That would have been Remy waking up inside my body. Manny knew how freaked out he had been when he suddenly found himself inside Remy's body in a strange world, and Remy must have felt just the same.

"Isn't that what you remember?" Mr. Gray lifted his glasses to the top of his head.

"Like I said, I don't really remember much about what happened that day."

Mr. Gray nodded. "You might have been in shock. I'm guessing the doctors decided you were well or else you'd still be in the hospital."

"Yeah, I'm okay," Manny agreed. "But what I was wondering about was whether I had dropped anything. On the floor."

"You had knocked a few books loose when you fell. And you left your backpack, but I returned that to your aunt."

"Was there a big, old book? With a faded, red leather cover?"

Mr. Gray scratched his nose pensively. "Hmm, no, I don't seem to recall any book like that. Just a few paperbacks. I shelved them again, of course."

"Nothing shiny?" Manny pressed. "Lying nearby?"

"Shiny?"

"Like a coin, maybe?" Manny bit his lip.

Manny met Mr. Gray's gaze. The clerk's pale eyes went dark and cold. It was startling enough for Manny to take a step back. His heart was racing.

But Mr. Gray smiled. "Come to think of it, I do recall something like that. Follow me." He turned and strode to the front counter. Manny hesitated, then followed him.

At the counter, Mr. Gray reached into a drawer and

pulled out a small wooden box. He slid it across the counter toward Manny. "I believe that's yours." Folding his hands, Mr. Gray raised his eyebrows expectantly.

Manny picked up the box. His heart was pounding so fast now that he was certain Mr. Gray could hear it, too. He held his breath and popped the box's lid off.

Inside the box, the golden coin gleamed.

"Is that what you meant?" said Mr. Gray.

"Yeah, this is it." Gingerly, Manny took the coin out of the box and studied it. The triskelion on one side and the young man in the laurel wreath on the other were exactly as Manny remembered. The coin seemed warm in his hand. And he couldn't be sure, but it felt like it might have been vibrating ever so slightly. Manny glanced at Mr. Gray as the clerk leaned over the counter and rested on his forearms.

"That looks very valuable," said Mr. Gray in a low voice. "I'd keep that close if I were you."

Manny looked at Mr. Gray again. There was something about him, some cold sense of age and presence, that reminded him of Merlin. "Who are you?" Manny demanded.

Mr. Gray cocked his head. "I'm a friend, Manny. Someone who means to keep an eye on you now that it's clear just how remarkable a young man you truly are." He lowered his glasses back onto his nose. "That's who I am."

The sense of power vanished and Manny blinked. All of a sudden, Mr. Gray seem ordinary again. Mr. Gray said, "Your parents would have been very proud of you."

Manny was sure he hadn't imagined the transformation. There was clearly something magical going on here. He said slowly, "You know about my parents?"

"Yes, they were mentioned in the papers. I'm sorry for your loss. It's clear they were quite remarkable as well." Mr. Gray sounded as if he really meant it.

Manny nodded. "Yeah, they were pretty cool. The coolest, actually." He put the coin back in the box, replaced the lid, and slipped the box into his pocket.

"I'd love to hear about them," said Mr. Gray. "If you ever feel like talking."

Manny glanced up. The clerk was smiling. His face reminded Manny of Etienne's chiseled features, his true features.

"Or we can just sit here for a while, if you want," added Mr. Gray. "There's no rush, Manny."

It made Manny remember how much he missed Adriana. "Okay," he said.

Then, taking a deep breath, Manny began to talk about his mother and father.

The End

SPECIAL THANKS TO:

Aaron Allston
Adrianne Middleton
AKASlaphappy
Al Clay
Aldwin Brooks
Alexander Huy
Alisha Kloc
Amanda Kaye Stein
Amber Zary
Andre Horn
Andreas Gustafsson
Antha Ann Adkins
AT Campbell
Avery
Ben Gibbs
Ben Hudson
Beth_gis
Bethany Scherbarth
Brad Cook
Brandon Salinas
Brian Anderson
Brian Miller
Brian White
Cameron Harris
Catherine Coker
Catherine Farnon
Chris McLaren
Christopher Buell
Christopher Valin
Chuck Wigginton
D Lohr
Donaithnen
Daniel Higdon
Daniel White
Danny Grossman
Dave Watson
David Lillie
Devin Harris
Diana Calder
Elizabeth Andrews
Elizabeth B Bizot
Emery Shier
Eric Fancis
Eric Norman Atkisson
Erin R Tingler
Exequiel Segovia
FA OSullivan
Gary Lee Webb
Gillian Dawson
Gordon Walton
Gwyn Case
Hall Hood
Harry Connolly
Hendrik Lesser
Hugh Sider
Isaac Dansicker

Ita Vandenbroek
Ivonne Z. Granados
J.R. Dijkstra
James Daly
James Glennon
Jeff Bent
Jeffrey Stevenson
Jennifer Douberly
Jennifer Hale
Jennifer Lane
Jennifer Skripac
Jesse Lawrence Morgan
John A
John Grigni
John Jackson
Jonah Rosestone
Joseph Hoopman
Josh Janoski
Judith Tarr
Juliana McCorison
Julie Kenner
Justine Etzkorn
Kaldronimamuchipaton
Karen Zieman
kassia
Kelley McCown
Huebner
Kellie Johnson
Kerry Stubbs
Kiai
Kirk Black
Kitt Hodsden
KLH
Krista Hoxie
Lars
Lauren Sheppard
Lawrence Schick
Linda Cast
James Sullivan
Jason Etheridge
Jason Smith
Jason Sperber
Jean Prior
linda kralowetz
Lisa Cohen
Lowell Berman
Lunin
Lynnea Glasser
Manny Hernandez
Marilyn Richmond
Mark Bennett
Mark Finn
Mark Han
Mark Himmelsbach
Marshall McAuley
Matthew Legare
matthurlburt
mbittner
Melanie Buckowski
Melita Kennedy
Michael B. Moe
Michael Bentley
Michael Blanchard
Michael Bowman
Michael Gilvary
Michael Mock
Michael Morlan
Michael Rigg
Michael Toler
Michelle Ossiander
Mindy King
Murray Triplett
Nancy Underwood
Natalya Alyssa Faden
Nathan Stohlmann
Neil Ferrin

Noel Rappin
Nova B
ozog
Patrice Sarath
Patricia Pooks Burroughs
Paul Bulmer
Persephone
Pete Newell
Peter Cline
Rob Rogers
Robert Harrold
Robin Faircloth
Ruth Riegel
S. Levy
Sanne Kaasen
Sara Felix
Scott Cupp
Scott Early
Sean L.
Sean Patrick Fannon
Sechin Tower
solardepths
Stephen Cheng
Steve Barr
Steven Holt
Sue Fruia
Susan Petroulas
Swordfire
Tara Smith
Terry Rossio
thanate Salamandra
Theron Bretz
Thomas Thrush
Todd Gdula
Troyce
Tyler Beusse
Vigilance Press
Vishal Bajaj
Will Cockrell
William C Smith
William Fisher
ZMiles

AUTHOR BIOS

Aaron de Orive:

A graduate of the University of Texas' film program, Aaron de Orive began his professional writing career in the video game industry, serving as a lead or senior writer on *Metroid Prime 3: Corruption, Star Wars Galaxies: An Empire Divided, Tabula Rasa, Anarchy Online,* and *Star Wars: The Old Republic.* He is also the creator of the fantasy role-playing game *SHARD: World of the False Dawn. Blade Singer* is his first novel. Aaron lives in Austin with his wife, daughter, and two very spoiled terriers.

Martha Wells:

Martha Wells is the author of a number of fantasy novels, including *The Cloud Roads, The Siren Depths, The Wizard Hunters, Wheel of the Infinite,* and the Nebula-nominated *The Death of the Necromancer.* Her YA fantasy, *Emilie and the Hollow World,* was published by Angry Robot/Strange Chemistry in April 2013, and the sequel, *Emilie and the Sky World,* was released in March 2014. Two collections of *Books of the Raksura* novellas will be published in September 2014 and Fall 2015. She has had short stories in *BlackGate, Realms of Fantasy, Stargate Magazine,* and *Lightspeed Magazine*and in the anthologies *Elemental, The Year's Best Fantasy #7,*

Tales of the Emerald Serpent and *The Other Half of the Sky*. She has essays in the nonfiction anthologies *Farscape Forever*, *Mapping the World of Harry Potter*, and *Chicks Unravel Time*. She has also written media-tie-in novels, *Stargate Atlantis: Reliquary* and *Stargate Atlantis: Entanglement*, and a *Star Wars* novel, *Empire and Rebellion: Razor's Edge*.

Made in the USA
San Bernardino, CA
18 August 2019